Graeme Macrae Burnet's second novel, *His Bloody Project*, was shortlisted for the Booker Prize 2016, and his fourth, *Case Study*, was longlisted for the Booker Prize in 2022.

'A triumph.' *Financial Times*

'*A Case of Matricide* demonstrates literary talent of the highest order … few writers can rival Burnet.' *Spectator*

'Wickedly funny … slyly playful … owes as much of a debt to Albert Camus as it does to Georges Simenon.' *Irish Times*

'Quirky … thought-provoking and entirely convincing.' *Guardian*

'A rewardingly tricksy novel full of literary games and misdirections … enthralling plot strands … compelling.' *Times*

'Pulls off the rare double of being emotionally involving as well as teasingly tricksy.' *Telegraph*

'An incredibly fun, cleverly crafted novel … works on so many levels.' *Eimear McBride, New Statesman, Books of the Year*

'A work of fine artistry; craftsmanship too … [Burnet is] a master of artifice.' *Scotsman*

'It's smart, quirky and fun.' *Los Angeles Times*

'You can gulp down *A Case of Matricide* in one sitting, as the prose style seems to demand. But linger over Burnet's novel, and its real pleasures emerge.' *New York Times*

Selected praise for the previous Gorski novels

'Extravagant talent.' *Mark Lawson, Guardian, Books of the Year*

'Clever, meandering and oh, so French … Burnet really has – a rare thing nowadays – a novelist's eye.' *James Marriott, Times*

'Highly accomplished … like something out of Greek tragedy but delivers as a proper police procedural too.' *Observer*

'Wry, intelligent and a lot of fun.' *Andrew Taylor, Spectator*

'A truly superlative tale … one of the most clever and compelling novels to be published this year.' *Lesley McDowell, Herald*

'Gripping and intelligent.' *Philip Pullman, Guardian*

'Classy … stylish … If Roland Barthes had written a detective novel, then this would be it.' *Philip Womack, Literary Review*

Selected praise for *His Bloody Project*

Shortlisted for the Man Booker Prize 2016

'A spellbinding piece of serious new fiction … Riveting, dark and ingeniously constructed.' *Edmund Gordon, Sunday Times*

'A smart amalgam of legal thriller and literary game that reads as if Umberto Eco has been resurrected in the 19th-century Scottish Highlands.' *Mark Lawson, Guardian*

'An astonishing piece of writing.' *Jake Kerridge, Telegraph*

'A fiendishly readable tale that richly deserves the wider attention the Man Booker has brought it.' *Justine Jordan, Guardian*

'Gripping, blackly playful and intelligent.' *Robbie Millen, Times*

'Its overarching themes are timeless.' *New Statesman*

'Darkly engaging.' *Sally Magnusson, Books of the Year, Herald*

'A brilliantly written story of rural hardship, fractured community and inescapable bloodshed.' *Ian Rankin, Guardian*

Selected praise for *Case Study*

Longlisted for the Booker Prize 2022

'A riveting psychological plot ... tortuous, cunning ... clever.' *Times Literary Supplement*

'A page-turning blast, funny, sinister, perfectly plotted … Rarely has being constantly wrong-footed been so much fun.' *Times*

'Encourages us to look more closely at the inherent instability of fiction itself … genuinely affecting … very funny.' *Guardian*

'Indecently entertaining.' *Telegraph, Books of the Year*

'A novel of mind-bending brilliance.' *Hannah Kent*

'Brilliant, bamboozling … burstingly alive and engaging.' *Telegraph*

'Bitingly funny and surprisingly moving … [A] barnstorming psychodrama … Consistently inventive, caustically funny … one of the finest novels of the year.' *Financial Times*

A CASE OF MATRICIDE

by

RAYMOND BRUNET

Translated and introduced by

Graeme Macrae Burnet

CONTRABAND

Contraband is an imprint of Saraband
Published by Saraband
3 Clairmont Gardens
Glasgow, G3 7LW
www.saraband.net

This paperback edition first published 2025

ISBN: 9781916812376

Printed and bound in Great Britain by Clays Ltd, Elcograf SpA.

FSC www.fsc.org MIX Paper | Supporting responsible forestry FSC® C018072

10 9 8 7 6 5 4 3 2 1

Contents

Foreword

Raymond Brunet was born in Saint-Louis, an unremarkable town of twenty thousand people on the French-Swiss border, in 1953. Aside from a short sojourn in Paris following the release of Claude Chabrol's screen adaptation of his 1982 novel *La Disparition d'Adèle Bedeau*, he spent his whole life in the town, before throwing himself in front of a train in 1992.

Until 2014, it was thought that *The Disappearance of Adèle Bedeau* was Brunet's only novel, something which undoubtedly contributed to its cult status, but in November that year a package containing two further manuscripts was delivered to the offices of Éditions Gaspard-Moreau in Paris. Shortly before his suicide, Brunet had lodged the two manuscripts with a firm of solicitors in the nearby city of Mulhouse with the stipulation that they be forwarded to his publisher only on the occasion of his mother Marie's death.

The first of these works, *L'Accident de l'A35*, was published in France in the spring of 2016. The novel was a fictionalised version of the 'minor mystery' surrounding the death of Brunet's father in a car crash in 1967 and contained certain revelations, which—if true—made clear why Brunet did not want the book to be published in his mother's lifetime.

Propelled by the 'lost manuscript' narrative skilfully promulgated by Gaspard-Moreau, *The Accident on the A35* was an immediate bestseller. The novel revived interest in Brunet, who had by then been largely forgotten, and spawned a great deal of speculation about the extent to which the events depicted in the book were true. Brunet thus enjoyed his greatest moment of success more than two decades after his death. Perhaps this would have suited him. He was a man ill at ease in the spotlight, temperamentally more comfortable with failure.

This current volume forms the concluding part of Brunet's trilogy of novels set in Saint-Louis and featuring the character of Georges Gorski. Given its title, Brunet's wish to delay publication until after his mother's death requires no explanation.

Une affaire de matricide was not published in France until October 2019, more than three years after *The Accident* had appeared. The excitement which had greeted the earlier book had long since dissipated. It would be an exaggeration to say that the final part of the trilogy met with indifference—Brunet's cult status ensured that that was not the case—but it certainly received a more muted response than the previous instalment. The delay in publication had led to speculation that the book was sub-standard or even unpublishable. These rumours were given credence when Christine Gaspard, head of Gaspard-Moreau, was overheard in the fashionable Paris restaurant Le Récamier loudly declaring that the editing process had become *un cauchemar*—a nightmare. Some construed that in discussing the project in such a well-known media haunt, Gaspard knew exactly what she was doing and was only seeking to revive waning interest in the book. Even were that the case, however, there was, as we shall see, an element of truth in what she said.

Regardless of the difficulties that may or may not have been involved in bringing *A Case of Matricide* to publication, the novel is a fitting conclusion to Brunet's trilogy, and one featuring all the elements that so captivated readers of his earlier work. It also, tragically, makes it all too clear why both Raymond Brunet's life and writing career ended in the way they did.

GMB, April 2024

A Case of Matricide

Il n'y a pas de villes maudites et la mienne, en tout cas,
est un modèle de petite bourgeoisie étriquée.

Georges Simenon

There are no cursed towns and mine is, in any case,
a model of petit bourgeois constraint.

It is three o'clock on a November afternoon in the town of Saint-Louis, Haut-Rhin.

The florist, Madame Beck, gazes out the window of her shop on Rue des Trois Rois. The day's bouquets have been dispatched and she is unlikely to receive more than a handful of customers before the shop closes. Rue des Trois Rois is not a busy thoroughfare, but even the few passers-by barely register in her consciousness. She is thinking about the piece of fish she will later cook for her husband and whether she might close a little early in order to catch the greengrocer's on Avenue de Bâle.

A short distance away, a man named Ivan Baudoin climbs the five steps to the police station on Rue de Mulhouse. He is leading a dog on a length of thin yellow rope, which he passes behind his back from his right hand to his left as he pulls the door open and enters. Earlier, he came across the dog wandering on Avenue de la Marne, where he lives. Monsieur Baudoin is not a well-off individual and he intends to leave his name and address with the police, lest the dog's owner be moved to offer a reward for his public-spirited act.

In the *salon de thé* on the corner of Avenue Général de Gaulle and Rue des Vosges, two ladies in their sixties discuss at great length the pastries they are eating. One of them, Thérèse Lamartine, unconsciously moves her hand towards her ankle where her little dog would once have been sitting. The dog is long dead, but Madame Lamartine keenly feels its absence on a daily basis.

In an inconspicuous street, parallel to Rue des Vosges, an elderly woman sits propped up in bed against embroidered pillows, listening intently while her son moves around on the ground floor below.

The hairdresser Lemerre is sitting in his own barber's chair leafing through the pages of one of the girlie magazines he supplies for customers to peruse while they wait. The pictures do not interest him much, but there is no other reading material to hand. In a few minutes, he will walk the short distance to the Restaurant de la Cloche to take his afternoon glass at the counter with Pasteur.

In the office of the Hôtel Bertillon, the proprietor, Henri Virieu, is caused to raise his eyes from his copy of *L'Alsace* by the sound of a guest placing his key on the counter. The guest does not so much as glance in Monsieur Virieu's direction, despite the fact that he is clearly visible behind the glass partition and the two men have previously exchanged some rudimentary pleasantries.

In the little park by the Protestant temple, a handful of pigeons peck at the dirt on the path between the benches. Around this time, a widow by the name of Agnes Vincent often passes half an hour watching the birds squabble over the breadcrumbs she scatters from a brown paper bag. Madame Vincent has not visited the park for three days. She is lying dead on the bathroom floor of the apartment on Rue du Temple that she shared with her husband until his death eight years ago. Her body will not be discovered for another week, when a neighbour notices an unpleasant odour in the corridor.

Through the window of Céline's, a ladieswear boutique overlooking the little park, the owner can be seen adjusting a display of lingerie too daring for the conservative womenfolk of the town.

On the corner of Rue de Huningue and Rue Alexandre Lauly, the Restaurant de la Cloche is experiencing the usual lull between lunchtime service and the end of the working day when the town's tradespeople gather for a post-work snifter and to catch up on the day's gossip. At the counter, the proprietor, Pasteur, leans over his newspaper, displaying his bald crown to the restaurant. His wife, Marie, surveys the dining room with satisfaction. Everything is in its place. The only customer is a commercial traveller who attempts to disguise his alcoholism through diligent attention to his order book. At his feet are the two suitcases in which he carries his samples. Later, he will walk unsteadily along Rue de Mulhouse to the Hôtel Bertillon, where he will spend the night.

At a table by the window, the waitress, Adèle, is smoking a cigarette. She has taken off her shoes and put her feet on the banquette. Marie would not tolerate this sort of behaviour from any other member of staff, but she indulges Adèle as she puts her in mind of her younger self.

In a large property on the outskirts of the town, a young widow, Lucette Barthelme, puts her ear to the door of her bedroom in order to ascertain the whereabouts of the housekeeper, this so that she can descend the stairs and leave the house without feeling the need to explain her movements. In the bedroom two doors along the landing, her teenage son, Raymond, sits on a straight-backed chair reading *The 120 Days of Sodom.*

It is three o'clock on a November afternoon in Saint-Louis.

It is three o'clock on a November afternoon in the town of Saint-Louis, Haut-Rhin.

The florist, Madame Beck, gazes out the window of her shop on Rue des Trois Rois. The day's bouquets have been dispatched and she is unlikely to receive more than a handful of customers before the shop closes. Rue des Trois Rois is not a busy thoroughfare, but even the few passers-by barely register in her consciousness. She is thinking about the piece of fish she will later cook for her husband and whether she might close a little early in order to catch the greengrocer's on Avenue de Bâle.

A short distance away, a man named Ivan Baudoin climbs the five steps to the police station on Rue de Mulhouse. He is leading a dog on a length of thin yellow rope, which he passes behind his back from his right hand to his left as he pulls the door open and enters. Earlier, he came across the dog wandering on Avenue de la Marne, where he lives. Monsieur Baudoin is not a well-off individual and he intends to leave his name and address with the police, lest the dog's owner be moved to offer a reward for his public-spirited act.

In the *salon de thé* on the corner of Avenue Général de Gaulle and Rue des Vosges, two ladies in their sixties discuss at great length the pastries they are eating. One of them, Thérèse Lamartine, unconsciously moves her hand towards her ankle where her little dog would once have been sitting. The dog is long dead, but Madame Lamartine keenly feels its absence on a daily basis.

In an inconspicuous street, parallel to Rue des Vosges, an elderly woman sits propped up in bed against embroidered pillows, listening intently while her son moves around on the ground floor below.

The hairdresser Lemerre is sitting in his own barber's chair leafing through the pages of one of the girlie magazines he supplies for customers to peruse while they wait. The pictures do not interest him much, but there is no other reading material to hand. In a few minutes, he will walk the short distance to the Restaurant de la Cloche to take his afternoon glass at the counter with Pasteur.

In the office of the Hôtel Bertillon, the proprietor, Henri Virieu, is caused to raise his eyes from his copy of *L'Alsace* by the sound of a guest placing his key on the counter. The guest does not so much as glance in Monsieur Virieu's direction, despite the fact that he is clearly visible behind the glass partition and the two men have previously exchanged some rudimentary pleasantries.

In the little park by the Protestant temple, a handful of pigeons peck at the dirt on the path between the benches. Around this time, a widow by the name of Agnes Vincent often passes half an hour watching the birds squabble over the breadcrumbs she scatters from a brown paper bag. Madame Vincent has not visited the park for three days. She is lying dead on the bathroom floor of the apartment on Rue du Temple that she shared with her husband until his death eight years ago. Her body will not be discovered for another week, when a neighbour notices an unpleasant odour in the corridor.

Through the window of Céline's, a ladieswear boutique overlooking the little park, the owner can be seen adjusting a display of lingerie too daring for the conservative womenfolk of the town.

One

Hôtel Bertillon was situated in an inconspicuous, whitewashed building at the intersection of Rue de Mulhouse and Rue Henner. Aside from a modest sign on the wall above the entrance, there was little to alert passers-by to its existence, and even this sign was in such a state of neglect that it was more likely to deter than entice potential custom. The bill of tariffs taped to the inside of the glass panel by the door was yellowed and torn. The surrounding paintwork was blistered, and bare wood was visible where it had flaked away altogether. A quantity of dry leaves had accumulated in the corner of the vestibule.

Inside, the establishment was no more appealing. The narrow foyer was dimly lit and smelled of stale carpet. The décor was tired.

Georges Gorski rang the brass bell on the counter. A man emerged from the office, which was partitioned from the counter by a rectangular glass panel, so that it resembled a large aquarium. He was very small and neatly dressed in grey slacks and a shirt and tie beneath a V-neck sweater. Around his shoulders was a pair of reading glasses on a chain. He had the grey pallor of a man who rarely exposed himself to sunlight. He had mentioned his name on the telephone, but Gorski had forgotten it, an increasingly regular occurrence.

Gorski held out his ID. 'Monsieur Bertillon?' he said, though he knew this was not correct.

'Oh no,' replied the little man. 'I am not Bertillon. Bertillon was my wife's name. Well, my wife's maiden name. The hotel belonged to her parents before … before it, eh, passed to us.' He paused, realising perhaps that Gorski was not in need of a history of the business. 'My name is Henri Virieu.'

'Yes,' said Gorski, as if refreshing his memory, 'Monsieur Virieu.'

There was a short silence. The man's fingers fidgeted on the counter as if playing a toy piano. His hands were bony and flecked with liver spots.

'You'll probably think me a dreadful busybody,' he said. 'It's just that, well, I suppose it seemed the right thing to do. In case, in case of, you know—'

'In case of what?' said Gorski. He had taken a dislike to Virieu on the telephone. He was a man who opened his mouth without having first formulated what he wanted to say. His explanation for calling had consisted of a string of meaningless half-formed phrases and fatuous aphorisms. 'Prudence is the mother of security, as they say,' he had wittered.

Ineffectual. He was an ineffectual little man, and meeting him in person only confirmed the impression.

Rather than answering Gorski's question, Virieu lowered his voice and, with a furtive glance along the passage, invited him into the office. 'There we can converse undisturbed,' he said, as if he was a member of the DST.* He raised the flap on the counter and ushered Gorski into his sanctum.

Everything was neatly arranged. Behind the desk were shelves of box files, each one clearly inscribed with the year. On the desk was a copy of *L'Alsace*, open at the page with the crossword, which was half-completed. There was a glass cabinet displaying a number of small trophies.

'From my chess career,' said Virieu, seeing Gorski glance towards them. He unlocked the cabinet and handed one to Gorski. It declared him champion of Haut-Rhin. It was thirty years old. 'I still play of course, but the mind, well, the mind isn't what it used to be. One finds oneself besieged by the young. Do you play at all? Perhaps we could have a game sometime.'

---

* Direction de la Surveillance du Territoire, the French internal security service – *translator's note*

Gorski shook his head.

A cat was asleep on the chair in front of the desk. Virieu tickled it behind the ear and murmured some soft sounds, before shooing it onto the floor. 'Our oldest employee,' he said, with a little laugh.

Gorski smiled thinly and took the cat's seat. The glass wall afforded a panoramic view of the foyer. Virieu sat down behind the desk, then immediately leapt to his feet.

'Perhaps you would do me the honour, monsieur, of sharing a glass with me.' From a filing cabinet he produced a bottle of schnapps. Gorski corrected his mode of address but did not decline the drink, which Virieu had in any case already poured. He resumed his seat.

'Your very good health, Chief Inspector,' he said, with an ingratiating emphasis on his title.

He knocked back his drink. Gorski did the same. Virieu refilled the glasses. It was half past nine in the morning.

'As I was saying, the business passed to my wife and I after Monsieur and Madame Bertillon took their leave of this world, but we were already running it in a de facto sort of way. My father-in-law had, I regret to say, become somewhat overfamiliar with the town's hostelries.' He redundantly mimed the motion of tipping a glass into his mouth.

Gorski now recalled hearing his own father occasionally refer to an acquaintance by the name of Bertillon. Perhaps they had even played cards together.

'It was,' Virieu went on, 'something of a relief when he, eh, passed away, and at that point—'

Gorski made a rotating motion with his fingers. 'If you don't mind, Monsieur Virieu.'

'Of course, my apologies. A man of your position, of your high office, must have much more pressing matters to attend to. Matters of great civic import, I mean.'

'As I understand,' Gorski said, 'you have some concerns about one of your guests.'

'As it happens the gentleman in question is currently our only guest. I say "our" only from force of habit. My wife passed away some years hence.'

'And these "concerns" are based on what?' Gorski interjected.

'They are based on the fact that he has been here for five nights.'

'Uh-huh?'

'And he shows no sign of leaving.'

'Anyone would think this was a hotel.'

Gorski's attempt at humour was lost on Virieu.

'We've never had anyone stay for so long,' he went on. 'It seemed irregular and so I felt compelled to report it; that it was my duty as a citizen. There's something about him. Something fishy.'

'Fishy how?' said Gorski wearily.

He should have put an end to this on the telephone. No crime had been committed or was even alleged. He should not be responding to the nebulous allegation of an individual being *fishy*. It was beneath him. Inspector Ribéry, Gorski's predecessor, would have told Virieu in the bluntest of terms not to waste his time.

The hotelier now seemed a little circumspect. He leant over the desk and lowered his voice. 'He speaks with an accent. And he does not appear to be in gainful employment. I asked him in the course of conversation what he did for a living, and he made a vague gesture and said, "This and that." I mean, if one has a legitimate profession, why conceal it?'

Gorski was beginning to find this neat little man quite objectionable.

'Perhaps he thought it was none of your business.'

'Why would someone stay for so long in Saint-Louis without a proper reason?'

Gorski tipped his head. This, he had to admit, was a reasonable point. 'Let me see his passport,' he said.

'I'm afraid I don't even know his name. Since my wife passed away, I do not always take care of the administrative side of things as diligently as I should.'

'That's very trusting of you,' said Gorski.

Virieu explained that the guest had paid upfront for three nights when he arrived, so there had been no need to ask for his passport or to fill out any paperwork. 'Since then he's paid for each subsequent night when he leaves the hotel in the morning.'

It was strange, Gorski thought, that he had never once seen Virieu before. In a town of twenty thousand people, this was unusual. He had passed the Hôtel Bertillon hundreds of times, yet he had never seen Virieu enter or leave. Clearly the man liked a drink, but he had never seen him in any of the town's bars. That said, he was the sort of mediocre character one could easily fail to notice.

Out of curiosity, he asked if he lived on the premises.

'We—I mean, *I*—have an apartment on the first floor.'

Gorski imagined Virieu in those gloomy rooms, sipping his schnapps and sadly shifting the pieces around a chessboard.

'So you must be well aware of the comings and goings of your guests?'

'It's not my job to snoop, Inspector.' He seemed offended by the suggestion.

'But you say there is something suspicious about this gentleman?' He allowed his tone to sharpen.

Virieu lowered his eyes. 'My apologies. I can see I've wasted your time. Business is rather slow. Perhaps I've been guilty of letting my imagination run away with itself. I assure you that my motives were quite sincere.'

Gorski could not help feeling a grain of pity for him. He waved away his apology and asked if the guest in question had already been down for breakfast.

'Unfortunately,' Virieu replied, 'we are unable to offer a breakfast service at the present time.'

Gorski exhaled heavily and asked for the room number. Virieu directed him to the elevator along the poorly lit passage.

The man filled the doorframe of Room 203. It was not that he was tall—he was a similar height to Gorski—but there was a certain physicality about him. He was about forty-five years old and had a large head like that of a horse, with heavy though not unpleasant features. His hair, greying slightly at the temples, was cut short. He was wearing dark brown trousers and a mustard-coloured shirt, open at the neck. His nose had been broken at some point and Gorski wondered if he had been a boxer. He had something of the air of a boxer or a butcher.

Gorski glanced down at his hands. They were big, weighty things, with thick fingers and prominent knuckles. Gorski's hands, like those of his father, were small and delicate. As a teenager, when he had spent a summer labouring on a farm, he had embarked on a concerted campaign to chafe and scratch them, but any effect had been temporary. As a young cop he had felt self-conscious about them. These were not the hands with which to rough up a suspect. Ribéry had to frequently upbraid him for keeping them in his pockets. Later, when he had his first intimate relations with his now estranged wife Céline, she had commented on his soft hands. She intended it as a compliment, but Gorski could not help feeling that she would prefer to be manhandled by a farrier or brickie.

'Yes?' said the man.

Gorski held out his ID and introduced himself.

The man pursed his lips, as if impressed or amused that he merited a visit from a high-ranking member of the town's police. 'What can I do for you?'

His French was correct, but as Virieu had indicated, heavily accented. He did not seem in the least disconcerted by Gorski's appearance. Why should he? There was no suggestion that he had done anything wrong. Still, in Gorski's experience, most people were discomfited by a visit from the police. Even the most blameless became flustered and tried to conceal their disquiet with inappropriate jokes or displays of servility.

'May I come in?'

The man stood aside.

The room was small. The double bed and an old-fashioned wardrobe occupied most of the floor space. Next to the bed was a nightstand and on the opposite side, beneath the window, was a wooden chair on which a jacket matching the man's trousers was hanging. On the pretext of looking out the window, Gorski stepped round the bed, but he only wanted to put a comfortable distance between himself and the occupant of the room. The window looked out onto Rue Henner. An elderly woman with a dachshund passed on the opposite pavement. It was beginning to rain. A few fat drops hit the windowpane. The woman paused to put up an umbrella while the dog waited patiently at her feet.

Aside from the jacket on the back of the chair, there was little to indicate that the room was occupied. There were no books or newspapers and, apart from a glass of water and a moderately expensive-looking wristwatch, there was nothing on the nightstand.

The man observed Gorski impassively. Gorski felt foolish, as if the tables had been turned on him, and it was he, rather than the guest, who was under scrutiny. He should never have acquiesced to the hotelier's request.

'It's a routine matter, Monsieur...?' he began. His rising intonation was intended as an invitation for the guest to volunteer his name, but he did not do so. He appeared to find this small-town cop amusing.

'It is my duty to inform you that if you intend to stay in the municipality for more than ten days, you are required to register your place of residence at the police station.'

Gorski was not even sure if this was true. He was vaguely aware that a regulation of this sort existed, but he had never had cause to enforce it, either because no one had ever stayed in Saint-Louis for long enough, or, if they had, they had done nothing to come to the attention of the authorities.

The man gave a little snort through his nose. 'This must be a very law-abiding town if the chief of police has nothing more urgent to attend to.'

'I was passing,' Gorski said, immediately reprimanding himself for feeling the need to explain his actions. 'May I see your passport?'

The man looked at him, as if weighing up whether to comply. The pause lasted long enough for Gorski to wonder what he would do if he refused. Eventually, the man asked Gorski to pass him the jacket hanging on the chair beneath the window. He took his passport from the inside pocket.

'Just like the old days,' he said, as he handed it over. '*Papiere, bitte*!'

The passport was from the Federal Republic of Yugoslavia. The man's name was long and complicated. Gorski stared at it for a few moments, trying to commit it to memory. If he then slowly turned the pages of the document, it was purely for show, to give the Slav the impression that he was engaged in some kind of formal procedure. Then he snapped it shut in a businesslike manner and handed it back without comment.

The man did not ask if everything was in order. Those unused to dealing with the powers-that-be invariably wish to demonstrate that they are not troublemakers. If they have failed to comply with any regulations, they are anxious to assert that they have done so inadvertently. This fellow, however, exhibited no such behaviour. He appeared to be entirely at ease.

'Can I ask the purpose of your visit to Saint-Louis?' Gorski felt the need to somehow wrest back the initiative.

'Must there be a purpose?'

'Isn't there a purpose for everything?' said Gorski.

'Do you mean in a theological sense?'

Gorski was uncomfortable with this turn in the conversation. 'I simply mean that you must have some reason for being here. Some business to take care of.'

The man shrugged. 'And what if I prefer not to say?' He paused for a moment before continuing. 'You will almost certainly put a negative construction on such an answer. You will think that if my presence in your town was innocent, I would be happy to tell you why I am here. However, you might also think that if I was here for some illicit purpose, I would make a point of answering your question in order to appear to have nothing to hide. But if I choose not to answer, it's simply because I do not think you have the right to ask me. France is supposed to be a free country, is it not? *Liberté, égalité, fraternité*, et cetera.'

Gorski had no answer to this. He shifted his feet a little on the floor. 'It's as you say,' he said. 'You're under no obligation. Nevertheless, I remind you that if you plan to stay longer, you must register your presence at the police station.'

'It seems,' said the man, 'that my presence has already been registered.' He took up his watch from the bedside table and calmly fastened it on his wrist.

Gorski wished the man good day.

He pulled on the jacket that Gorski had moments ago passed to him. It was a little tight around the shoulders, as if it had been borrowed from a smaller man. 'I was just leaving myself,' he said. He opened the wardrobe door and took a light-coloured raincoat from a hanger. On the shelf above, a suitcase was neatly stowed.

Gorski made his way along the corridor. The walls were painted pale green. The man followed at his shoulder, which made Gorski feel that he was being escorted from the premises. The carpet was sticky beneath his shoes. Not wishing to squeeze into the tiny lift, he followed the signage to the stairs.

When Gorski emerged into the foyer, Virieu looked up from behind the counter.

'Well?' he said, before catching sight of the guest behind him.

Gorski did not know what to say. He did not want the Slav to think that he had made this visit at Virieu's behest. The conversation had been uncomfortable enough without having him think that he, the chief of police, was at the beck and call of the meddlesome proprietor of a third-rate hotel.

Without breaking step, he simply said, 'Everything's in order, monsieur.'

On the pavement outside, Gorski stopped to light a cigarette, assuming that the man would walk off, but he did not do so.

Instead, he too paused, apparently waiting to see which direction Gorski was going. Inside, Virieu craned his head over the counter and shamelessly observed what was unfolding. Gorski felt that it must look that he was now in cahoots with the Yugoslavian.

Without a word Gorski set off. The Slav fell into step beside him. They walked side by side along the narrow pavement of Rue Henner before turning into Rue de Mulhouse. The Slav made no attempt to initiate conversation. After a few minutes, Gorski could not restrain himself from pointing out one of the half-timbered buildings, characteristic of the region. He did not do so out of civic pride, but simply to break the silence between them. The Slav obediently looked in the direction of the unremarkable building and nodded.

As they approached the police station, he paused at the foot of the steps.

'Well,' said Gorski, 'perhaps I'll see you in a few days. In the meantime, enjoy your stay in Saint-Louis.' He did not want the man to think he was unwelcome in the town, but neither did it do any harm for him to think that the authorities had their eye on him.

He did not move away, but watched Gorski climb the steps and disappear inside.

Schmitt was at his usual post at the counter. He looked up, but seeing it was Gorski, returned his gaze to his newspaper. From the small waiting area, Gorski glanced back through the glass panel of the door. The Slav was loitering on the pavement outside. It was now his turn to take out a cigarette and light it. There was no apparent reason for him to remain there.

Gorski concealed himself behind the doorframe. Schmitt looked up for a second time.

'Are you lost?' he asked. It never failed to irk Gorski that Schmitt addressed him with the familiar *tu*. It was a provocation, but he had never had the nerve to confront the issue. Schmitt would be sure to laugh it off, and Gorski would only make himself look petty. In any case, Schmitt regarded the reception area as his personal fiefdom and exercised the right to challenge anyone who lingered on his territory.

Ignoring his question, Gorski inched his head forward. The Slav was still there. Gorski retreated to his office on the first floor. He sat down behind his desk and lit another cigarette. The incident had left him feeling foolish. He had behaved stupidly and now, here in his own office, he felt as though he was somehow under siege, as if this Slav was standing guard over him. So as to demonstrate that he was not intimidated, he got up and paced around the room. He paused by the window, which looked out onto the car park behind the building. He half-expected to see the Slav below, gazing up at his window. Of course, there was nobody there.

He summoned Roland. On account of his long face and gangly limbs, the older officers had nicknamed the young cop The Foal. If Gorski now and again singled him out for certain tasks, it was not because he displayed any particular aptitude or talent, but because he, alone among the staff, seemed to have some respect for him. He was young and eager for advancement. He stood, as he always did, with his hands clasped behind his back, as if he was still in military service. Gorski instructed him to leave the building by the front entrance and walk to the *tabac* on Place de l'Europe, buy a packet of cigarettes, and return by the same route. He wanted to know if a man was skulking outside the building.

Roland took out his notebook and jotted down the description Gorski gave him.

'What kind of cigarettes should I buy?' he asked.

'It doesn't matter,' said Gorski. 'The cigarettes are just a pretext.'

'Yes, I see,' said Roland. 'But all the same.'

Gorski realised that he had never seen Roland smoke. He rummaged in his pocket and handed him a banknote. 'Gitanes,' he said. 'Get two packs.'

'Two packets of Gitanes,' the young man repeated earnestly.

He was soon back with a detailed account of his mission. He had seen no one answering the description Gorski had given, but he placed the two packets of Gitanes on the desk, along with the change. Gorski dismissed him. He shook his head to himself. It was ridiculous to think that this Slav had been watching him. Nevertheless, when he left for lunch, he did so by the exit at the rear of the building.

Two

Later that afternoon, as Gorski left the police station, Schmitt was arguing with a man with a stray dog. 'This is not a dog pound,' the desk sergeant was explaining in a world-weary tone. The mutt sniffed at the hems of Gorski's trousers, causing him to become entangled in the thin yellow rope tied around its neck. Neither man so much as glanced at him as he extricated himself.

Rue Saint-Jean was in the middling part of Saint-Louis, an area consisting neither of the squat post-war apartment blocks surrounding the railway station, nor of the draughty mansions of the well-heeled on the outskirts of the town. This was the kind of neighbourhood to which Gorski's work brought him least frequently. The poor generally confine themselves to robbing and assaulting each other. They are as accustomed to the sound of sirens as they are to shouting matches taking place on the other side of the flimsy walls of their apartments. The upper classes, on the other hand, have no qualms about sending for the police over the most piffling matter. For them, a cop is just another servant to be summoned, like the butler or the maid.

The petite bourgeoisie, however, regard contact with the police as something shameful and to be avoided at all costs. Attending incidents in streets like Rue Saint-Jean, Gorski was routinely asked not to park outside the house in question. When residents of such neighbourhoods fall victim to a crime, they are inclined to believe that they themselves are responsible for their misfortune. Had they properly secured their windows or doors, the incident would never have occurred. A passing burglar cannot be blamed for taking advantage of such negligence. This tendency explained the mania among these people for domestic security devices. The installation of such alarms had less to do with deterring crime than assuaging the guilt felt by victims. Certainly, in Gorski's experience, no housebreaker worth his salt was put off by the rudimentary gadgets peddled by door-to-door salesmen. Indeed, circumventing such systems appealed to their professional pride and, furthermore, suggested that there might be something worth stealing inside, which was rarely the case.

26 Rue Saint-Jean was an ordinary semi-detached house with little to distinguish it from its neighbours. The woodwork was painted white. The lawn was neatly cut. The windows were hung with voile curtains to discourage prying eyes. In such streets, residents habitually clutter their lawns with amusing garden ornaments, plant pampas grass or cultivate a bent for topiary, all in an effort to assert a modicum of individuality. It does not do to stand out too much, but conversely a desire for anonymity is regarded as suspect. Number 26 was notable only for the absence of embellishment or ornamentation. Clearly, the occupants were inclined to keep themselves to themselves.

Gorski had visited the premises before. The incident had seemed of such little consequence that he had not troubled to file a report. But now as he stepped up the path for a second time, he regretted not having done so. Was that not the entire reason for making a report? To create a record for future use. To verify that one had been present. And, above all, to guard against forgetting.

The elderly resident had reported some garden tools missing. After a rudimentary search, they had been located in the shed. No crime had been committed, but that was not the point. Perhaps some detail Gorski had noted at the time was now lost. It is not possible to know what apparent triviality may later turn out to be significant. Even if asked when the incident had occurred, Gorski would be hard-pressed to say. A year ago certainly, but perhaps it had been two. Without a record of the event, he had no way of knowing. It was a free-floating memory unconnected to anything that might anchor it in time.

Ribéry had scorned all note-taking and report-writing. 'If it's important, you'll remember it,' he would say, tapping a crooked finger to his temple. But still, it bothered Gorski. He had failed to adhere to his own credo: that intuition had no place in police work. It was not for a cop to exercise discretion, but rather to follow the procedures which had evolved precisely for the purpose of eliminating human error. He had been negligent.

The sound of the doorbell transported Gorski back to his earlier visit. It had the harsh tone of a school or prison bell and had, previously, been followed by the yapping of a small dog; a detail, Gorski noted, that he had until that moment failed to recall. Today there was silence from within and he had the impression that the house was holding its breath.

He rang the bell a second time. After a minute or so, there was some movement inside and a dark shape became visible through the frosted glass panel of the door. It was opened by a man of around forty. His dark hair was neatly cut and parted. He was wearing a white shirt, black slacks and brown slip-on shoes. Gorski had an aversion to slip-on shoes and, for reasons he had never properly examined, felt that those who wore them were not to be trusted. The man did not fully open the door, but peeped out from behind it so that only half his face was visible.

'What is it?' he said by way of greeting.

Gorski pointedly wished him good day and held out his ID.

The door remained no more than ajar.

'What can I do for you?'

'We received a call from this address. From a Madame Duymann.'

'Ah,' said the man.

'And you are?'

'Robert Duymann. Her son.' The latter words were spoken with the resigned tone of one who knew it was an admission of failure for a man of his age to be living with his mother. Duymann now opened the door enough to reveal the other half of his face. It offered nothing in the way of surprises. No scars or birthmarks. But he still did not invite Gorski inside.

'I'm sorry you've wasted your time, Inspector. I'm afraid Maman is quite gone in the head.' He circled his index finger to the side of his forehead to emphasise the point.

'Nevertheless,' said Gorski.

'Nevertheless what?'

'I'd like to speak with her.' He took a step closer to the threshold.

'I don't think that's such a good idea,' said Duymann.

Gorski firmly stated that whether he thought it was a good idea or not was neither here nor there.

Duymann appeared to recognise that there could be only one outcome to this minor stand-off. He shrugged and stood back from the door to allow Gorski in.

'You won't get any sense out of her.'

The two men stood too close to each other in the cramped hallway. Duymann cupped his hand over his mouth and breathed into it. Apparently satisfied that his breath did not smell, he surreptitiously wiped his hand on the thigh of his trousers.

Gorski observed him placidly. The man's discomfiture interested him, and he saw no need to alleviate it by speaking. It is in moments like this that individuals reveal themselves. We are all practised liars. Rare is the person incapable of improvising a fib or parrying unwelcome questions, but there are always tell-tale signs: the hand unconsciously placed over the mouth, the avoidance of eye contact, the redundant offers of beverages. Silence strips us naked, which is why people under duress habitually seek refuge by engaging in garbled chit-chat. Silence was the most potent weapon in Gorski's arsenal. All but the most habitual criminals crumble when faced with a lull in conversation.

This was not an interrogation, but what had begun innocuously had already become more intriguing. The most obvious conclusion one might draw from Duymann's gesture was that he was a secret tippler embarrassed to be caught drinking shortly after three o'clock in the afternoon. But the fact that his breath did not smell made the gesture more notable. Here was a man who, even when having done nothing wrong, acted as though he was guilty of something.

Upstairs, Gorski found Madame Duymann's bedroom to be quite unlike that of his own mother. Madame Gorski's room felt like a relic from an earlier age. It was barely big enough to house the brass bedstead and the oversized wardrobe in which, twenty years after his death, Gorski's father's clothes still hung. The oppressively patterned wallpaper, unchanged in forty years, was discoloured by decades of tobacco smoke. The windowsill and shelf above the bed were cluttered with ornaments of neither aesthetic nor monetary value. These gewgaws had once been diligently dusted, but each now bore a mantle of dead human cells. If Gorski had not taken it upon himself to clean these trinkets, it was because his mother would have experienced this as a kind of admonishment; an acknowledgement that she no longer had the will or inclination to carry out such chores.

As a boy, Gorski had never been explicitly forbidden from entering his parents' room, but he never did so of his own volition. He knew instinctively that this was a place where things that were not spoken of took place—he occasionally heard muffled noises through the wall—and when he was sent to fetch an item from the bedside table, he did so with the anxiety of a trespasser and lingered no longer than necessary. The room had a sour, metallic smell that caught in his nostrils and which, to this day, he associated with certain acts. Now that he was more frequently in his mother's room, he was less conscious of this odour. No doubt he had become inured to it.

There was no such smell in Madame Duymann's room. Here it was light and airy, but still Gorski felt ill at ease entering the bedchamber of an elderly woman. A large window overlooked the garden with the shed in which Gorski had found the missing tools. The wallpaper had a pattern of flowers in various shades of lilac, a colour scheme taken up by the bedspread and soft furnishings. Beneath the window was a faux Louis Quatorze dressing table set out with face powders and other cosmetics. On the bedside table was an array of brown medicine bottles, the sole point of commonality with his mother's room.

Madame Duymann was sitting up in bed, propped up by a number of embroidered pillows. Her eyes were alert, but the skin of her face and neck had grown loose, so that she resembled a newly hatched nestling. In the V of her nightdress, her clavicles protruded like wishbones.

'How nice of you to call, Inspector Gorski,' she said. 'What a pleasant surprise!'

Gorski gently reminded her that it was she who had telephoned the police station barely an hour before. The fact that she remembered his name, however, suggested that she was not as gone in the head as her son had insinuated.

'Yes,' she said. 'But I didn't expect you to arrive with such haste.'

'Given the allegation you made, I could hardly do otherwise.'

Madame Duymann had claimed that her son was going to murder her.

'Oh, it's not an allegation, Inspector. Just this morning he said he was going to fetch the spade from the shed and break my skull like an eggshell.'

She gave a sharp nod as if to assert the truth of her statement.

Gorski found himself glancing towards the floor, where Robert Duymann was likely pacing around below. There was something in the precision of the phrase she had used that lent it the ring of truth.

'And why would your son want to kill you?' he asked mildly.

'He's always hated me. He's trying to poison me. He insists on cooking all my meals, but I don't touch a thing.'

Just then she looked down and realised that her nightdress was loosely fastened. She gathered the garment around her neck with her left hand and glanced at Gorski with the expression of a mischievous schoolgirl.

'You must think me a terrible flirt, Inspector,' she said. Then she asked him to pass her a woollen shawl that was draped over the stool by the dressing table.

'He's already killed Bibiche,' she said, as she arranged it modestly around her shoulders. Bibiche, Gorski now recalled, was the name of the yapping dog.

'I see,' he said.

'He kicked her to death.'

Gorski looked at the old lady. The room was oppressively warm. He sat down on the edge of the bed.

'What are you going to do about it, Inspector?'

'I'll have a word with him,' he said.

'Can't you arrest him? I'm frightened.' Madame Duymann held out her hands in desperation and Gorski took them in his. Her grip was surprisingly strong.

He explained that he could not arrest her son without any evidence.

'But I've told you what he said to me.'

'Even so, I'm afraid—'

'So you're just going to wait until he murders me?'

Gorski shook his head. He did not doubt that Madame Duymann believed every word she said. 'Of course not,' he said. 'I promise you'll be perfectly safe.'

He wrested his hands from her grip.

Robert Duymann was waiting in the hallway at the foot of the stairs.

'I suppose she told you that I'm planning to kill her.'

'Yes,' said Gorski.

'I must apologise. As I said, she's completely gaga.'

'She said you threatened to smash her head in with a spade.'

At this Duymann gave a little snort through his nose. 'I'm sure we all say things we don't mean now and again.'

Gorski looked at him. He could not imagine saying such a thing to his own mother.

'She said you killed her dog.'

Another snort. 'The mutt had to be put down. It had cancer. It was shitting all over the house.'

Gorski nodded. It was a perfectly plausible explanation.

'Nevertheless, I'll call back in a day or two. Just to make sure all's well.'

He had no intention of doing so, but he had taken a dislike to Duymann and it did no harm to put him on his guard.

As soon as the door to the house on Rue Saint-Jean closed behind him, Gorski lit a cigarette. He stood for a few moments on the pavement, looking at the patch of grass which constituted the front garden. He wondered if Madame Duymann employed someone to cut it, or if her son carried out this task. He turned his back to the house and looked up and down the street. If he did not move off immediately, it was not because he was lost in contemplation, but rather that he wanted to unsettle Duymann. He was sure to be lurking behind the voile curtains. Why, he would wonder, was the cop not leaving? Perhaps he would think that Gorski was going to have the house placed under surveillance. Gorski finished his cigarette and dropped the butt through the slats of a drain cover. He turned and took a last look over the house, as if committing it to memory, before walking slowly off.

As he happened to be passing, Gorski dropped into Le Pot and took what had become his usual place. It was no longer necessary to order or even perform his little *une pression* mime. Yves brought his beer and wordlessly placed it on the oblong Formica table, which like the four others was bolted to the floor in front of the banquette. This was not a precaution against theft, but to prevent the inebriated from overturning them as they rose unsteadily from their seats. Le Pot was an establishment in which no judgement was passed upon those who chose to drink themselves into oblivion. Instead, measures were taken to mitigate the likely consequences of such behaviour. Gorski found this reassuring. Even to the regulars who attempted to engage Yves in conversation, no favour was shown. There were no tabs or drinks on the house here. In Le Pot, everyone was equal. If the communists ever took over, all bars would be like Le Pot.

Gorski took a mouthful of beer. There was no need to hurry

back to the police station. No pressing business awaited him there. His visit to the house in Rue Saint-Jean had unsettled him. He realised he had unthinkingly dismissed Madame Duymann's allegations. But in doing so, was he not guilty of a certain prejudice? That he regarded the claims of a bed-bound old woman as less credible than those of a younger, more vigorous person? If a young woman in one of the blocks in the vicinity of the railway station had alleged that her husband was threatening to do away with her, he would have been derelict in his duty if he had simply shrugged and left. Yet that was precisely what he had done. He had allowed his prejudices to determine his course of action. But what if he was mistaken, and in the coming days, weeks or months, Robert Duymann killed his mother, and it became known that the chief of police had visited the victim's home and taken no action?

There was, moreover, the awkward demeanour of the son, but he did not read too much into that. Even the most blameless individuals are apt to behave suspiciously in the presence of a cop. It was not a crime to be maladroit. Again, Gorski was obliged to examine his prejudices. Had he not taken against this fellow from the off? And this on account of being guilty of no more than the offence of wearing slip-on shoes. And yet, there was something incongruous about those shoes. They were too smart, too *dressy*, to wear around the house, yet Duymann did not appear to have just arrived home. Nor had he given any indication that he was about to go out. The word that had first attached itself to Duymann—*shifty*—could not be shaken off. Regardless of the questionable grounds of his dislike for Duymann, Gorski realised that having attended the incident, he would be obliged to follow it up: to do something.

He had finished his beer and looked up to catch Yves' eye. This was unnecessary as the proprietor had already spotted that his glass was empty and was drawing another beer from the tap. It troubled Gorski that Yves assumed he would take another, but he could not blame him. It was hard to say for sure, but it was doubtful that he had ever left Le Pot after a single glass. Certainly, he had not done so for months. Even so, it irked him to be taken for granted. He would leave after this beer. Or better still, throw Yves off by ordering something out of the ordinary: a marc or a glass of the rough cider which he sourced from a local farmer.

The beer was delivered and acknowledged with a brief nod of gratitude.

The corpulent hairdresser, Lemerre, came in. He glanced around but did not greet Gorski. If a notable case had made it as far as the pages of *L'Alsace*, Lemerre would not hesitate to furnish him with his theories, but otherwise he did not bother to exchange pleasantries. Instead, he unhurriedly drank the glass of wine set on the counter for him with a peeved air, muttering and shaking his head to himself. Of course, he was trying to lure the proprietor into asking him what was up, but Yves refused to take the bait. Lemerre was permanently disgruntled, and his conversation consisted entirely of enumerating the day's sources of aggravation.

When he had drunk two-thirds of his second glass, Gorski rummaged in his pocket for change. He made a neat stack of coins on the table. Naturally, he knew the exact price of a beer in most of the town's various hostelries. He rounded the sum up to the nearest franc, this being adequate acknowledgement of Yves' services, while not being extravagant enough to be regarded as flash. This early intervention was intended to communicate that he did not wish to have another. Had Yves supplied him with a third beer before he had set out his little stack of coins, Gorski would have accepted it. It was not that he did not want another beer. He would quite happily have sat there until the bar closed, but he wished to exert some control over the situation, or at least appear to do so. In any case, once he had left Le Pot he would pass the Café de la Gare, and it was reassuring to know that the option for one more was there should the fancy take him.

He lit a cigarette and took a long draw and watched the smoke coil up towards the rectangular window high in the exterior wall. Outside, the sky was beginning to darken. Gorski experienced this as a kind of relief. He did not like to be seen emerging from Le Pot in the hours of daylight. It was, in any case, too late to bother going back to the station. He would buy a couple of cutlets from the butcher on Rue de Mulhouse before returning to the apartment on Rue des Trois Rois.

The only other customer in the bar, a former schoolteacher who had left his post after an allegation of sexual misconduct, got up and left with the briefest of nods in Gorski's direction. This prompted Yves to emerge from behind the counter to collect his glass and wipe down the table. On his way back, he scooped Gorski's stack of coins into his hand and asked, 'Sure you won't have another?'

Gorski looked at him. For the sake of respectability he glanced at his watch, and then after a moment's consideration replied, 'Why not? One more can't do any harm.'

Yves nodded, as if he had known all along that Gorski would capitulate. He could not help feeling that he had lost a minor battle of wills. Yves waited for Gorski to finish his current beer before bringing the fresh one. To do otherwise would be unseemly, even in Le Pot.

Three

Gorski took a detour past the Hôtel Bertillon. He wanted the Slav to know he had his eye on him; that he was on his turf. It was an empty gesture, of course, as the visitor was nowhere to be seen. There was only the dimmest of lights in the foyer. Previously, the establishment had barely registered in Gorski's consciousness. Even a cop—whose trade it is to notice things—can struggle to describe the streets he walks on a daily basis. Whether one frequents the grand boulevards of Paris or the nondescript thoroughfares of a provincial town, we mostly go about our business preoccupied with the petty concerns of our lives, seldom raising our eyes from the pavement.

Gorski, in any case, disliked hotels and rarely had occasion to stay in one. The more attentive the staff, the more ill at ease he became. He did not enjoy having another man carry his suitcase. Not that the Bertillon was an establishment in which such services would be offered. It was a place for salesmen to hunker down for the night, or for a *cinq à sept* for couples too ardent to be concerned about the shabby surroundings.

In the first year of their marriage, Gorski and his wife had vacationed in Nice. When Céline had proposed a holiday, Gorski had dismissed the idea. Such a thing was out of the question on his modest salary, but she had laughed off his objections: 'Oh, I know that, silly,' she had said. 'Daddy will take care of it.' 'Daddy' was Jean-Marie Keller, at that time the town's deputy mayor.

Gorski had mumbled something to the effect that he wasn't sure he was comfortable with such an arrangement, but Céline affected not to hear him. 'You wouldn't want me spending the summer cooped up in boring old Saint-Louis, would you?'

In the event, Céline passed the month of August in a hotel, Le Negresco, on the Promenade des Anglais. Gorski joined her for the second fortnight and found that she had already established her clique among the guests. Her routine consisted of tennis in the morning, a light lunch, then an afternoon sunbathing and swimming on the beach, before an *apero* on the hotel terrace. In the evenings they dined with other couples staying at the hotel. The lingua franca of Le Negresco was English, and Gorski was obliged to laugh along at witticisms he did not understand. Whenever he replied to an enquiry about his profession, Céline would make it clear that his current role was only temporary and that her husband's ambitions lay in the law or in politics. Nonetheless, there were frequent jokes about a murder taking place in the hotel and Gorski assuming the role of Hercule Poirot or Inspector Maigret. Gorski felt obliged to point out that even if such a crime were to occur, it would fall under the jurisdiction of the local police, but his protestations were cheerfully ignored. He was no fun.

Gorski was not used to vacations. Aside from Sundays and national holidays, his father never took a day off. There were no relatives to visit, and a fortnight in a boarding house by the sea or a lake would have been well beyond his parents' means. He was not sure either of them had ever even seen the sea. He himself had never learned to swim.

Now with two weeks of empty days ahead of him, Gorski had not known what to do with himself. The mornings were straightforward enough. He could linger over breakfast and read the day's newspapers on the terrace overlooking the promenade. Céline did not object if he had a glass of wine at eleven o'clock, but she had to remind him that he did not have to apologise to the staff if he was 'in their way'. He was a guest. Sometimes, he watched her play tennis. She had an athletic, boyish figure and she played with gusto and determination. As in all things, she liked to win. Sometimes she took a lesson from the handsome professional, who would draw her hand aloft and place his palm against the small of her back while attempting to improve her service action.

In the afternoons, he refused to go to the beach. The idea of sitting practically naked with his torso slathered in tanning oil struck him as the sort of activity in which only men of certain inclinations would indulge. Accompanying Céline to the beach would, furthermore, have meant admitting that he could not swim. In their courting days, when they walked by the Petite Camargue to the north of Saint-Louis, Gorski dreaded the idea that Céline might suggest going for a dip. Often he hastened to the business of love-making solely to avoid this eventuality.

Instead, he took long walks along the esplanade. He watched weather-beaten anglers casting their lines from the harbour walls. He admired their capacity to pass hour upon hour doing nothing more than gazing at the water. Before he was required back at the hotel, he would enjoy a glass of beer or two at a backstreet café and watch the locals play boules. He bought a picture postcard and wrote to his parents, but he did not send it. Monsieur and Madame Gorski would not approve of their son squandering money on hotels and restaurants, and he would have been ashamed to admit that he was not paying for any of it. For them—and indeed for Gorski—the Riviera was a sort of mythical place; somewhere for other people. It was not for the likes of them, and those that tried to rise above their station in life only invited ridicule.

One evening, he persuaded Céline to take a drive along the coast. They dined in a tiny restaurant in a nearby village. 'If you die of botulism, don't come running to me,' she said cheerfully as they were shown to a rickety table. The waxcloth was sticky. A group of local men played cards at a table beneath the awning. They wore canvas trousers and straw hats. Their hands were misshapen from a lifetime's manual labour. Gorski felt embarrassed by the doughiness of his own hands. They were served sardines from the grill, then thick chops with cloves of garlic, rosemary and fat green olives. The wine was supplied in a carafe upon which the proprietor marked the amount consumed with a pencil. Once the alcohol took effect, Céline relaxed and set about the chops with her hands, allowing the juice to dribble down her chin. She giggled and leant over the table so that Gorski could see down the front of her blouse. They drank a second, then a third carafe of wine.

On the drive back, Gorski pulled the car into a layby among a copse of olive trees and clumsily kissed her. The tang of wine and herbs was still on her lips. The gearstick dug into his thigh. Céline was game. She undid Gorski's trousers and masturbated him, her face a study in earnest concentration. She seemed amused when Gorski discharged himself on her blouse, admonishing him in the manner of a stern schoolmistress. Gorski liked it when she called him a 'naughty boy'. Then she manoeuvred Gorski's hand between her legs and he roughly kissed her neck as she brought herself to a climax.

Afterwards they sat for some minutes while their breathing subsided, their clothing still disarrayed. Then Gorski turned the key in the ignition and drove back to the hotel. In their room, he tried to undress her. He was still aroused. Céline told him to get into bed and disappeared into the bathroom, but his ardour dissipated and by the time she emerged he had fallen asleep between the linen sheets which were changed daily by a heavy-set chambermaid who spoke only rudimentary French.

On the morning of their departure, as Gorski returned the key of their suite, the manager tactfully informed him that 'everything had been taken care of'. Gorski knew that this would be the case. A few days earlier he had caught sight of the hotel's tariff. His monthly salary would barely have stretched to a weekend in one of the most basic rooms. What made things worse than the supercilious smile on the lips of the manager was the fact that Céline had reminded him not to forget to leave a tip. Gorski had no idea what sort of amount would be appropriate. Nor did he understand the mechanics of how such a tip might be disbursed without embarrassment to one or both parties. Should he place some banknotes under the palm of his hand and slide them across the counter while looking the manager meaningfully in the eye? Or should he attempt to slip them to him in the course of a handshake? In the event, the manager asked affably if there was anything else he could do for him. Gorski put his hand to the inner pocket of his jacket, then touched his fingers to his forehead to suggest how absent-minded he was.

'Ah, forgive me, monsieur,' he said. 'My wife has my wallet. I believe she has just stepped outside with our luggage.'

The manager nodded graciously. Gorski made his way towards the entrance and slipped out, all the time making a show of looking for Céline. Needless to say, he did not go back inside.

When he returned to work, his colleagues made fun of him for weeks on account of his deep tan. Such displays of health and affluence did not go down well in Saint-Louis. Schmitt insisted on referring to him as 'the Negro'. Gorski bore all this stoically. His suntan would fade. In the meantime, he peppered his speech with coarse turns of phrase and made a show of smoking the cheapest brand of cigarettes.

The following year, the vacation followed the same pattern. Céline left at the beginning of August and by the time Gorski joined her, she was already tanned and had her routine and clique established. For the first time since they were married, Gorski wondered if she took advantage of his absence to fool around. Certainly there was no shortage of available men with whom she might enjoy a dalliance. As they ate dinner, he began to picture each of the men around the table in bed with his wife. It was not so much that he thought Céline had an insatiable sexual appetite, it was more that he could not imagine her putting up much resistance to any advances. She would think it vulgar to turn down sex on the grounds of 'being married'. Such scruples were the preserve of the petite bourgeoisie. It was clear that Céline could have done far better than him, so who could blame her if she now and again had some fun elsewhere? Still, Gorski struggled to banish such thoughts from his mind.

One evening, he and Céline were dining with an English couple two decades their senior. The Davidsons lived in a 'frightful pile' in Sussex and had been coming to Le Negresco for years. Mr Davidson did something in finance and dressed in the tourist uniform of blazer, slacks and deck shoes. Mrs Davidson spent the meal moving her hand up Gorski's thigh. By dessert she had reached his crotch. Later, as Céline was removing her make-up at the dressing table, Gorski told her what had been going on. She laughed and expressed the view that Mrs Davidson was still very beautiful. It was true that the Englishwoman was not unattractive, but Gorski felt no desire for her. He found himself wondering if, in the society in which he now found himself, he was expected to present himself at her bedroom door at a time when it was known that her husband was gone from the room. Of course, he did not do so, and as the fortnight wore on Mrs Davidson cooled towards him. Whether this was on account of Gorski's failure to fulfil her expectations or simply because he could not hold his own in English conversation, he did not know.

He did his best to take advantage of the attractions of Nice. He spent his days walking along the seafront, stopping at cafés for a snifter and to read a few pages of a novel picked up from the spinner in the foyer of the hotel. Now, as well as watching the old salts by the harbour, he became aware of the young women who sunbathed topless or in the skimpiest of bikinis. Of course, it would not do to linger in a spot where one might be thought to be deliberately observing these young women, but if, while strolling along the esplanade, one's eyes happened to alight on a young female body, one could hardly be accused of voyeurism.

He realised too that, as one ventured further from the seafront, there were certain narrow streets where altogether earthier women plied their trade. In Saint-Louis, Gorski was aware of one or two apartments in the nondescript blocks by the railway station in which certain services were available, but a degree of discretion was maintained. In a small town, neither those providing nor availing themselves of such services had any desire to advertise the fact. Here, however, there was no such need for furtiveness. Everything was out in the open and if, quite by chance, Gorski found himself among this labyrinth of alleyways, he experienced a quickening in his throat. The air was indolent, heavy with the odour of rotting food and marijuana. Gorski politely declined the coarse propositions of the women clustered in the shadows and kept his eyes, insofar as possible, fixed on the pavement. Often he could hear their laughter as he scuttled away. It was not that he had any moral objection to such transactions. It was more that he feared he would not be able to perform in the manner expected. Even so, he found himself getting lost in these alleyways more and more often. It was a relief, he told himself, to find some shade from the intense Mediterranean sun.

One evening, as he and Céline were preparing to go downstairs for dinner, Gorski suggested that they drive instead to the village they had visited the previous year. Whether from the intoxicating atmosphere of his afternoon stroll or from the couple of wines he had already consumed, he was feeling light-headed. Céline replied that the Davidsons and another couple were expecting them, but she did so without conviction and a few minutes later they were racing along the D559, laughing like a pair of schoolkids that had bunked off school. The little restaurant was unchanged. They sat at the same table and were brought the same food. Gorski drank more wine than before and when they left, Céline suggested that she should drive. Gorski would not hear of it. Céline shrugged. Perhaps the idea of dying in a car plunging from a coastal road appealed to her. As they approached the layby among the copse of olive trees, Gorski slowed the car. The windows were open and the heavy scent of mimosa and the Provençal earth caused his sex to stiffen. He glanced across at Céline, but her eyes were fixed on the road. She showed no sign of wishing to recreate the scene of the previous year. Nevertheless, Gorski pulled into the layby and started to kiss her on the mouth and neck. He fumbled with the buttons of her blouse, tearing one off. He was momentarily filled with a desire to force himself on her. Wasn't she always chiding him for being too passive? Then quite suddenly he realised how boorishly he was behaving. Céline fended off his advances with the efficiency of a governess dealing with an unruly pupil. There was still time, she said, to have a nightcap with the other couples on the terrace. She got out of the car and shoved Gorski onto the passenger seat. He meekly complied. She removed her heels and drove barefoot, throwing the car into the clifftop bends with abandon.

Back at Le Negresco, he pretended to pass out on the bed while Céline changed her blouse before going downstairs to enjoy what was left of the evening with the couples they had earlier snubbed. Through the open window, amid the sound of the cicadas, Gorski could hear their laughter from the terrace below.

The following year, Gorski was due to join Céline in Nice as usual but was prevented from doing so by the murder of a fifteen-year-old girl, Juliette Hurel, in the woods on the outskirts of Saint-Louis. And so the tradition was broken, but for the duration of their marriage, Céline continued to spend August in Nice at her father's expense. Their daughter, Clémence, would be left in the care of her grandparents, and for a month Gorski would experience a freedom of which he made no use.

Four

The little brass bell above the door to the florist's beneath his mother's apartment tinkled when Gorski entered. It was attached to the door by a pewter chain and dated to when the premises had been his father's pawnbroker's. The sound never failed to transport Gorski back to his boyhood, returning from school to the dimly lit shop with its special aroma of dust, varnish and cracked leather. Now the smells were quite different, but it remained the case that the apartment above could only be accessed via the staircase at the back of the shop.

Madame Beck had already turned the sign in the window to *Fermé*. She was sweeping petals and leaves into a pile. She always kept the shop immaculately tidy. A musty aroma of soil mingled with the heady perfume of cut flowers. Madame Beck was around forty-five. She had a slim willowy figure and a particular way of standing at her counter with her hip thrust slightly to one side. Her light brown hair was often dishevelled, and the crow's feet that had lately appeared around her eyes only made her more attractive. She stopped what she was doing and leant on her brush. She had a melancholy way of smiling at Gorski that suggested she understood exactly what he was feeling.

'Closing early?' he asked.

'I wanted to catch the greengrocer,' she replied.

Gorski was carrying a brown paper package from the butcher whose name he could never remember on Rue de Mulhouse. He briefly held it aloft to indicate that dinner was taken care of in the Gorski household.

'Cutlets,' he said.

She smiled at him. Then, casting her eyes towards the ceiling, said, 'She seems a little tired today.'

Madame Beck looked in on Gorski's mother once or twice a day. *Tired* was a euphemism they had come to use when referring to her state of mind.

When he entered the tiny hallway of the apartment upstairs, Gorski heard his mother call weakly from the living room, 'Albert? Is that you? I've been waiting for you.'

Albert was Gorski's father's name, but he had given up correcting her. It seemed a pointless cruelty to continually remind her that her husband had been dead for twenty years. He went into the poky living room and asked how she was.

'Oh, I'm fine,' she said, her tone more cheerful for seeing him.

At first it had troubled Gorski to play along with his mother's mental aberrations. He felt he was deceiving her and, worse, that by not correcting her, he was conspiring in her decline. Doctor Faubel had set his mind at rest. There was nothing to be gained by pointing out the truth. Such a strategy would do nothing to alter the course of her disease and would only serve to distress her. Gorski hated hearing the word 'disease' used in relation to his mother, but he had grown accustomed to going along with whatever gibberish issued from her lips. To do otherwise was, in any case, exhausting.

He realised, moreover, that with the passage of time, he had increasingly come to resemble his father. He had always shared his verbal tics, as is usual enough among family members, but since his own hair had begun to grey and the lines on his forehead had deepened, he could understand his mother's confusion. Perhaps this was what happened to all sons. They spent their youth rebelling against their fathers and their middle years returning to them, as if reeled in by an invisible cord. These days, were Madame Beck to give up the shop below, Gorski could think of worse things than reclaiming it and spending his remaining years haggling over pieces of bric-à-brac in a brown store coat.

He kissed his mother on both cheeks. The room was, as always, overheated. The electric bar fire, which burned from morning to night, made the air smell scorched. He had asked her many times not to sit so close to it, but as with all else she either forgot or simply did not heed his advice.

'I brought some cutlets.'

'I like a cutlet,' she said, but Gorski knew she would barely touch it.

He went into the kitchenette and uncorked the bottle of wine left over from the previous evening. He poured himself a glass and smoked a cigarette at the table in the living room. His mother's head drooped towards her chest. Her hair was thinning and unkempt. Tomorrow he would call Mademoiselle Huber and make an appointment to have her come and wash and set his mother's hair. It was the one thing that seemed to perk her up these days. He opened the window to allow a little fresh air into the room.

In the kitchenette, he peeled some potatoes and trimmed some beans before putting them on to boil. Then he fried the cutlets in butter with some salt and pepper, first setting them on their side to render the fat. It was only since he had returned to his childhood home that he had started to cook, and he found these moments at the stove served to empty his mind for a few minutes. It made him feel closer to his mother to stand on the spot where she had spent so much time that her slippers had worn away the pattern on the linoleum.

He laid the table and gently roused his mother.

'Time to eat,' he said.

She insisted that she hadn't been asleep.

He helped her from the armchair to the table.

'Cutlets! How lovely!' she said.

Gorski had cut her meat into small pieces and crushed three small potatoes with the back of a fork. She took a mouthful of lamb and chewed it in the leisurely manner of a cow at the cud. She still had a respectable number of teeth.

Gorski reached for the salt. The porcelain cruet set had occupied the same spot on the dining table for as long as he could remember. It consisted of matching salt and pepper cellars and a little mustard pot with a lid which had at some point been broken and glued back together. The original mustard spoon had been lost and replaced by a wooden one, the stem of which was too broad to allow the lid to close properly. Each piece bore the coat of arms of Haut-Rhin with its six crowns set on a scarlet background traversed by a band of gold. The three pieces sat on a saucer with indentations to keep each of them in their place. As a boy, Gorski had thought of these indentations as the pieces' homes, and at the end of a meal it had given him a feeling of deep satisfaction to return them to their rightful places.

For some reason Gorski believed the cruet set to have been a wedding gift, but aside from the fact that it had been there for as long as he could remember, there was no evidence for this. It could equally have been an item Monsieur Gorski had brought up from the shop, by way of a present for his wife. Monsieur Gorski had not been a man given to amorous declarations, and even as a boy Gorski had understood that it was through these little gifts that he communicated his affection for his wife. As a result, in the early days of his own marriage, Gorski had felt remiss if he did not once or twice a week present Céline with some trinket or a bouquet of flowers.

Gorski looked at his mother. She had finally swallowed her mouthful of meat and had set aside her fork. On the mantelpiece behind her shoulder was a photograph of his parents' wedding. His mother was not wearing a wedding dress, but a matching tweed skirt and jacket with a wide-collared white blouse underneath. His father was in a dark suit. It must have been a windy day, as his mother had planted her hand on top of her little hat and the hair around it blew loosely. His father's tie had blown over the shoulder of his jacket. They were looking into each other's eyes and laughing.

Once, when he was a teenager and his parents were gone from the house, he had, without quite knowing why, removed the picture from its frame. On the back of the photograph was written 'May 12, 1932', a mere six months before Gorski had been born. The Gorskis never celebrated their wedding anniversary, no doubt to avoid mention of this embarrassing circumstance. Gorski did not even know where his parents had been married, nor indeed where he had actually been born. He assumed he was a native of Saint-Louis. He *felt* that he was, and yet he had no evidence for this. No doubt his place of birth would be recorded on his birth certificate, but he had never seen this document. He assumed it was in the wooden coffer beneath the windowsill in which his father had kept papers deemed to be of a certain importance, but if he had never troubled to look for it, was it perhaps on account of a vague fear that he might turn out to be from elsewhere? That he might, in some sense, not be who he thought he was. Were he not a true son of Saint-Louis—a proper *Ludovician*—it would not seem proper to occupy the position of chief of police. He would feel like an impostor, with no right to hold a position of authority over his fellow citizens.

'Perhaps you would like a little mustard with that, Maman?'

She looked at him.

'With your cutlet,' he said. 'You've hardly touched it.'

'I'm full.'

Gorski nodded. He took a little mustard for himself. Unconsciously, he glanced at his mother as he did so. It was the sort of inadvertent gesture which, had it been made by a suspect, Gorski would have taken as an indication of guilt.

When he was eight or nine years old, the original porcelain mustard spoon had fallen to the floor. It was a delicate object, resembling the bone of a small animal. It had come to rest next to Gorski's shoe and he had, quite deliberately, put his foot on it and pressed downwards. As soon as he felt the tiny snap, he experienced a rush of an emotion he later learnt was called guilt. He did not know why he had acted as he did. It was a malicious impulse that he had not paused to suppress. He glanced from his mother to his father. They were oblivious to the crime that had taken place.

Gorski had forced himself to finish his meal, all the time keeping his foot on the broken pieces. Then, when his mother had gathered the plates and taken them to the kitchenette, he knelt down and under the guise of retying his shoelace slipped the shards of china into his pocket. His mother returned with the dessert, and it was only when this had been eaten and the table cleared that the absence of the mustard spoon was noticed. At first the search was quite calm—the little spoon could not have got up of its own accord and walked off!—but soon his parents became more mystified and agitated. Monsieur Gorski got down on his hands and knees and ran his hands over the rug. Perhaps it had somehow rolled under the sideboard. A torch was fetched from the shop downstairs, but nothing could be seen. Then Gorski's mother asked him, 'Have you seen it, Georges? It can't just have vanished into thin air.' He shook his head, but he felt his cheeks colour and placed his hand over his face in an attempt to conceal this manifestation of guilt.

The following day, on his way to school, Gorski made a detour along Rue du Temple and, having first ascertained that he was not being observed, dropped the pieces between the slats of a culvert.

For days the missing spoon was the sole talking point in the household. Eventually, the little wooden spoon was accepted as an imperfect replacement, but for what seemed years afterwards, Monsieur Gorski would shake his head in bemusement and wonder what had happened to the original. And even now, as he reached for the mustard, Gorski felt that his mother knew; that she had *always* known and had only lacked the evidence with which to confront him.

Gorski cleared the plates. Thankfully, Madame Gorski was still able to take care of her ablutions and ready herself for bed. Gorski was well aware of what would happen when that was no longer the case. He could not bear the idea of undressing his mother or helping her take care of her toilet.

He waited until she was installed in bed before slipping out. She would probably not sleep until he returned, but he found the thought of spending the evening in his father's chair intolerable. His parents had never owned a television set, and the idea of acquiring one for the apartment at this late stage did not seem appropriate. Gorski, in any case, did not like television. Instead, of an evening, if there was a case ongoing, Gorski would use that as an excuse to call on a witness or two. More often than not, he would drop in on a couple of the town's bars, assiduously avoiding any semblance of routine which might elicit tittle-tattle about the drinking habits of the town's chief of police.

The move back to his mother's apartment had been a purely short-term measure. Céline, he told himself, was sure to come to her senses. It had been through the act of separating, however, that Gorski had come to *his* senses. Their marriage had been a sort of conspiracy: they had colluded in the pretence that they were a happy couple. This act of denial had been partly to fulfil the expectations of their respective families, but it was also a way of avoiding the realisation that they were ill-suited and should never have married in the first place.

It had taken Gorski longer than Céline to comprehend this, but even now, in full possession of this knowledge, he would readily embrace the chance to return to their former charade. Gorski regularly heard colleagues or itinerant drinkers lament the constraints of married life, but now that he had his freedom, he had no use for it. What, for example, would he do if one day Madame Beck asked him to join her for a glass? Or if she confessed—as he suspected was the case—that her own marriage left her frustrated? Most likely, instead of grasping her shoulders and kissing her—as he had often thought of doing—he would foolishly brandish a parcel of cutlets and use his mother's dinner as an excuse to scurry away. 'Another time, perhaps,' he would say. But Madame Beck would take it as a snub and not humiliate herself by asking again. Even in his daydreams he was a spineless piece of work.

It was less demeaning to be deprived of one's freedom by an unhappy marriage than to admit that one lacked the mettle to make use of it.

On the first night back at his childhood home, Gorski had returned from Le Pot to hear his mother call his father's name from her bed. He closed the door and stood in the little hallway, barely daring to breathe, waiting for his mother's cries to subside. But they only grew more urgent and plaintive. She was weeping. Eventually he had pushed open the door of her bedroom.

'Maman,' he said tenderly.

'Albert,' she sobbed. 'I thought you'd gone.'

She held her hands out towards him, her fingers grasping the air.

Gorski took her hands and sat down on the bed beside her.

'It's all right,' he said. 'I'm here.'

Madame Gorski put her thin arms around him. He gently pushed her back against the pillows and sat with her for a while. Then, perhaps because he was a little drunk, he lay down beside her. He intended to remain only until she fell asleep, but he awoke in the morning lying next to her, one arm draped across her skinny chest.

Over the following week or so, a pattern emerged. Gorski would come home and climb into the bed in his childhood room. Then through the thin walls he would hear his mother sobbing or calling out to her husband. It was unbearable. Gorski gave up trying to sleep in his own room. At first, it felt wrong sleeping next to his mother, but as he had once read somewhere, *Man is a beast; he can get used to anything*. We are capable of justifying anything to ourselves. It was his own fault, Gorski told himself, for disrupting his mother's long-established routines. She was not used to having another person in the apartment. In any case, what harm was there in it? The situation was only temporary.

Naturally the subject of their sleeping arrangements was never broached. Madame Gorski always fell asleep as soon as Gorski climbed into bed next to her, and she was up and about long before he awoke in the morning. The old don't sleep much.

Five

The following morning, Gorski paused on the pavement outside the apartment and surveyed the street. It was a grey, chilly morning. He lit a cigarette. He had half-expected the Slav to be waiting for him on the corner, but of course he was not. It was a ridiculous thought: the stranger had no way of knowing where Gorski lived. A pair of schoolboys, satchels slung carelessly over their shoulders, made their way along the opposite side of the narrow street engrossed in conversation. The shoelaces of the taller boy were undone. It was only a matter of time before he tripped up, but Gorski did not alert him to the danger.

Madame Beck pulled up in the little van she used to make deliveries and bumped it onto the pavement. Gorski bid her good morning. It must have looked like he was waiting for her. She returned his greeting cheerfully, brushing a loose strand of hair from her face as she did so.

'Did you manage to catch the greengrocer?' Gorski asked.

'I'm sorry?' she replied.

'You said you were closing early to go to the greengrocer's.'

'Oh, yes. I did. Thank you.' She seemed bemused that Gorski saw fit to enquire about such an inconsequential matter. Or perhaps she thought he was trying to catch her in a fib. Either way, he regretted the question. His intention had only been to prolong the encounter for a moment or two.

'I'm glad to hear it,' he said idiotically, before wishing her a pleasant day.

On Rue de Mulhouse, the travel agent Vinçard was hoisting open the metal shutters of his shop. He spotted Gorski across the street and raised his hand. Gorski returned the gesture in a manner intended to suggest that he was a man with a hectic schedule who could not afford to dally.

At the police station, he proceeded briskly to his office, this to avoid becoming embroiled in small talk with his colleagues. He sat down behind his desk and leafed through his mail. There was nothing that demanded his attention. This demeaned him. A sense of purpose bestowed worth on an individual. He recalled an argument with Céline which she had concluded with the words, *What are you even for, Georges?* He had had no answer.

He could only hope that somewhere in Saint-Louis a crime was being committed, preferably a violent, dramatic one that would attract a decent amount of newspaper coverage. That was the sort of thing that impressed Céline. The law-abiding nature of Saint-Louis should, in theory, have been a source of satisfaction to the chief of police. But without some larceny or the occasional outburst of violence, Gorski had no function.

He picked up the telephone and placed a call to the Hôtel Bertillon. Virieu picked up on the second ring. He attempted to engage Gorski in small talk, but he cut him short and asked if his guest had already left.

Virieu asked which guest he was referring to. Gorski reminded him that he had previously said he only had one guest.

'That is no longer the case,' Virieu replied. 'Since we spoke the hotel has seen an increase in occupancy.'

Gorski held the receiver away from his face for a moment.

'I was referring,' he said eventually, 'to the gentleman who was the subject of our conversation yesterday.'

'Ah,' the hotelier replied. 'I haven't seen him leave, but as I explained yesterday, it's not my job to—'

Gorski put down the receiver. It was impossible to leave the building without passing Virieu's glass cage.

He had Roland sent to his office. When Gorski made his start as a uniformed officer, Ribéry had made a habit of pulling him from the rota to entrust him with an errand or accompany him to a crime scene. This led to ribbing from his colleagues, which although ostensibly jocular, revealed their resentment about the favouritism Ribéry showed him. This ribbing commonly took the form of insinuations about the men's sexuality, and Gorski frequently overheard Schmitt refer to him as Ribéry's 'bumboy' or simply as 'The Bumboy'. If Ribéry had been aware of any of this, he would have laughed it off or retorted with a more offensive slur. He was more than capable of holding his own in workplace banter, and when called upon to say a few words on the occasion of a colleague's retirement or similar occasion, he did so with humour and good grace. He was clubbable, and for this reason both his subordinates and the bigwigs in the town hall were prepared to overlook the fact that he spent his afternoons making the rounds of the town's bars. This, he explained to his young protégé, was in the service of intelligence-gathering. 'You will not find the riff-raff,' he liked to explain, 'in the boulangerie, the butcher's shop or on the pews of the Protestant temple. No, no, my boy, the riff-raff gather at the counter of the bar. And if that is where the riff-raff lurk, then that is where we must also lurk.' The conclusion of this sermon was invariably marked by the draining of his glass and a nod to the proprietor for a refill. The landlords of Saint-Louis never charged Ribéry a centime for his drinks. When Gorski replaced him, he was extended the same courtesy, but he declined these favours. No matter how innocently such gestures were intended, the chief of police could not be beholden to anyone. If Gorski had thought that the act of paying for his drinks would meet with the approval of the town's bar-owners, he was sorely mistaken. They resented him for it. He had broken the code that bound them together.

Roland shifted his weight from foot to foot. Gorski appeared to have forgotten he was there. He instructed Roland to take up a vantage point outside the Bertillon. 'I want you to follow the man I described to you yesterday.'

Roland was delighted by being entrusted with this important assignment. 'Can I ask what he is suspected of?'

Gorski shook his head, as if to suggest that he was not at liberty to say.

There was no justification for placing the Slav under surveillance. Gorski was not really concerned with what he was doing in Saint-Louis. It was more that he felt that this outsider had somehow got the better of him the previous day.

Roland asked if he should go home and change out of his uniform. Gorski told him that would not be necessary. Even in civilian clothes, Roland's presence would not go unnoticed. He lacked the experience to tail someone without being detected. That, however, was precisely what Gorski wanted. He wanted the Slav to know he was being watched; to be aware that he was on Gorski's turf and that it was he who was in charge.

With nothing more to distract him, Gorski's thoughts returned to his visit with the Duymanns. He typed up a rudimentary report. Unless Madame Duymann's allegations were vindicated, no one would ever read it, but that was not the point. He was following procedure. Furthermore, he felt that the writing of such reports somehow justified his existence. They constituted a tangible record of what he had done. He turned to the telephone directory. He had given himself no choice but to attempt to corroborate Robert Duymann's story about the dead dog. There were four veterinary clinics in Saint-Louis. He made a note of the addresses, pulled on his raincoat and headed out. It was as good a way as any of occupying himself until lunchtime.

Beiderbrecke & Son was located in the same building as the legal firm of Barthelme & Corbeil on Avenue Général de Gaulle, and as this was closest to the Duymanns' home, Gorski made it his first port of call.

The waiting room on the first floor was cramped and had a smell of hay and dung, an aroma that reminded Gorski of the summer he had spent labouring on a farm as a teenager. Torn posters advertised worming tablets and flea powders. Three plastic chairs were arranged against the wall opposite the counter. On the middle of these was a young woman with a cardboard box on her lap, her arms tightly clasped around it.

A middle-aged receptionist sat behind a glass partition, her hair secured in a tight bun. She showed no reaction when Gorski held out his ID. She had the air of someone from whom life had crushed any capacity to experience surprise. He asked if he could see Monsieur Beiderbrecke.

The receptionist perused the ledger and informed him that no appointments were available until the afternoon.

'It's a matter of police rather than veterinary business,' he said.

The young woman glanced up from her box. She pressed her lips close to the slat and murmured some comforting words to whatever creature was inside.

The receptionist stared at Gorski. He stared back. On her blouse she wore a brooch in the shape of a treble clef. Gorski imagined her at home in a gloomy parlour cluttered with antiquated junk, listening to Chopin and thinking of a young man she had once admired from afar. She probably lived with her mother.

Grudgingly, she said she would see what she could do.

The young woman shuffled onto the adjacent seat to make room for Gorski and gave him a wan smile. Gorski had never had a pet, even as a child. He had considered getting a cat as company for his mother, but she was now well beyond even looking after herself. In any case, she had never shown any particular liking for animals.

He asked the young woman what was in the box.

'It's my rabbit,' she replied in a forlorn voice. 'He's got a runny eye.'

'I'm sure the vet will sort it out,' Gorski said. He creased his face into the sympathetic expression he used when informing individuals of the death of a family member.

'I hope so,' she said and started to cry.

Some minutes passed. Gorski looked at his watch. It was quarter to ten. He was already thinking of lunch at the Restaurant de la Cloche, or more specifically of the *pichet* of wine he would drink.

The door to the surgery opened and a man with a huge black dog emerged.

The young woman wiped her nose with her sleeve and stood up.

The receptionist held up her hand, in the manner of a traffic cop. 'Did I call your name, mademoiselle?' she said rhetorically.

No matter how pitiful one's dominion, Gorski reflected, we are none of us able to resist the urge to indulge in a show of power.

She picked up her telephone and held a whispered conference with the vet. She put down the receiver and told Gorski that Monsieur Beiderbrecke would see him. The young woman looked imploringly at him. He imagined a scenario in which the rabbit's life could have been saved if it had been examined a few minutes earlier.

'You go first,' he said. He did not want a dead bunny on his conscience.

The young woman thanked him and cast a triumphant look at the receptionist. The consultation did not take more than a few minutes. She emerged with a look of relief.

Beiderbrecke was in his late fifties with thinning grey hair. He wore a white coat with well-established ink stains around the pocket. He was wiping down the examination table.

'How's the rabbit?' Gorski asked.

'It'll live.' He rested his knuckles on the table. 'To what do I owe the honour of a visit from our chief of police?'

'I wanted to know if you recently put down a dog belonging to a Madame Duymann of Rue Saint-Jean?'

The veterinarian seemed amused. 'Are you investigating the death of a dog, Inspector?'

'It relates to a wider investigation,' Gorski replied curtly.

'I don't remember seeing Madame Duymann for a while,' he said. 'But I remember the dog, a yappy little mutt. Bib or something.'

'Bibiche,' Gorski reminded him.

'Yes, that's it. I can't remember offhand the last time I saw it though.'

'But you'd remember if you'd put it to sleep?'

'I kill a lot of dogs, Inspector,' the vet replied with an air of great ennui.

'It would have been her son, Robert, who brought it in.'

Beiderbrecke shrugged. 'If I destroyed the dog, there'll be a record of it. You can ask Mademoiselle Cherville,' he said. 'But if you don't mind—' He gestured towards the door.

'Yes,' said Gorski. 'You have rodents to attend to.'

'I have my work, Inspector, and you have yours.'

Mademoiselle Cherville looked up the dog's record. It had been over two years since Bibiche had been brought in and then only for a routine renewing of vaccinations. There was no mention of cancer.

Outside, Gorski lit a cigarette and set off in the direction of the second practice on the list. It didn't necessarily mean anything. Robert Duymann could have taken the dog to any of the town's veterinary practices. Until Gorski had spoken to all of them, it would be premature to draw any conclusions. He glanced at his watch. Strictly speaking, it was too early for a drink, but as he was passing Le Café de la Gare, he stopped in for a snifter. He asked first for a packet of cigarettes and then, as if it was an afterthought, added, 'And give me a cognac. It's chilly out there.' He rubbed his palms together to emphasise the point.

The proprietor placed the drink and the cigarettes wordlessly on the counter. He was a large man with hooded eyes that gave him the air of a somnambulist. During the day the place existed mainly to sell cigarettes, service those who placed bets at the PMU counter* and cater to those having a quick schnapps or coffee on their way to the railway station. Unlike Le Pot, it was not a serious drinking den. One did not linger there.

Despite the fact that he had an open pack in his pocket, Gorski

---

* ***Pari mutuel urbain:*** the French system of placing bets on horse racing – ***translator's note***

unwrapped the cigarettes and lit one. From the counter, you could faintly hear the sound of passing trains. Gorski smiled ruefully. What was to stop him walking out of here and simply getting on a train? People disappeared all the time. Naturally his absence would be noted. Naturally, he thought wryly, it would be reported to the police. But no crime would have been committed and once it had been ascertained that he was not the victim of an accident or murder, there would be nothing to investigate. Would he even be missed? In due course a new chief of police would be appointed. His daughter, Clémence, might miss him for a short time, but in a few months she would be off to university and would rarely give him a thought. At la Cloche, his disappearance would fuel the gossip for a week or two, but it would soon be forgotten. His place on the banquette at Le Pot would be occupied by another solitary drinker. There was only Maman. Her mind was so far gone that it was unlikely she would comprehend what had occurred, but his departure would nevertheless have a profound effect on her existence. There would be no question of her remaining in the apartment. She would be taken away and incarcerated in a nursing home. Gorski imagined her crying out for him, pleading to be taken home. And that was that. If he did not walk out of the bar there and then and step onto the first train leaving Saint-Louis, he could think of nothing else to prevent him than this. He knocked back his drink and left.

By the time he arrived at the Restaurant de la Cloche, Gorski had resigned himself to the necessity of paying a return visit to the Duymanns. None of the town's veterinarians had any record of putting down Madame Duymann's dog.

He had given up struggling against *la patronne* Marie's desire to seat him at what had formerly been Ribéry's table. The feeling that he had allowed himself to slip into his predecessor's place troubled him. It was not that it mattered where he sat. Indeed, it made Marie's life easier if the regulars sat in their designated places. But he was left with the nagging feeling that he had failed to resist; that he had spent his life submitting to whatever course of action caused the least friction. He exerted no agency over his life. He subordinated his own desires to those of others, and every time he did so he eroded his sense of who he was. Each time he squeezed himself onto the banquette behind Ribery's table he became less of an individual. In a certain sense, he existed a little less.

During lunch service Marie did not herself take orders or bring dishes from the kitchen, but instead coordinated operations, directing the waitresses to any unattended guests and taking a moment to exchange pleasantries with the regulars. If la Cloche had been in Paris, she would have been called the maître d', but in Saint-Louis such a designation would be considered inexcusably pretentious. Her husband, Pasteur, never ventured from behind the counter. His temperament was ill-suited to the glad-handing and bonhomie required of front-of-house staff. Instead, his duties were limited to the dispensing of drinks and settling of bills, which, in order to facilitate the swift turnover of tables, was taken care of at the counter.

The waitress, Adèle, was working the tables on the other side of the room, so Gorski's order was taken by Marie's niece. This was always a relief. Adèle had once found herself the subject of a police investigation and although this was never acknowledged between them, it lent an awkwardness to their interactions. There was nothing of this sort with Marie's niece. She was a timid girl with uncombed yellow hair and pale blue eyes. Her name was Nathalie, but she was invariably referred to as The Niece. She had been working the lunchtime service for some time, but she had never cast off the harassed air of an employee on her first shift. She made no pretence of remembering orders, earnestly writing everything longhand in a spiral-bound notepad, the tip of her tongue peeping from the corner of her mouth. Gorski had never once witnessed Adèle address a word to her.

Gorski ordered the *fromage de tête* followed by *couscous marocain*. The *fromage de tête* was a departure from his usual order, but The Niece did not register even a flicker of surprise. When she had finished writing, she said, 'And a *pichet*!'

She glanced briefly at him from beneath her brow, as if she expected special praise for remembering this part of Gorski's order.

A single glass of wine was included in *la formule*, but Gorski was never charged extra for his *pichet*. He did not know if this was on account of his status or if all the regulars were afforded the same courtesy, but he knew better than to draw attention to the fact.

Gorski poured himself a glass of wine and unfolded his copy of *L'Alsace*. It was only when The Niece brought his *fromage de tête* that he looked up and saw the Slav at a table on the opposite side of the room. Adèle was taking his order, but as soon as she turned away, the Slav looked in Gorski's direction as if he had all the time known he was being observed. He inclined his head in greeting. Gorski nodded back. He could hardly do otherwise. He was disconcerted to find the Slav here in la Cloche, as if he was purposefully intruding on his territory.

Gorski turned his attention to his food. He regretted ordering the *fromage de tête*. It was a peasant dish. But had it not been for this very reason that Gorski had ordered it? To demonstrate that despite being the chief of police, he was not stuck-up. His father enjoyed nothing more than a slice of *fromage de tête* washed down with a glass of rough cider. But now, on account of the presence of the Slav, he felt that he was betraying his lowly origins. Why should it concern him what inference this stranger might draw from what he was eating? In any case, it was not even possible to see what he was eating from the other side of the room.

The Niece brought Gorski's main course before he had finished his entrée. Customers of la Cloche were expected to eat at the pace determined by the establishment. The Slav did not appear to be aware of this. He had tucked his napkin into the collar of his shirt and was consuming his meal at a leisurely pace.

At a certain point, the stream of customers abated. Marie took the opportunity to take a turn around the dining room. She paused to have a few words with Lemerre, who was at his table by the door, eating in his usual pig-at-the-trough manner. As she approached Gorski's table, he nodded in a manner intended to express that he was open to engaging in a little conversation. He wished it to be apparent to the Slav that he was a person of note with whom a few banalities would be exchanged. Marie continued in his direction but passed his table and took up the pole used to open the upper section of the window looking onto Rue de Huningue. As she rotated the pole which operated the window's mechanism, her backside was only inches from Gorski's face. When the operation was concluded, she did not turn and excuse herself or even acknowledge Gorski's presence, but carried on around the room, pausing here and there to enquire if everything was to her customers' liking.

Gorski fixed his eyes on his newspaper. He preferred not to know if the Slav had observed this humiliating spectacle. After a minute or so, he felt it was safe to look up. Marie was leaning over the Slav's table. Over the hubbub of the restaurant, Gorski could not hear their conversation, but she had the palm of her hand pressed to her bosom as if to express her pleasure at some compliment he had paid. Then he must have said something humorous or charming as Marie coquettishly tossed her head back and giggled like a schoolgirl. She patted the stranger on his forearm in playful admonishment. Gorski glanced towards Pasteur, who was observing this grotesque spectacle with similar distaste. As Marie moved away, the Slav turned his head very deliberately towards Gorski. His expression was neither smug nor triumphant. It did not have to be. It was sufficient to communicate that he knew that Gorski had witnessed what had occurred.

Gorski was confident that the odd drink during the day did not impair his abilities. Only the first drink of the day had any noticeable effect. After that, nothing. If anything, any subsequent drinks only made him feel him more solid. That was the word he used in his own mind: *solid*. He saw things with more clarity and felt more decisive. The idea of being inebriated on duty horrified him. He would certainly not tolerate any of his men indulging in such behaviour, but thankfully he seemed to be immune to the effects of alcohol. Even so, he would not necessarily have wished it to be known that after lunch at la Cloche, he had stopped off at Le Pot. And if, later on, he had entered the police station by the back entrance, it was not at all because he felt a little unsteady on his feet.

He summoned Roland.

'Well?' he said.

The young constable took out his notebook. He had made copious notes.

'Do you want to know everything?' he asked.

'Everything,' Gorski replied. 'It may be that some detail that seemed of no significance to you is of great importance.'

Roland nodded earnestly. He drew a deep breath, then began: '08.55: I take up position on the corner of Rue de Mulhouse opposite the entrance to Hôtel Bertillon. 09.10: Postman delivers mail. 09.12: Subject emerges from hotel. He is dressed in a brown suit and light-coloured raincoat. He is approximately five feet eight inches tall with—'

Gorski made a rotating gesture with his finger. 'I know what he looks like,' he said.

'You said you wanted to hear everything.'

Gorski conceded the point and told him to carry on.

'Approximately five feet eight, with neatly cut hair, greying at the sides. He was not wearing a hat or carrying a briefcase. Subject proceeds along Rue de Mulhouse. At 09.16, he enters the boulangerie. He buys something, a croissant or a pain aux raisins perhaps—I was too far away to see—and eats it while standing at the window of the shop.'

'Inside the shop?' Gorski asked. The boulangerie was across the road from the police station. Now and again Gorski purchased a pain au chocolat there for his breakfast.

'Yes, sir. Inside the shop.'

This was quite irregular. It was not the done thing to consume goods inside the boulangerie, but the man was a foreigner and could not be expected to understand the local customs.

'And where were you at this point?'

'I continued past the boulangerie, then crossed the road and took up a vantage point behind the shrubbery at the little park by the Protestant temple.'

Gorski nodded. Roland must have been there when he left the police station. He asked if Roland had seen him walk past.

'Yes, sir, I did.'

Gorski gestured for him to continue.

'Shortly afterwards, the subject emerges from the boulangerie and proceeds along Rue de Mulhouse in the direction of Place de l'Europe. He then turns right into Avenue Général de Gaulle. I was a little bit behind and when I turned the corner, I thought I had lost him.'

'Ah,' said Gorski.

'But then I spotted him in the Café des Vosges on the corner of Rue des Vosges.'

'I know where it is,' said Gorski curtly.

It was directly opposite Beiderbrecke's veterinary practice.

'He purchases a cup of coffee or tea, certainly a hot beverage of some sort, and sits down at a table in the window. After about twenty minutes, he leaves and walks back along Avenue de la Marne.' Roland turned a page of his notebook. 'He continues onto Rue de la Gare, where he remains among the trees at the edge of the car park for twenty minutes or so.'

'What was he doing?'

'He did not seem to be doing anything in particular. He smoked two cigarettes.'

And so it went on. Gorski could not fault the diligence with which his protégé had carried out his duties. Finally, when he reached the point at which the Slav entered the Restaurant de la Cloche, Gorski interrupted: 'Tell me,' he asked, 'what would your explanation of the man's movements be?'

Roland seemed embarrassed to answer. 'He appeared to be following you, sir.'

Gorski nodded. There was a brief silence. Then Roland added, as if suddenly emboldened, 'Actually, at some points, it was difficult to keep track of who was who.'

'How so?' Gorski asked.

'Just because you and he look quite similar.'

Gorski frowned. Perhaps there was a vague resemblance, but somehow the idea offended him, as if Roland had called into question his individuality.

'What about his nose?' he said.

'His nose, sir?'

'Yes, his nose. It's flattened like a boxer's.' He demonstrated by pressing his own nose to one side.

'Yes, I see what you mean. Now you look even more alike.'

Gorski waved him away. What did it matter if they resembled each other? It was of no consequence.

Six

When Gorski arrived home, Clémence was already in the apartment, setting the table for the evening meal. She found it easier to busy herself with a chore than attempt to engage her grandmother in conversation. She greeted her father warmly, relieved that he had arrived. He kissed her, conscious of the beery smell on his breath. Gorski went into the kitchenette and splashed water on his face, then dried it with a dishtowel draped over the handle of the oven.

Clémence looked skinny. She bore no resemblance to her grandmother, who had coarse features and thick ankles. Physically, Clémence was very much a Keller. She had the same slim boyish figure as her mother. There were dark circles under her eyes, but he knew better than to pass comment on her appearance.

He crossed the room and kissed his mother.

'Clémence is here,' she said.

'I see that,' said Gorski. He apologised for being late.

Madame Gorski described how during the afternoon two well-dressed young men had broken into the apartment and stolen all the cutlery. They had been Americans. Gorski pulled open the drawer in the sideboard and showed her that the knives and forks were still there.

'Well, they must have brought them back,' she said with irrefutable logic. 'None of it's worth anything. I don't know why they would have taken it in the first place.'

Clémence and Gorski exchanged a rueful smile.

'I brought sea bass,' Clémence said in a cheerful tone. 'And some fennel.'

'Fennel?' he said. 'I'm not sure I know what to do with that.'

Clémence made a flatulent sound with her lips. 'Don't ask me!'

She couldn't cook and had no interest in learning. Gorski vaguely understood this to be a matter of principle. Whatever the reason, it was this disinclination that had given rise to this weekly ritual: Clémence brought some ingredients and Gorski made dinner. He was grateful for these visits. Officially, Clémence was coming to see her grandmother, but this was no more than a pretext.

The fish was on the worktop of the kitchenette. Fronds of fennel sprouted from a cone of newspaper. Gorski picked it up and put it to his nose. The aniseed aroma reminded him of something. Pastis, of course, but there was something else. He passed it to Clémence. She inhaled deeply. 'Le Midi,' she said. Yes, of course, Marseille, the villages along the coast from Nice. It was a smell from elsewhere.

'Maman,' he said, brandishing the foliage in her direction, 'what should I do with this?'

'What is it?' she croaked.

He brought the vegetable across the room and held it inches from her face. Her eyesight was beginning to fail.

'Fennel,' she said without hesitation. 'Braise it, you idiot. Braise it!'

Gorski looked at Clémence. 'I think I'll braise it,' he said. They laughed.

He poured two glasses of wine. Clémence stood in the doorway and watched her father get to work. He turned on the oven, then seasoned the fish with salt and pepper. Clémence pointed out that there were potatoes as well. He hadn't noticed. He put a pot of water on to boil.

He unwrapped the fennel and looked at it with exaggerated puzzlement. He took a knife and trimmed off the feathery tops. Then he cut the bulbs into quarters.

He looked to Clémence. 'What do you think?'

She shrugged. He set a roasting tin on the hob and poured in a glug of olive oil. He crushed a few cloves of garlic with the blade of the knife and threw them into the oil. The fennel followed. Secretly, he knew what he was doing. He had seen his mother do it often enough. He was not sure that anything had ever given him more pleasure than that moment: tossing fennel and garlic into the sizzling oil while his daughter looked on.

He gave it all a grind of pepper, then, adeptly opening the oven door with the toe of his shoe, shoved in the tray, before kicking it shut.

'Nice work, Pops!' said Clémence.

Gorski concealed his emotions by taking a swig of wine. He loved it when Clémence called him Pops.

The potatoes were chopped and deposited in the pot of boiling water. Now there would be a hiatus before the fish could be cooked. He and Clémence looked at each other. She retreated from the doorway.

'Perhaps your grandmother would like a little wine,' he said.

Clémence poured some into a tumbler and brought it to her grandmother. While her back was turned, Gorski refilled his own glass.

When they eventually took their places at the table, Gorski was pleased with his efforts. The fish was tasty and the fennel nicely browned at the edges. He placed a small portion in front of his mother.

'Thank you, Albert,' she said.

The first time Clémence had heard her grandmother call Gorski by his father's name, she had instinctively corrected her, but of course it had done no good. Now she too played along, as if everything was normal. And because they pretended it was normal, it had become so.

Now that there was no other activity to distract them, Clémence chatted. She told them about some minor incidents at school. A boy had been suspended for reading passages by the Marquis de Sade aloud in the assembly hall. A teacher's car had been sprayed with paint. She and her friends had formed a study group. She was worried about not getting the grades she required in the approaching *bac*. She was planning to study philosophy in Strasbourg. Gorski knew nothing about this subject, but he approved of her plan. He understood that she had to escape Saint-Louis, but Strasbourg was not so far. Perhaps she would still visit now and again.

She described her progress and difficulties in various subjects. Gorski was aware that she was performing for the benefit of her grandmother, regardless of whether she was able to follow anything that was said. In the past, when Gorski and Clémence had been required to dine alone, they had mostly done so in awkward silence.

He was relieved that his daughter had not inherited his lack of social graces. From what he could gather, she was popular at school. In this respect she was her mother's daughter. Céline could talk to anyone. She could charm anyone. And she was beautiful. It was a mystery to Gorski that she had, at least for a time, seemed to have been so taken with him. Even as a boy he had had difficulty making friends. At school he had observed his classmates congregate in their cliques in the playground. He had no idea how one gained entry into these mysterious factions. It was not that he was explicitly excluded. It was more that he seemed to be invisible. His peers simply did not notice him. Once, in the latter years of elementary school, a new boy had joined the class mid-term. There was nothing exceptional about him, and yet by the end of the week, he was in a huddle in the playground, haggling over picture cards of football players.

Gorski wondered if his exclusion was on account of his unusual name, but plenty of other kids had funny-sounding names and it did not appear to impede their acceptance. He wondered if his difficulties stemmed from being an only child, but again, he was not alone in this affliction. There did not appear to be any explanation, and after a while he accepted that he was destined to be an onlooker rather than a participant in life. Later on, he wondered if this was why he had become a policeman: that he had chosen a profession in which the ability to remain on the margins and observe a situation was an asset. He had not realised that becoming a policeman would further exclude him from society. People do not like policemen. They do not like to be around those who, as they see it, make it their business to snoop on them.

When he was thirteen or fourteen, Gorski finally befriended a boy named Jiři Holub. He had arrived from Czechoslovakia and spoke French with a heavy accent. His name meant 'pigeon' in his own language, and so that was what Gorski called him. Perhaps on account of the merciless ribbing he received, Pigeon had developed a stutter, but as Gorski was not much of a conversationalist, this was no impediment to their friendship. It was not that Gorski particularly liked Pigeon, and he did not know if Pigeon actually liked him. But they recognised the mutual benefit of sticking together. At weekends they took walks in the woods around the Petite Camargue or fished in the canal that runs between Saint-Louis and Huningue.

The friendship was to come to an abrupt end when they were sixteen. The two boys were sitting on a bench in the little park by the Protestant temple, doing no more than scuffing their feet in the dirt. A girl named Janet Hassemer appeared with her friend Isobel Arnaud. Janet was a tall, flat-chested girl, with a long, slender neck that Gorski often admired as he sat behind her in history class. She stood with her hand on her hip and one foot resting on its heel.

'I don't know why you hang out with st-st-st-stutterer here, G-g-g-gorski,' she said.

Gorski looked at Pigeon. He was blushing at the mere presence of the two girls. Gorski realised that any benefit he had derived from their alliance was at an end. It was time to jump ship.

'I've been asking myself the same question,' he said.

'So?' said the Hassemer girl. She tipped her head in the general direction of the town centre. 'Coming?'

Gorski got up and followed the girls. 'Catch you later,' he said to Pigeon.

Pigeon never spoke to him again. Gorski's betrayal bought him no more than the privilege of walking the girls as far as the café on the corner of Rue des Vosges, where they made it clear that he was not welcome to join them. Aside from an unfortunate incident at a party a couple of years later, that was the extent of Gorski's relationship with Janet Hassemer. Isobel Arnaud now lived on Rue des Trois Rois and they sometimes passed one another in the street. If she remembered him from school, she did not acknowledge it. Perhaps she too was shamed by her role in this episode and preferred to pretend that it had never happened. After he left school, he never saw Janet Hassemer again. Most likely she had moved away.

In the months after their falling out, Pigeon's silence weighed heavily on Gorski. It came as a relief when he heard that he had been killed when his father's car stalled on a level crossing outside the nearby village of Bartenheim.

Madame Gorski's chin had slumped to her chest. Clémence and Gorski both noticed this at the same moment. Perhaps she had been asleep for some time. She had at least eaten a reasonable amount of food. For a while they continued the conversation as if nothing was amiss.

'How's my friend Walter?' Clémence asked.

'Walter' was Sergeant Schmitt. When she had been a little girl, Gorski would occasionally take his daughter into the station to show her his office. Schmitt kept a bag of caramels under the counter at the reception and he would make her guess which hand he held one in. If she chose incorrectly, he would theatrically produce a sweet from behind her ear and present it to her. As a result, Clémence was fond of him. She thought he was funny.

'His usual grumpy self,' Gorski replied.

Gorski, for his part, relayed some minor details from his week. Clémence laughed when he told her he had been reduced to investigating the suspected murder of a lapdog. She pressed him for more details.

'Duymann?' she repeated. 'The writer?'

Gorski shrugged. He hadn't asked what the man did for a living.

'Robert Duymann?' she asked.

'That's him.'

'He's famous. Or he was. I thought he was dead.'

'He's alive and well and living with his mother in Rue Saint-Jean.'

Duymann, Clémence explained, had written a novel set in Saint-Louis, but she could not remember the title. She was not sure if he had ever written anything else.

'I'll ask him next time I see him,' said Gorski.

Madame Gorski woke with a start. Gorski got up and helped her back to her armchair. Clémence cleared away the plates. Now the roles were reversed. Gorski watched as she washed the dishes and cleared up the mess he had made in the kitchen. This was the final act in their weekly ritual. Once the dishes were put away, Gorski would run her back to the house on Rue de Village-Neuf.

Gorski poured the last of the wine into his glass. As she scrubbed the tin in which the fennel had been cooked, Clémence said in an offhand manner that she had been chatting to Madame Beck downstairs.

'She's nice,' she said.

'Yes, she is,' Gorski agreed.

Clémence looked up from her scrubbing. 'She told me what a nice man you are.'

'She did?' Gorski felt the colour rising to his face and touched his glass to his cheek. He often felt that he was intruding on Madame Beck's domain when he traipsed through her shop on his way in and out of the apartment. At other times he felt that his attempts to make conversation fell flat. He did not know what to make of this information, and he could not help but feel that Clémence had some motive for passing it on.

They sat for a few minutes outside the house on Rue de Village-Neuf. Céline's BMW was in the drive. Clémence asked him if he wanted to come in and say hello.

'Probably best not,' he said.

She thanked him for dinner. Gorski thanked her for coming. He would have liked to tell her how much her visits meant to him, but he did not do so.

'See you next week?' he asked.

She nodded. He watched her walk up the path to the front door. She turned and waved as she let herself in.

Seven

An ambulance idled in the pot-holed car park of the concrete factory on the outskirts of Saint-Louis. The siren that had announced its arrival had been switched off, but the blue lights continued to rotate. Two paramedics stood smoking by the rear doors. The need for urgency had passed. Fat drops of rain splatted into the puddles.

Gorski climbed the breeze-block steps into the prefabricated cabin which served as the factory owner's office. Inside, the walls were plastered with year planners and out-of-date calendars with photographs of young women in varying states of undress. Every surface was strewn with papers, empty glasses and coffee cups. Over-stuffed ring-binders spilled their contents onto the floor. Had he not visited the premises on a previous occasion, Gorski would have assumed the place had been ransacked.

Marc Tarrou had fallen backwards onto a smoked glass coffee table, the tubular metal frame of which had collapsed, so that it cradled his body in an asymmetric 'M'.

Roland, who Gorski had brought along to take photographs, loitered by the door. The only other person present was Doctor Faubel, who had pronounced the victim dead fifteen or twenty minutes before.

Gorski asked who had found him.

'The secretary,' Faubel replied. He was standing by one of the small windows, filling his pipe.

A young woman in a short skirt and knee-length white boots huddled outside under a transparent dome-shaped umbrella.

Faubel was nearing retirement and could not be relied on to

be either observant or conscientious in the performance of his duties. Despite this, Gorski asked if he had noted any external injuries to the victim.

'Looks like a heart attack to me,' he replied, tamping down the tobacco in the bowl of his pipe.

Gorski was glad no one else was there. He disliked going about his business under the scrutiny of a crowd. Thanks to novels and television shows, onlookers these days believed themselves to have some expertise in police procedure, and Gorski sometimes found himself acting in imitation of his fictional counterparts in order to fulfil the expectations of his audience. But there was no need for any of that on this occasion. Faubel was entirely occupied with getting his pipe going and was, in any case, entirely unconcerned. Roland, on the other hand, observed him with the fervour of a neophyte.

Gorski set about his inspection of the scene in his usual methodical way. Tarrou's right hand rested on his chest; his left was above his head as if he had been staggering backwards to catch a ball. The body was still warm. He was dressed in a royal blue suit with a sheen to the fabric. His shirt had come untucked from his trousers, the flies of which were half-open. He was only wearing one shoe. The other, a grey patent-leather slip-on, lay two or three feet from the body.

There was no bruising around the face or neck. Nor were there any abrasions around the wrists or ragged fingernails. His clothing was not torn. There was nothing to indicate that there had been a struggle. Even so, there was something curious in the positioning of the body.

'This is exactly as you found him?' Gorski asked.

'Well, he hasn't moved since I got here.'

'Would you say that this is a usual posture for a man who has suffered a heart attack?'

Faubel turned from the window. 'Sorry?' he said.

'It looks as if he might have been pushed. As if he was propelled backwards with some force.' He held his left hand above his head in imitation of the dead man and took a couple of steps backwards.

Faubel stared at him blankly. 'People having heart attacks generally fall over,' he said drily.

Gorski stood back from the body. Faubel was probably right. There was no reason to suspect that anything untoward had taken place. People drop dead all the time, whether at work, at home or in the street. In the end, all bodies cease to function and generally require no outside interference to do so. They carry around the source of their own demise for years, the clogged arteries, the lurking embolism, the predisposition to cancer. In most cases, it's a miracle they function for as long as they do.

Was there even any real reason for Gorski to attend such an incident? In all likelihood, no crime had been committed. Nevertheless, it was his role to determine whether that was the case: to perform the administrative task of declaring that no foul play had occurred; that the individual in question had expired of natural causes, and there was thus no reason for alarm among the citizenry. For sure, he could have delegated the task to a minion, but Tarrou was a bigwig, well connected to the worthies of the town. The death of such a personage is not treated in the same way as a down-and-out found dead from exposure by the railway tracks. The idea that everyone is equal in the eyes of the law is a fairytale, even in death.

Gorski had previously encountered Tarrou in the course of his investigation into the death of a local lawyer, Bertrand Barthelme. He had clearly been a man of big appetites, the sort who would habitually be described as larger than life. Now, sprawled limply on the floor of this draughty prefabricated hut, it was strange to see what little was left of him.

Gorski indicated to Roland that he could start taking photographs.

'If you don't need me, I'll be on my way,' Faubel said. His pipe was filling the Portakabin with a dark nutty aroma that never failed to remind Gorski of his father.

He asked the doctor to have the post-mortem report sent over as soon as possible.

As Roland went about his business, Gorski took a turn around the office. He could not imagine working amid such disorder. It would be impossible to tell if some incriminating item of paperwork had gone missing.

He made sure Roland did not neglect the kicked-off shoe. It leant a minor note of drama to the scene.

'Details,' he said. 'It's the details that are important.'

Roland nodded earnestly, committing this nugget of wisdom to memory.

Outside, the secretary was hopping from foot to foot to keep warm. A crowd of employees had gathered on the opposite side of the car park. The factory was an ugly affair of recent construction. There had been some objections when it had been built, but these had been summarily dismissed by the powers that be. No doubt the correct palms had been greased. And in any case, the area needed the jobs.

Gorski told the paramedics they could remove the body. Despite the rain, he did not think it wise to invite the secretary back inside and question her while they went about their business. He lit a cigarette and offered her one. She was an attractive girl of about twenty or twenty-one. From what Gorski knew of Tarrou, it was probable that he was in the habit of employing pretty girls.

He asked her name.

'Anna Petrovka,' she replied.

'And you found him at what time?'

A sob rose in Mademoiselle Petrovka's throat. Then the tears came. Gorski waited patiently. He did not have a handkerchief to offer her. She dried her eyes and then wiped her nose on the sleeve of her coat. Her blonde hair fell across her face. She brushed it aside, then drew on her cigarette and forced out a little laugh.

'I don't know why I'm crying,' she said. 'I didn't even like him.'

She glanced up at Gorski, as if concerned that he would disapprove.

'Me neither,' he said to reassure her. 'If you could just tell me when you found him.'

She looked at her watch as if the time would somehow be recorded there. 'I couldn't say exactly.'

'Not to worry,' Gorski said gently.

He asked instead when she had last seen him alive.

'When I arrived this morning, I took some dictation and then went back to my desk to type it up. That would have been about half past nine.'

'So your desk is elsewhere?'

She gestured towards the main building.

'And you didn't see him again until you called for the ambulance?'

'Nope.'

'Had he complained of feeling unwell?'

She shook her head. 'He was his usual self.'

The paramedics emerged with Tarrou's body. There was a kerfuffle as they manoeuvred the stretcher through the narrow door. Roland stepped in to lend a hand. The onlookers gathered in the car park inched forward to get a better view.

Gorski asked Anna Petrovka to show him where she worked.

Her desk was in an open-plan office on the ground floor of the main building. The windows overlooked the car park, but from where she sat it was not possible to see Tarrou's cabin. She had worked at the factory for a year and half. Tarrou had interviewed her himself. She had shorthand and could type eighty words per minute, but he had not seemed overly interested in any of that. Anna could not recall if she had left her desk during the course of the morning, but she was certain she had not seen anyone enter Tarrou's office.

'But someone could have visited without you knowing?'

'I suppose so,' she replied. 'People came and went all the time. Women, a lot of the time. I suppose that's why he kept his office separate from the main building.'

'You said you didn't like him,' Gorski said.

She seemed reluctant to repeat her earlier assertion.

'Why was that?' he persisted.

'You know how men are.'

'Well, not really,' he said.

'He was all hands. Always trying to touch you up.'

'I see.' Knowing what he did of Tarrou, it hardly came as a surprise.

'If I told him to keep his paws to himself, he would just laugh and tell me that if I didn't like it, I should find another job. It was a kind of game for him to see how far he could go. Some of the other girls just played along. Maybe I'm a prude.'

Gorski shook his head.

'You said before that women would often visit his office. You mean for the purposes of business?'

'Depends what you mean by business.'

'So they came to … to have sexual relations with Monsieur Tarrou?'

She looked at Gorski as if he was slow in the head. 'Uh-huh.'

'Did you ever—?'

'Catch him at it? Now and again.' She shrugged as if to suggest that such behaviour was perfectly normal. 'He liked to tell me he was a dirty dog. He thought it was funny if I walked in.' She made a face.

Gorski remembered now. A '*marseillais* mongrel' was how he had described himself when they had met before. Perhaps a disgruntled husband had paid Tarrou a visit and a struggle had ensued.

He took down Mademoiselle Petrovka's address and advised her to take the rest of the day off. She started to explain that there were more letters to be typed up, before stopping herself.

Outside, the ambulance had gone. It was only at this point that Gorski noticed his father-in-law, Jean-Marie Keller, on the far side of the car park, leaning against the door of his BMW. Gorski made a point of having a word with Roland before making his way over. He did not want to give the impression of being at the beck and call of the mayor. The two men shook hands silently.

'Is it a matter for the town hall?' Gorski asked.

'Is it a matter for the police?' Keller replied.

'It might be.'

Keller lit a cigarette.

'So you just happened to be passing?' said Gorski.

'Tarrou was a pal. I thought I should come and see what was going on.'

Gorski did not ask how he had heard of his friend's demise.

'Faubel called me,' he said, as if reading Gorski's mind. 'He didn't seem to think it was a police matter.'

'Faubel!' said Gorski. 'Hardly a byword for diligence.'

'Unlike yourself, Georges. But I don't think there's anything to get your knickers in a twist about here.' He patted him on the upper arm. 'There's a good chap!'

He got into his car and drove off, splashing pale clay mud onto Gorski's trousers. Gorski took a series of slow breaths, before returning to where Roland was waiting. He instructed him to call the station and have a couple more men sent down. On no account was anyone to be allowed to enter Tarrou's office.

A huddle had formed around Anna Petrovka, who had emerged from the building. She was clearly enjoying her status as an authority on what had happened. Gorski instructed Roland to tell the employees that they were to return to the main building and not leave until they had been questioned. With the crowd dispersed, Mademoiselle Petrovka trotted across the car park towards a bashed white *deux chevaux*. Gorski followed her and knocked on the passenger side window. She leant across and let him in. The seat was damp and he shifted his weight.

'Sorry,' she said. 'It leaks.'

The floor at Gorski's feet was littered with soggy cigarette packets. He asked her if she could drop him off in town. The little Citroën lurched across the rutted car park. She halted at the exit and started to rummage in her bag. Gorski lit two cigarettes and handed her one. She leant over the steering wheel, her face almost touching the windscreen before pulling out onto the A35. The interior filled with smoke.

'I was wondering if you recognised the man I was speaking to just now in the car park,' Gorski asked.

'The mayor?' she replied. 'Of course I recognise him.'

'Because you've seen his picture in the paper?'

'Because he's here all the time.'

Anna Petrovka drove with the fingertips of her left hand lightly resting on the lower part of the steering wheel. Her right hand was reserved for smoking and occasionally grappling with the gear lever. Slowing down to take a corner did not seem to occur to her.

'What do you mean by "all the time"?'

'Once a week. More sometimes. He's as bad as Monsieur Tarrou. Worse, in fact.'

'In what way?'

'For touching you up. Making remarks. A creep.'

This was not a side of his father-in-law Gorski was familiar with.

'And what did he and Monsieur Tarrou have to talk about?'

She blew out a long plume of smoke. 'I couldn't tell you. Deals, I suppose. I didn't pay much attention.'

'What sort of deals?'

'Oh, I don't know. They would stop talking if I came in. Or they would change the subject.'

Gorski nodded. 'And did Monsieur Tarrou keep any money on the premises? Large amounts of money, I mean.'

'I wouldn't know. I mean, I never saw any.' It was the sort of answer people gave when they wanted to conceal something or were afraid of revealing something they shouldn't. 'There's a safe in a compartment under his desk,' she added.

'And what did he keep in there?'

'No idea.'

Gorski asked if she knew the combination. She didn't.

She took the roundabout at the Hôtel Bertillon without lifting her foot from the accelerator. Gorski asked her to drop him outside the police station. She pulled up in a screech of brakes. Gorski thanked her and got out, but he did not go inside. He waited until she had pulled away before heading to Le Pot.

There, he downed his first beer in two or three swallows. Yves wordlessly brought him another. That was the thing about Yves. He didn't care how plastered anyone got. There were no chummy remarks. No *You must be thirsty today, monsieur.* As long as his customers could pay for their booze, it made no odds to him if they collapsed in the gutter outside. The pavement was beyond his jurisdiction. The only other person in the bar was the former schoolteacher who had left his position after a pupil had made some unsavoury allegations. They had exchanged a rudimentary nod as Gorski took his place on the banquette.

Gorski was in good spirits. Something had happened. Something important enough for the town's mayor to feel compelled to make an appearance at the scene. Had it not been for Keller showing up, Gorski might have thought no more about it. In all probability, Tarrou had died of natural causes, but until that was confirmed, there was no harm in indulging in a spot of conjecture. Indeed, was it not his duty to keep an open mind? Something about the whole incident bothered him. If he could not yet put his finger on what it was, that did not mean his concerns should be dismissed. He imagined Ribéry mocking him: *What you are experiencing, my boy, is a hunch.* He was right. At this point it was no more than a hunch, but until he was presented with evidence to the contrary, it was perfectly legitimate to entertain the hypothesis that something untoward might have occurred.

He took a sip of his second beer, lit a cigarette.

He enumerated what he knew.

A man in apparently good health had been found dead. The doctor attending the scene had felt the need to inform the town's highest-ranking official, who had then in turn seen fit to turn up at the scene and pronounce that the affair did not concern the police. Then there was the odd position of the body, the loose shoe, the unfastened flies of the victim's trousers. Perhaps a female visitor to the Portakabin had taken against his advances and shoved him backwards. While this could not be ruled out, it seemed unlikely. Tarrou was a sizeable, vigorous man and it would have taken a powerful individual to overcome him. From that point of view, the idea that there might have been a scuffle with a disgruntled husband was more plausible, but in neither case was it likely that such a confrontation would have proved fatal. It had to be borne in mind, moreover, that there were no injuries of the sort that might have been sustained in a tussle. Furthermore, neither of these scenarios would have been any concern of the mayor. What possible motive could Keller have for so shamelessly seeking to draw a veil over the matter?

Gorski leaned back on the banquette. He tapped another cigarette from his packet and lit it. For sure, there was nothing wrong with indulging in a little hypothesising, but he was in danger of letting himself get carried away. He was guilty of interpreting what he had seen in a certain way because he wanted it to be so. He *wanted* something untoward to have happened. Not because he wished misfortune on Marc Tarrou, but because such a crime gave him a sense of purpose. In the eyes of the townspeople, it bestowed a certain gravitas. The chief of police should not be reduced to asking questions about the death of a lapdog or harassing innocent visitors to the town.

Even so, he must be disciplined in his thinking. He re-examined the facts. First of all, he did not know whether Tarrou had been in vigorous health. Perhaps he had had a heart condition for years, and it had only been a matter of time before he had a cardiac arrest. Secondly, he did not actually know if Faubel had called the mayor. He only had Keller's word for that. Perhaps the mayor had been calling on Tarrou for one of their regular powwows and, for some reason, had wished to explain his presence at the scene. As for the position of the body or his disarranged clothing: there was nothing in that. Tarrou could easily have kicked off a shoe while in the throes of a heart attack. One hand had even been clutching his chest, supporting Faubel's theory. And as for the unfastened flies: most likely Tarrou had recently visited the WC and forgotten to do them up.

Gorski shook his head to himself. He gave Yves the nod for another beer. Just as his drink arrived, Lemerre came in for his mid-afternoon snifter. His shop was a short distance along the street. He did not, as was his habit, head to the counter, but spotted Gorski and planted himself on the stool at his table, his thighs splayed apart. There was a greasy stain on the crotch of his trousers.

'I didn't expect to find our esteemed chief of police in here today of all days,' he said.

Gorski drew his mouth into a tight smile. Had he not had a fresh beer in front of him, he would have made his excuses and left.

Yves placed a glass of white wine in front of Lemerre. He picked it up daintily by the stem and downed it, then slid the glass to the side of the table to indicate that he would take another. He pulled his seat closer, forcing his thighs further apart.

'Quite a story about this Tarrou fellow,' he said.

Gorski made a face to indicate that he was unconcerned about the matter. 'Is it?' he said.

'I didn't know the bloke myself,' Lemerre went on, 'but from what I hear, he had his finger in a lot of pots of jam. And not just his finger, if you know what I mean.' He gave a lewd wink.

Yves refilled Lemerre's glass. Uncharacteristically, he lingered at the table. The former schoolteacher in the corner kept his eyes firmly trained on the newspaper spread in front of him.

'So what's the story, Inspector?' Lemerre said, with a special emphasis on the final word.

Gorski gave a little shake of his head. 'There is no story.'

'No story? Come on, mucker! A guy like that doesn't just drop dead all of a sudden.'

Gorski remained tight-lipped.

'I get it,' said Lemerre, turning to Yves. 'He can't tell us anything. Ongoing investigation and all that.'

Yves retreated behind his counter. Lemerre set his forearms on the table between them. His breath stank of stale Riesling.

'Seriously, Inspector, we all know what Tarrou and his cronies in the town hall are mixed up in. You're not telling me that this is some kind of accident, are you?'

Gorski swallowed. 'I can't tell you anything,' he said enigmatically.

The trouble was, he had no idea what Lemerre was talking about. He could hardly admit that a gossip-mongering hairdresser knew more about what was going on in the town than he did.

He downed his beer.

'You'll have to excuse me,' he said. He rose from the banquette and rummaged in his pocket for some change, but Lemerre held up his hand.

'It's on me,' he insisted. 'It's not every day I get to share a glass with the Big Cheese himself, is it?'

Gorski did not protest. As he made for the exit, Lemerre suggested that it was time he popped in for a trim. 'Unless you're frequenting one of those fancy places in Mulhouse these days.'

On the pavement outside, Gorski ran his fingers through his hair. Lemerre was right. He was due a haircut. He always put off his monthly visit to Lemerre for as long as possible. He dreaded the twenty minutes in his company. It was, however, unthinkable to take his business elsewhere.

Eugène Vinçard stares out the window of his travel agency on Rue de Mulhouse. He has not had a single customer all day. Since the death of his wife, the business has been failing. There has always been competition from the larger outfits in Basel and Mulhouse. That has not changed. Rather, Vinçard suspects that people are embarrassed to buy a holiday from a widower. He decides to close up early and have a snifter round the corner at the Café de la Gare. As he pulls down his shutters, the attractive florist from Rue de Trois Rois passes in her little van. He raises his arm in greeting, but she fails to notice him.

At half past three, Raymond Barthelme, who has recently been suspended from school for the *acte gratuit* of reading aloud from the Marquis de Sade during assembly, is loitering at the corner of Avenue Général de Gaulle and Rue des Vosges. He is waiting for Clémence Gorski. He is intrigued by her. She has a boyish figure and an otherworldly air, and he has often seen her reading serious books. As she passes, he greets her and asks if she would like to join him for a pot of tea. They are right outside the Café des Vosges. Across the table in a booth at the back of the café, he tells her, 'I mean to become a nihilist.' Clémence looks at him sceptically. 'Surely you either are a nihilist or you're not,' she replies. 'It's not something you become.'

Lemerre is cutting the hair of Maître Corbeil, who has his office nearby on Avenue Général de Gaulle. The hairdresser keeps up a steady stream of chitchat while he snips away, but the solicitor makes only the most perfunctory responses. His hair is beginning to grey at the temples and Lemerre does not forego the opportunity to point this out. 'Perhaps in the future,' he says, 'we might need to consider a little colourant.'

Henri Virieu is roused from a nap at his desk by the sound of the brass bell on the counter of the Hôtel Bertillon. A couple are standing by the desk. They are laughing about something, but Virieu cannot hear what through the glass. They are both in their late thirties. The man has his arm tightly round the woman's waist. When Virieu emerges from his office, the man asks for a room. Just for one night, he replies in response to Virieu's question. Virieu assumes they are not married, or at least not to each other. They already reek of booze, but with business the way it is, he is in no position to be choosy about his guests.

In the little bookstore on Avenue de Bâle, Aude Poiret rings up a sale of *Madame Bovary*. There are no customers in the shop. It's for herself. Every year since the age of fifteen, she has bought herself a new edition. On her shelf at home there are eleven copies. This will be her twelfth.

Gervaise Dutheil turns the sign on the door of her little bar on Rue de Huningue to *Ouvert*. She only lights the candles if a customer comes in. No sense wasting wax. She deliberately drags her feet as she makes her way back to the table at the rear where she has already dealt out a hand of patience. She enjoys the scuffing sound the soles of her slippers make on the tiled floor.

At the house at 26 Rue Saint-Jean, Robert Duymann is sitting at his desk typing. From her bedroom upstairs, his mother has been calling for him to bring her some tea for half an hour. He ignores her. She's perfectly capable of coming downstairs and making it herself.

certain feeling of trepidation that he now did so. As a teenager, he had devoured detective novels, imagining himself a future Maigret, but as an adult his interest had waned. He no longer saw the point in spending his time in the company of characters that didn't exist or following events that had not occurred. His father had been different. For Albert Gorski, reading had been a kind of sacred duty and there was only one author: Émile Zola.

A leather-bound edition of the Rougon-Macquart cycle occupied a shelf of the alcove next to the fireplace, and every two years or so Monsieur Gorski methodically worked his way through the twenty volumes. *This is France*, he liked to say. *If you want to understand France, you must read Zola*. In the latter part of his life, he struggled with the tiny print, hunching over the pages with a magnifying glass, but he refused to purchase a more modern edition, or to contemplate reading any other author. The suggestion offended him.

'There *are* no other authors!' he would invariably declare.

Gorski admired his father's dedication. Since he had returned to live in the apartment, he had once or twice opened random volumes, but after a few pages of painstaking description, he found his attention wandering.

Robert Duymann's novel was certainly less dense than those of Zola. The sentences were short, and he did not indulge in long-winded descriptive passages. The pace, though, was leisurely and the depiction of Saint-Louis every bit as unflattering as the journalist in *L'Alsace* had suggested. Ludovicians were described as a 'mediocre tribe who clung stubbornly to an unwarranted pride in their municipality'. The establishment of the title was clearly based on the Restaurant de la Cloche and fictionalised versions of Marie, Pasteur and even Lemerre, who appeared in the guise of a local butcher, were unmistakeable. The book's protagonist was a former schoolteacher who had been forced to leave his post after a pupil made some unsavoury allegations. He lived with his mother and spent his days drifting between the town's bars, eavesdropping on the inconsequential conversations of the townsfolk. After fifty pages, nothing of note had happened and Gorski dozed off. He awoke with a start in the middle of the night and climbed into bed beside his mother without troubling to brush his teeth.

Robert Duymann did not seem surprised to see Gorski again. There was no reason that he should. Gorski had, after all, said he would return, and the pool of potential visitors to the house on Rue Saint-Jean was unlikely to be large. The novelist was dressed, as before, in a white shirt, black slacks and grey slip-on shoes. A creature of habit.

He stood back from the door to allow Gorski to enter.

'I'm sorry to disappoint you, Inspector, but my mother is still in the land of the living. At least she was the last time I looked,' he added with an unappealing snigger.

'Glad to hear it,' said Gorski.

'Really?' he said. 'I had the impression you might be grateful to have a murder on your hands. I imagine the life of a detective in a town like Saint-Louis must be rather uneventful.'

Gorski scrutinised him. Duymann repeated the action of cupping his hand to his mouth and smelling his breath. He looked and behaved as before, but Gorski's perception of him had changed. He no longer saw him as a mere oddball tied to his mother's apron strings. The knowledge that he had had a career, however brief, as a writer made him more intriguing. And his remark suggested an insightfulness he would not previously have expected. He remembered a detail from the opening pages of his novel. Duymann had described how the character of the butcher—for which Lemerre was clearly the prototype—had, while awaiting a glass of wine, gently stroked the cleft of his upper lip with the forefinger of his left hand. At the time it had seemed inconsequential, but he now realised that this was a characteristic gesture of Lemerre's, and yet in all these years Gorski had never noticed it. He found himself wondering if he too had some tic of which he was unaware.

Duymann said that he would let his mother know that Gorski was here.

'Actually, there's something I'd like to clear up with you first.'

Duymann suggested they step into the living room.

A French window gave out onto the patchy lawn. The shed in which Gorski had located Madame Duymann's missing garden tools was in need of a coat of creosote. During the summer he had laboured on a farm as a teenager, Gorski had spent days creosoting the disintegrating slats of a barn. He had found the task satisfying, and to this day found that the reek of creosote evoked the memory of the clumsy sexual experiences he had had there. In the corner of the room was an old-fashioned writing table with a typewriter on it. A stack of pages rested under a glass paperweight.

'Perhaps, Inspector, you would like something to drink.'

Duymann was standing by a sideboard, quite modern in design, already wielding a decanter. Among the inhabitants of streets like Rue Saint-Jean it is considered vulgar to serve booze straight from the bottle in which it has been purchased. A decanter bestows respectability on daytime tippling. Gorski did not object, but Duymann had in any case taken it upon himself to pour two measures. He handed one to Gorski and sat down on the sofa. Gorski took the armchair. Had he wished to intimidate Duymann, he would have remained standing with his back to the window so that his face would have been partially obscured. But that was not the correct approach here. He did not want Duymann to feel that he was being interrogated. Gorski swirled the contents of his tumbler and nosed the drink. Whisky. He took a sip.

'Very nice,' he said.

'Johnnie Walker's,' Duymann replied. Then after a moment, 'Perhaps you would like a little water or some ice?'

'A little water perhaps,' said Gorski. He proffered his glass.

Whether he had water or not was neither here nor there, but it interested him that Duymann appeared to be so keen to play the amenable host. He disappeared into the kitchen and returned with a small jug, which he placed on a coaster on the coffee table between them. He made a gesture for Gorski to help himself.

They settled back into their seats.

'A drop of water loosens it up,' said Duymann. 'I'm glad you didn't ask for ice. A dreadful American habit. Anyway, I don't have any. Ice, I mean.' He gave a little laugh.

He crossed his legs. Gorski noticed that he was wearing silk socks of the same colour as his shoes; an affectation he had picked up in his time in Paris, no doubt. But it was curious that he would indulge this minor vanity when he seemingly had no reason to leave the house.

'I owe you an apology, Monsieur Duymann,' Gorski began. 'I didn't realise on my previous visit that you are something of a local celebrity.'

'More of a black sheep, I'd say,' he replied.

'Well, the assistant in the bookstore on Avenue de Bâle is quite a fan of your work.'

'A fan? I'm surprised she's even heard of me.'

'She described your novel as a masterpiece.'

'A masterpiece?' he murmured. 'Really?' He could not conceal his pleasure. He drained his glass.

'That was the word she used. She said it was a shame that you'd never written anything else.'

Duymann got up to fetch the decanter from the sideboard and refilled their glasses.

'Why would that be?' Gorski asked.

'Why would what be?

'That you've never written another book.'

He did not answer.

'Perhaps you'd exhausted what you had to say?' Gorski suggested amiably.

'It's not that,' Duymann responded sharply. 'It's a misconception to think that a novelist must have something to say.' This last phrase he pronounced with great disdain.

'So, can we expect some new work from you soon?' Gorski asked.

'The world is not holding its breath for another novel by Robert Duymann.'

'But I see you're working on something.' He nodded in the direction of the typewriter in the corner of the room.

'No,' said Duymann firmly. 'I'm not working on anything.' His right foot had begun to tap on the carpet in an agitated fashion.

'The woman in the bookstore will be sorry to hear that.' Gorski allowed a few moments to pass. He sipped his whisky. 'How did you enjoy your time in Paris?' he asked.

'I was only there a few months. It wasn't for me.'

'Why was that?'

'People there are different. All they care about are fancy restaurants and champagne and *being seen*.'

'That doesn't sound so bad,' said Gorski.

'I don't like being seen,' he said. 'I didn't fit in. I belong here.'

'And yet the picture you paint of Saint-Louis is hardly flattering.'

Duymann drained his glass for a second time and reached for the decanter, which he had left on the table between them. 'I didn't realise you were a literary critic, Inspector.'

'You're quite right,' he said. 'I'm afraid I've allowed my curiosity to get the better of me. It's not every day one meets a renowned author.' He apologised if he had offended him.

A few moments passed in silence. It was Duymann who broke it.

'You said there was something you wanted to clear up.'

'Ah, yes,' said Gorski as if it had slipped his mind. He held out his glass, which Duymann obediently refilled. 'It regards this business with your mother's dog. Bibiche, wasn't it?' He adopted a tone suggesting it was a matter of no consequence.

Duymann's demeanour altered almost imperceptibly. His nostrils flared slightly. His eyes narrowed. He drew his chin towards his chest.

'You said when we spoke previously that the dog had been put to sleep. Unfortunately, though, none of the town's veterinarians seem to have any record of carrying out this procedure. I wonder how you would explain that?'

He spread his hands as if he and Duymann were mutually engaged in trying to resolve a conundrum.

Duymann shook his head. 'I don't know what you expect me to say. If the vet can't remember putting the dog down, I don't know what you want me to do about it.'

Gorski maintained his breezy, almost apologetic, tone. 'If I may, Monsieur Duymann, it's not a question of *remembering*. The problem is that there is no record of the dog being put down, and it is a foible of mine that I am something of a stickler for record-keeping. Now perhaps there is a perfectly innocent explanation—'

Duymann now cut him off. 'To be frank, Inspector, I would have thought you'd have more important things to deal with.'

'That may be so, but I'm afraid that when an allegation is made, no matter how trivial it may seem, we are obliged to look into it. As officers of the law, we cannot allow our own feelings to dictate what we choose to investigate. Procedures have to be followed.' He shrugged, as if to convey that this was something over which he exercised no control. 'So, you would be doing me a great service if you were able to tell me which vet carried out this task. It's one of my flaws that I have a kind of mania to resolve things. I don't like loose ends. Perhaps it's the same for a novelist. I just need the name of the veterinarian.'

Duymann looked at him without expression. He was assessing his possible courses of action. He should at this point have admitted defeat. *You're right, Inspector*, he ought to have said. *I never took the dog to the vet. I lost my temper and kicked out at it. Of course I didn't mean to kill it, but I did. I'm not proud of it.*

Gorski would have understood. He didn't blame Duymann for his initial lie. It was perfectly understandable not to wish to admit to such an act. But now that his lie had been exposed, he would have been better advised to abandon it.

But that was not what Duymann did. Instead, after an interval of some duration, he simply said, 'I don't remember.'

'You don't remember?' Gorski said. He took the notebook from the inside pocket of his jacket and calmly recited the names of the four vets to Duymann, who shook his head after each one.

'Perhaps you took the dog elsewhere? Somewhere outside Saint-Louis?' Gorski suggested helpfully.

Duymann's cheeks were now flushed. The grip on his glass had tightened. 'Look, Inspector,' he said, with exaggerated calm, 'the mutt's buried in the garden. If you want to dig it up, you'll find the tools in the shed.'

Gorski said that he didn't think that would be necessary.

Duymann got to his feet. The amenable host of a few minutes before had gone. He had had enough of the conversation. 'I've got better things to do than answer inane questions about a dead dog,' he said.

Gorski downed the remains of his whisky, placed his glass on the table and thanked him for his time. Before he left, however, he would like to look in on Madame Duymann. 'That is if I haven't imposed enough already.'

Duymann took a moment to compose himself. While he went upstairs to tell his mother that she had a visitor, Gorski took the opportunity to step over to the desk with the typewriter. The paperweight bore the six crowns of the crest of Haut-Rhin. On the uppermost page of the stack of typed sheets, the title had been underlined in blue pencil: *A Case of Matricide*.

Upstairs, Madame Duymann was in bed, propped against her pillows. She was delighted to see Gorski. There was a make-up bag and hand-mirror on the bed beside her. She must have asked her son to fetch them so that she could apply a little rouge to her cheeks. In her younger days, Gorski's mother had never left the house without make-up. She called it *putting on her face*.

'How nice of you to call again, Inspector,' she said.

Gorski sat on the edge of the bed. 'I thought I should make sure that you hadn't been murdered,' he said.

Madame Duymann patted him on the arm. 'You shouldn't listen to a silly old woman like me. Robert's a good boy. I couldn't ask for a more dutiful son. I'm sure he'd be happy to bring us some tea. Shall I ask him?'

Gorski shook his head. The room was warm and there was a heady aroma of lavender. The whisky had made him drowsy. He could not resist closing his eyes. There was something else mingled with the smell of lavender, the sour tang of sweat, perhaps. When he opened his eyes, he could not be sure that he had not dropped off for a few moments. He realised the sour smell was that of his breath. Madame Duymann's hand was resting lightly on his.

He rose from the bed and walked over to the window. At the foot of the garden was a little mound where Bibiche must have been buried. That Duymann was capable of kicking his mother's dog to death did not speak well of him. Nor did the fact that he had threatened to crack in his mother's skull with a spade. But both these acts suggested that he was quick-tempered rather than calculating. Gorski did not really believe that he was planning to kill his mother. Still, the title of the novel downstairs had piqued his interest. In itself, it was no more than circumstantial. In all probability it was the book's name that had put the idea into Madame Duymann's head in the first place.

Gorski turned back to the old lady. She smiled at him.

'And how is your own family?' she asked.

Gorski did not respond. Instead, he assured her that he would call again. Madame Duymann asked if he was sure he wouldn't have some tea. It was really no trouble.

'Perhaps next time,' he said.

As he passed through the hallway at the foot of the stairs, he could hear the clack of typewriter keys in the living room.

Nine

A market took place once a week in the square adjacent to the Restaurant de la Cloche. It consisted mainly of stalls selling fruit and vegetables, cheese, charcuterie and so forth, manned by ruddy-faced women with brawny forearms. In the past, these women would greet Ribéry with lewd remarks, and he would stop and engage them in rounds of increasingly vulgar badinage. No such banter was forthcoming as Gorski made his way through the throng on his way to lunch. His presence was politely acknowledged, but no more than that. It was perfectly possible for Gorski to avoid the market by making a detour along Rue de la Synagogue and approaching la Cloche from the opposite direction, but if he did not do so, it was because he felt that as the chief of police he should not be closeted away in his office. It was necessary to be seen.

The market's most coveted pitches were those at the entrance to the square on Rue de Huningue. Pitches could not be bought or sold but were passed down through generations. The only mechanism to obtain a better pitch was to wait for a stallholder to die and hope that their offspring had resisted the pressure to continue the family trade. This was rare, but when a vacancy arose, each remaining trader shifted one pitch closer to the entrance. It was in this way that the passage of time was measured in Saint-Louis.

Towards the back of the square, agricultural produce gave way to a number of stalls selling household goods and bric-à-brac masquerading as *objets d'art*. Gorski had learned enough from his father to know that nothing of any value was sold at these stalls. The same tat was packed and unpacked every week for years. It was impossible to imagine these traders turning any sort of profit and Gorski assumed their motives were social rather than commercial.

By a distance, the busiest stall in this part of the market was that of Eugène Maloin. Beneath a sign bearing the word *Quincaillerie*, Maloin's trestle tables were strewn with random hinges, window locks, brackets, clamps, fishing weights and reels, padlocks, pocket-knives, assorted lengths of chain and mousetraps; none of it in any discernible order. Little cardboard boxes, so old that their sides had become as pliable as animal pelts, contained odd screws, nuts and bolts, lengths of fuse wire, old keys, cogs and spindles of various sizes. If it began to rain, Maloin, who was well into his seventies, would unfurl the tarpaulin and unhurriedly clamp it to the metal carapace above the stall. He kept a three-legged stool behind the tables, but rarely used it, preferring to preside over proceedings from a standing position.

There was invariably a clutch of pot-bellied men huddled around his stall, doggedly picking through the contents of the boxes in the hope that they would eventually unearth whatever it was that would allow them to complete the repair of an ancient wireless, camera or clock. They paused at intervals to examine a screw or spindle, sometimes wordlessly proffering it to their neighbour in a leathery palm. If, after due consideration, it was deemed to be suitable, a price would be sought. Maloin inevitably waved away such enquiries. *Just take it, you'll be doing me a favour*, he would say. *It's not worth a thing.*

Maloin had been a friend of Gorski's father. Once or twice a week, when Gorski returned from school, the two men would be sitting in the office at the back of the shop, sharing a pot of coffee and arguing about the value of a carriage clock or an antique firearm. On market days, they would share a glass or two in la Cloche with the other traders.

Gorski stopped at the ironmonger's stall. Maloin greeted

him, as he always did, as 'Young Georges' and made a point of reaching across the table to shake his hand. Gorski asked how business was going.

'I can't lie,' Maloin lamented. 'Things are a little slow. Trouble is, everyone just throws stuff away these days. Nobody fixes anything anymore.'

This complaint was belied by the bustle around the stall, but Gorski nodded his agreement. Their conversation ran along similar lines every week. They were interrupted by an elderly gentleman asking if Maloin had a bracket matching one he held out.

'If I do, it'll be in the box over there,' he replied, wagging a gnarled finger towards the far end of the table.

Gorski hung around. He enjoyed this weekly exchange with Maloin. Sometimes, for no other reason than to prolong his visit, he picked a few items off the stall and made a show of examining them. After his father's funeral, Maloin had made a point of taking him aside at the little reception held in the apartment above the shop. He had been a little drunk. *Your dad probably never told you himself*, he had said, gripping Gorski by the elbow, *but he was proud of you.*

Arsène Susselin appeared at the end of the stall. He exchanged a cursory handshake with Maloin.

'My dear Inspector,' he said, inclining his head to Gorski. 'To what do we owe this pleasure.'

Susselin was the bursar of the market. Each week he made his rounds, collecting the stallholders' dues in a battered leather satchel which he kept on a strap under one shoulder. It was this accessory which gave him his nickname. He wore a peaked cap, which Gorski was sure he had acquired at a costumier's to give himself an air of authority. This authority, however, was not altogether illusory. On paper, Susselin was no more than a lackey of the town hall, but, in reality, the market was his private fiefdom. It was common knowledge that he siphoned off a portion of the stallholders' fees, but no one was ever foolhardy enough to lodge a complaint. The Satchel alone had the power to decide what dues were to be paid. He could raise rents on a whim, and he had, moreover, a book of regulations governing the size of awnings, what may or may not be sold, mandatory hours of business and a myriad of other matters, all of which could be invoked to levy fines or even to threaten eviction. In the distant past, these regulations had been issued to the stallholders, but no one had ever troubled to read them. Thus, when The Satchel scribbled some violation into the notebook he carried for this purpose, no one had a clue what regulation they may or may not have contravened. Susselin's authority over such matters was thus absolute. He was not a popular figure.

Susselin had inherited the position of bursar from his father a decade before. His first act had been to announce a general rise in rents. It was true that there had been no increase for many years, but that was beside the point and a strike was organised. No trader was foolhardy enough to be identified as the ringleader—though rumour had it that Maloin was the agitator-in-chief—and no formal announcement was made. Instead, on a particular day in September, not a single trader showed up at their stall and a list of demands was pinned to a tree where Susselin could not fail to see it.

The following week, Susselin had the square roped off. Signs were erected citing a regulation stating that any pitches left vacant for three consecutive weeks would be reallocated without further consultation. Such draconian measures were unnecessary, however. The stallholders had assumed that Susselin would capitulate at the earliest opportunity, but they had miscalculated. There was a long waiting list for pitches and Susselin could, in theory, charge newcomers whatever he wanted. After the second week of action, solidarity among the traders fractured. It was all right for those at the back of the market selling bric-à-brac. They could, theoretically, hold out for as long as they wished, but the same could not be said for those selling perishable goods. If the farmers and artisans could not sell their produce, it would go to waste.

Susselin knew he only had to wait things out, but he was shrewd enough to understand that he needed to allow the stallholders a way of saving face, and at a meeting called in the town hall, he let it be known that the proposed increases in rents would be introduced incrementally. Thus, both sides were able to claim victory and the following week the market resumed, albeit with a simmering resentment that had never entirely dissipated.

Gorski was well aware of how Susselin operated. When Ribéry retired, The Satchel invited him for a glass at a corner table of la Cloche. After some banalities, he wordlessly slid an envelope across the table and left. The sum was not large, but if multiplied by the number of weeks in a year, it would not be insignificant. The following week Gorski handed the envelope back to Susselin, making sure he did so in full view of the holders of the most coveted pitches. This act did not have the anticipated effect, however. In refusing to have any part in Susselin's scheme, he placed himself outside the system in which the entire market colluded. He was thus treated with suspicion by both Susselin and the traders.

Susselin was careful not to be too brazen about his illicit gains, but it was clear that he lived beyond the means of his municipal salary. He drove a Mercedes, his three daughters dressed in the latest fashions and he and his wife regularly dined in upmarket establishments in Basel and Strasbourg. Such things did not go down well in Saint-Louis.

If Susselin habitually affected a certain obsequiousness in his dealings with Gorski, it was perhaps because he thought that the cop might one day bring an end to his petty venality. But in this he was mistaken. What he did not understand was that Gorski simply did not care.

The three men now stood in an uneasy triangle. Gorski determined that he would not be the one to move off. Maloin stroked his moustache with his thumb and forefinger.

Susselin held a palm out and suggested that it would soon rain. Then he tapped his famous satchel. 'Well, these dues aren't going to collect themselves, are they?'

He bid the men good day and moved off.

'Asshole,' Maloin muttered, loudly enough for Susselin to hear him, but quietly enough for him to deny that he had said anything.

The Restaurant de la Cloche was rowdier than usual. The market generated something of the atmosphere of a minor holiday. The farmers' wives and other stallholders who made their weekly pilgrimage to the metropolis greeted one another exuberantly. Conversations were carried on between adjacent tables and even bellowed from one side of the restaurant to the other. These interlopers drank more than the regulars, wiped their mouths on their sleeves, and made liberal use of certain earthy turns of phrase. Lemerre was sitting alone at his table by the door looking even more disgruntled than usual.

This influx naturally had an impact on the seating arrangements, but despite the annoyance it caused, Marie guarded the regulars' tables zealously. The regulars, in turn, held up their side of the bargain by bolting their meals with even greater haste than usual and not lingering over coffee or schnapps.

As Gorski ate his *salade de viande*, he slowly turned the pages of *L'Alsace*. If he kept his gaze fixed on his newspaper, it was not because he had a pressing interest in the affairs of the region but, rather, to avoid being drawn into conversation. On an inside page, there was a short account of the death of Marc Tarrou. He was described as a 'prominent industrialist' and 'colourful character'. A photograph showed him as a younger man. He was exceptionally handsome. A journalist had called Gorski and he was quoted as saying there was no reason to suspect foul play. Tarrou, the article ended by stating, was survived by his wife, Alice, which came as a surprise to Gorski as he had not been wearing a wedding ring.

That morning Gorski had returned to Tarrou's office with a locksmith, who had the safe open in seconds. '1-2-3-4,' he laughed. 'The guy hadn't even gone to the trouble of changing the factory setting.' The safe was empty. Did this mean that the contents had been stolen or just that Tarrou had never used it? Gorski tried to recall what Anna Petrovka had said. It was a point he would need to clarify. But it would be strange to go to the trouble of installing a safe if one had no intention of using it.

On the opposite page, the newspaper carried an article about a champion egg-laying chicken. A photograph showed the bird—a medal draped around its neck—being held aloft by a grinning farmer. 'She's a phenomenon,' he was quoted as saying. 'Eight, ten eggs a week. I've never known anything like it.'

Although he had not yet finished his entrée, Adèle arrived to take Gorski's plate. He did not protest. As he glanced up, he saw that the Slav had come in. Then something extraordinary occurred. Despite the fact that there were a dozen or so people waiting to be seated, he gestured towards the empty chair at Gorski's table. Marie shook her head firmly, but the Slav waved away her objections and made his way across the restaurant, with Marie in his wake. Several diners looked up from their meals to observe the drama.

It unfolded in a matter of seconds.

'You don't mind, do you, Inspector?' said the Slav. 'I assured Madame that you wouldn't. If you'd rather eat alone, please say so, but it hardly makes sense to have empty seats when the place is so busy.'

Marie was standing by the table with her hands on her hips. There was an indisputable logic to his statement. Gorski felt he had no choice but to comply, even though he felt that he was somehow betraying Marie. In any case, the fellow had already installed himself at the table and it would only cause further disruption were Gorski to refuse.

'Be my guest,' he said, with an open-handed gesture.

Marie walked off shaking her head, as if anarchy would surely ensue. Adèle set a place for the Slav with characteristic docility, unmoved by the violation of convention that had taken place.

Gorski folded his newspaper and placed it on the banquette

next to him. Not only was there now no room for it on the table, it would have been ill-mannered to continue reading when he had a dining companion, even an uninvited one. As the Slav settled himself, his knee bumped Gorski's beneath the table. The Slav did not withdraw, however, and in order to prevent their legs touching, Gorski was forced to shift his to the left, like a woman riding side-saddle.

Adèle's blouse was, as usual, loosely fastened and the lace edging of her brassiere was clearly visible. As she laid the Slav's place, he gave Gorski a little wink, as if the two men were complicit in a moment of voyeurism. Gorski lowered his eyes to his plate, the colour rising to his cheeks like a schoolboy caught looking up Teacher's skirt.

He took a mouthful of wine, emptying his glass. Why did he feel that he was being scrutinised, that the Slav was somehow mocking him? He was not obliged to say anything. He had not invited the Slav to join him. The onus was on him to initiate conversation. Nevertheless, despite the hubbub, the silence between them weighed heavily, and it was all he could do to restrain himself from making some fatuous observation about their surroundings, just as previously he had found himself pointing out minor points of architectural interest as they walked along Rue de Mulhouse.

After a minute or two, Adèle returned to take the Slav's order. He must have sensed Gorski's discomfiture, because he pushed back his chair with an unpleasant scraping sound and began to gather up his coat.

'Actually,' he said, 'I can see I have made an error and intruded on the Inspector's lunch. I'll wait for another table.'

Gorski was now forced to insist there had been no such intrusion and that the Slav was most welcome. He even apologised for not being more hospitable, making the excuse of having a pressing case on his mind. The Slav was placated and resumed his seat. Adèle regarded this tedious pantomime with indifference. She tapped her pencil against her notebook. The Slav perused the menu on the blackboard above Gorski's head.

'Perhaps you would be so good as to recommend something, Inspector?'

As it would seem odd to recommend something other than what he had ordered himself, he suggested the meat salad and the *baeckeoffe*, a speciality only available on market days. The Slav nodded his assent and Gorski took the opportunity to order a second *pichet*. Somehow the first one was already empty.

Their dishes arrived almost immediately. The Slav studied his salad, lowering his head over it as if he was short-sighted. He took up his fork and pushed one of the chunks of meat around the plate as though it was a dead mouse. Then he speared it and put it in his mouth. He chewed for a few moments before spitting it into his napkin and pushing his plate aside. Gorski hoped that Marie had not witnessed this affront.

'It's something of a regional speciality,' he said. 'I suppose it's not to everyone's taste.'

The Slav looked at him blankly. 'Evidently,' he said.

Adèle made no comment as she took away his plate.

Not wishing to let the silence reassert itself, Gorski asked how the Slav was enjoying his stay in Saint-Louis.

'I like your town very much,' he replied solemnly.

'Thank you,' Gorski said stupidly, as if it was he who had been paid a compliment.

'I hope,' the Slav went on, 'that you have forgiven my little joke the other day.'

'What joke was that?'

'Tailing you around town. I saw at once that you had put a man on me—well, a boy—and I thought it would be amusing to, so to speak, turn the tables on you. I hope you took it in the spirit in which it was intended.'

'Of course,' Gorski said. He creased his face into a smile but knew that it had been very far from being a joke. Clearly the Slav had wished to demonstrate that he was not to be pushed around by any small-town cops.

The Slav tucked into his main course with some enthusiasm. 'This is excellent.'

Gorski felt a sense of relief, not only that the Slav approved of the dish, but for the change of subject. He explained that the dish was originally cooked through the day in baker's ovens. The Slav replied that there was a similar dish in his own country. He told Gorski the name, but he didn't catch it.

Perhaps the Slav had, after all, not intended to cause any awkwardness. It could be that in Yugoslavia it was customary to share tables in a restaurant. Indeed, were there not certain workers' canteens in France where people squeezed onto benches next to people they did not know? And it had to be admitted the Slav's earlier statement was reasonable: it did not make sense to have unoccupied places when there were hungry people waiting. That, Gorski supposed, was the logic of the communist.

The Slav ate methodically. Twice Adèle appeared at the table to see if he had finished, only to be forced to retreat. In such a situation, any other customer would have hurriedly polished off his food or simply given up his plate, but the Slav was a foreigner and could not be expected to know how to behave. Then, quite abruptly, he laid down his cutlery. Despite his apparent appreciation of the dish, he had not finished it. This troubled Gorski. He had been brought up to never leave a scrap of food on his plate. Nevertheless, he did not make any remark. It was a matter of no consequence and did not concern him.

Only when Adèle had returned and taken his plate did the Slav lean forward slightly in his chair.

'I believe that some condolences are in order.'

He spoke with the air that this had all along been his purpose; that it was this he had come to say.

Gorski made a face to indicate that he did not know what he was talking about.

'On the death of your friend, Monsieur Tarrou.'

'Tarrou was not a friend of mine.'

'Not a friend perhaps, but—' said the Slav. He made a gesture with his hand. Clearly he did not feel it should be necessary to explain himself to a fellow man-of-the-world. 'I gather he was an influential person hereabouts. And as you too are an influential man, I assume you must have been bound by some mutual interests.'

'I wouldn't describe myself as an influential man,' said Gorski. He immediately regretted this response. Why was it always his instinct to diminish himself?

'Just because an individual chooses not to exercise the power at his disposal, it does not mean that he is not powerful.'

Gorski chose to ignore this cryptic formulation. 'So you were acquainted with Monsieur Tarrou?' he asked instead.

'Me?' He pursed his lips and shook his head. 'How could I be? I'm a stranger here. I read about his death in that newspaper of yours.' He gestured towards the copy of *L'Alsace* on the banquette. 'And, of course, one can't help overhearing certain conversations. I'm afraid I have a weakness for eavesdropping.'

Gorski felt that the Slav was trying to entice him into making some statement about the case or to enquire about what it was he had heard. He had often used such fishing tactics himself. He began to wonder if the Slav was himself an investigator of some kind.

'Of course, I understand that you cannot comment on an ongoing investigation,' he went on in an affable tone. 'I merely wanted to offer my condolences, but I see that those were not required.'

'And what makes you think there is an ongoing investigation?'

'I assumed this was the "pressing case" that you mentioned was on your mind.'

'You assumed incorrectly,' said Gorski.

'So there is no investigation?'

'I didn't say that. I merely asked what made you think there was.'

The Slav adopted an innocent expression. 'The fellow seems

to have died in mysterious circumstances. I suppose I thought something like that would be of interest to the police.'

'If you have any information relating to the case, I'd be happy to hear it.'

'I'm sure you don't need a stranger to tell you what people in your own town are saying.'

Gorski made a face to indicate that he was indeed fully appraised of any rumours that might be circulated. 'I try not to pay attention to tittle-tattle,' he said.

'Very wise, I'm sure,' said the Slav.

Gorski took a swig of wine. He had already finished the second *pichet*. Adèle arrived with a slice of *tarte aux pommes* for each of them. The Slav protested that he had not ordered it. Adèle informed him in a bored tone that it was included in the *formule*. If he didn't want it, she would take it away. For the taciturn waitress, this constituted a major speech.

The Slav indicated that she should do so, then, to Gorski's relief, pushed back his chair.

'I shall leave you to your *tarte*, Inspector.'

He was already familiar enough with the rituals of la Cloche to know that bills were settled at the counter.

It was only when Gorski went to pay his own bill that he noticed that Lemerre was wearing a black armband. 'What's up with him?' he asked Pasteur.

'Petit popped his clogs. Seems he'd been dead for days before anyone found him. The old bastard's pretty cut up about it. They'd been friends since they were at school.'

'What happened?'

Pasteur made a fist and jerked it out from the side of his neck while making an unpleasant strangulated sound in the back of his throat.

Gorski nodded. He glanced across at Lemerre. His great heavy head was bowed over the table. He appeared to be sobbing.

'You'd think his dog had died,' said Pasteur.

On his way out, Gorski paused at Lemerre's table. 'Sorry to

hear about Petit,' he said.

Lemerre raised his head. His eyes were red and watery. The shoulders of his V-necked sweater were speckled with large flakes of dandruff.

'Well, that's us a man down for Thursdays,' he said.

He was referring to the weekly bridge game which had taken place at the corner table of la Cloche for as long as anyone could remember. Gorski's own father had once been a participant, although whether this predated Lemerre's involvement, he did not know.

'Perhaps you'd be interested in making up the numbers, Inspector,' Lemerre went on.

Gorski smiled thinly. 'I don't think so,' he said. 'But thank you.'

Outside, Gorski wondered if it would really be so bad to take part in the card game. It was not as if he had anything better to do with his evenings.

Ten

Gorski smelt smoke from the landing at the top of the stairwell. He found his mother on her chair by the electric heater, her chin slumped to her bosom. For a moment he thought she was dead, but when he called out to her, she stirred a little.

In the kitchenette, a dishtowel had caught fire on the hob. A thin stream of smoke advanced along the ceiling towards the window. Flames were scorching the wall above the cooker. Gorski came to a halt in the doorway. The ancient wallpaper started to burn. Then the fire spread with sudden rapidity across the ceiling. The paint melted into globules and dropped onto the linoleum below. Gorski stepped into the tiny room and closed the door behind him. He tossed the burning dishtowel to the floor and stamped on it. Then he filled a pan with water and tossed it at the flames on the ceiling, which subsided momentarily then reignited and continued their progress towards the window. He heard his mother cry out from behind the door, which was never normally closed. Another two or three panfuls of water put paid to the flames. He threw more water on the charred wall above the cooker.

There was an acrid chemical smell from the burnt paint. Water dripped from the ceiling. It was a mess. Gorski opened the window and put his head out for some fresh air. His heart was beating rapidly. An elderly woman passed by on the opposite pavement with a dog. She did not look up. He recalled the moment when he had entered the apartment and thought his mother was dead. For a brief moment, he had felt a sense of relief; that this was for the best? He now felt ashamed for having entertained such a thought, however briefly. One did not think such things.

He patted the pockets of his jacket for his cigarettes, but they were in his raincoat, which he had thrown down in the hallway.

With a clean dishtowel, he wafted away as much smoke as possible. Then he opened the door.

'Are you all right, Maman?' he asked.

She looked at him, quite alert. 'Georges,' she said, 'what are you doing in there?'

It irked him that she chose this of all moments to recognise him. He reassured her that everything was now under control, but she did not seem the least bit disturbed by what had occurred. Probably she didn't understand what had happened. There was no point enlightening her.

It was only then that he noticed Madame Beck standing in the doorway.

'I smelt burning,' she said by way of explanation. She still had a pair of secateurs in her hand and was a little out of breath. She must have run up the stairs.

Gorski was pleased to see her.

'There was a fire,' he said.

Madame Beck looked into the kitchenette. With the blackened wallpaper and dripping ceiling, it looked a good deal more dramatic than it actually had been. Still, there was no need to articulate what would have happened if Gorski had not returned when he did.

The florist asked Madame Gorski if she was all right.

'Oh yes, my dear,' she replied. 'Georges must have been careless with his cigarette.'

Madame Beck stepped into the kitchen and began to clear up the mess. Gorski begged her not to, but she ignored him, and he stood uselessly behind her. She seemed to know where everything was kept. Once the floor and surfaces had been wiped down and dried, there was not much more that could be done.

'That's all ruined,' she said, gesturing towards the walls and ceiling.

She squeezed past him into the living room and retrieved her secateurs. Gorski followed her out into the tiny hallway. He didn't want her to go.

'You know,' he said in a stage whisper, 'I could really do with a drink.'

Madame Beck looked at him. They had never stood in such close proximity. She smelt earthy, like moss on the forest floor. Gorski hoped she could not smell alcohol on him. Below, the little bell above the shop door tinkled. Madame Beck stepped towards the stairwell and called down, 'I'm sorry, we're closed.'

The pair held their breath until they heard the bell signal that the customer had departed.

'Give me a few minutes to tidy up,' she said, before disappearing down the stairs.

Gorski returned to the living room. The smoke had dispersed, but the acrid chemical smell lingered. Nevertheless, he stepped across the room and closed the window. Madame Gorski hated to be cold. She eyed him suspiciously.

'Albert,' she said, 'there's a customer downstairs. I heard the bell.'

'Yes,' he replied. 'I'm just going to attend to him.'

In the tiny bathroom, he splashed water on his face and ran his damp hands over his hair. He brushed his teeth, then swilled mouthwash. He examined himself in the mirror. There was stubble on his chin, but there was no time to rectify that. Perhaps, in any case, it made him look more rugged. He straightened his tie and then, on second thoughts, took it off and put it in his pocket. That was better. He looked more relaxed; less like a buttoned-up petty bureaucrat.

In the short time he had remained upstairs, Madame Beck had managed to sweep the floor of the shop and, Gorski noted, apply a little lipstick. She was standing with her slim buttocks against the counter where she cut and prepared her bouquets, and which dated from Gorski's father's time. The wood had a pleasing patina and sometimes, as he passed it, Gorski ran his palm over the surface, enjoying the sensation of the undulations against his skin. They stood for a moment in awkward silence, as if in recognition of the momentous step they were about to take. Or perhaps it was only significant in Gorski's mind. Perhaps Madame Beck had only agreed to have a drink because she felt sorry for him after his distressing experience and there was nothing more to it than that.

'So, where are you taking me?' she asked.

Gorski puffed out his cheeks. The most natural thing would have been to head to la Cloche, but that would only set the tongues of the town's gossipmongers wagging. Entertaining Madame Beck in Le Pot was clearly out of the question. Women rarely set foot in the place. The Café de la Gare was more respectable, but would mean walking some distance along Rue de Mulhouse and inevitably encountering someone they knew. The atmosphere, in any case, lacked intimacy.

Gorski was at a loss. 'Wherever you like,' he said.

Even now he was incapable of taking control of the situation. He felt that in some way he had already disappointed Madame Beck.

She seemed unperturbed, however. 'There's the little place on Rue de Huningue,' she said.

Gorski knew the place she meant but had never been inside. It gave every appearance of being abandoned. More importantly, getting there would not entail walking along any of Saint-Louis' main thoroughfares. Gorski could not help but think that this was why Madame Beck had suggested it.

They turned left outside the shop and walked along the narrow pavement of Rue des Trois Rois in silence. When they reached Rue du Temple, they paused to let a car pass. As they stepped off the kerb, Madame Beck slipped her hand into the crook of Gorski's elbow. She did it so naturally that Gorski might have thought there was nothing to it; that no particular meaning should be attached to it. He pretended not to have noticed. Gorski never passed along this street without recalling the precise culvert into which, at the age of eight, he had dropped the broken pieces of the little mustard spoon. Even now he directed his gaze in the opposite direction, as if to feign ignorance of what had occurred there.

They made a right turn. 'I think it's up here,' Madame Beck said. It was clear that she had never been to the place either.

That they were engaged in something illicit was now undeniable. Gorski felt apprehensive. Were they embarking on some kind of affair? After a glass or two of wine, perhaps Madame Beck would expect him to propose they remove to a nearby hotel. He imagined turning up at the Bertillon and asking Virieu for a room. He felt pinpricks of perspiration on his forehead. Madame Beck, for her part, seem perfectly composed. Perhaps she engaged in such assignations on a regular basis.

The place was called Chez Gervaise. It was sandwiched between a hairdressing salon and a shoe shop. Yellowing voile curtains concealed the interior from prying eyes. Gorski held open the door and gestured for Madame Beck to lead the way. The floor was tiled black and white. There were half a dozen tables covered in checked waxcloth with mismatched wooden chairs. On the walls was a miscellany of faded prints, depicting, among other things, a toreador slaying a bull; a girl with a fat tear rolling down one cheek; a group of English horsemen in red hunting jackets. The pictures might have been bought in a job lot from a box in Gorski's father's shop. At the back was a counter, behind which various bottles were arrayed on a shelf. There were no beer taps. The place had the air of a converted living room. A woman of about sixty—presumably Gervaise—was sitting at the rear-most table with a glass of pastis, playing patience, a cigarette burning in the ashtray besides her. There were no other customers.

Gorski and Madame Beck glanced at each other and silently agreed to sit at the table by the wall, midway between the window and the counter. Gorski gallantly helped Madame Beck out of her coat and hung it on the stand by the door. The card player rose and unhurriedly made her way across the room. She was wearing what appeared to be men's carpet slippers. She welcomed them cordially and asked what she could get them. Before they had the chance to reply, she shuffled back to her table and retrieved a box of matches. Her slippers made a pleasant sound on the tiles, like sandpaper lightly rubbing on wood. She returned at the same leisurely pace and lit the candle secured in a wickered wine bottle on the table.

'There!' she said. 'A little ambience.'

Gorski glanced at Madame Beck. She was smiling charmingly at the proprietress. She asked for a glass of white wine.

Gervaise enumerated the small number of options and nodded her approval at Madame Beck's choice. Gorski indicated he would have the same.

'Then I might as well bring you a bottle,' she said. 'You don't look like you'll be going anywhere for a while.'

Gorski agreed without seeking Madame Beck's approval. What harm could there be in it? If they didn't finish the bottle, so what? He was the chief of police. He could afford to show a little largesse.

On her way back to the counter, the proprietress paused to light the candles on the other tables. As they waited, Gorski fingered the drops of wax that had coagulated around the neck of the bottle. There was no point initiating a conversation before their wine arrived, but in the silence the question of what they were doing there hung heavily between them.

'Well, here we are!' he said stupidly.

'Here we are,' replied Madame Beck. She seemed amused by his discomfiture.

The proprietress arrived with the wine, along with two green-stemmed glasses. They touched glasses and drank.

'I really should thank you,' Gorski said.

Madame Beck looked questioningly at him.

'I know how often you look in on Maman. It's appreciated.'

While what he said was true, he regretted opening the conversation this way. It made it seem as if this was the reason for their assignation. Mentioning his mother dissipated the intimate atmosphere between them. The playful expression which had been playing on Madame Beck's lips faded away.

'It's no trouble. I'm happy to help.' She paused and took a sip of wine. 'But you know things can't go on as they are. Today only proved that. If you hadn't arrived when you did—'

Of course he knew it was inevitable: the nursing home. Doctor Faubel had said so months ago, but his mother would not countenance the idea. *I will die in my own bed, thank you* was her mantra. Gorski had even visited a suitable place in the countryside near Bartenheim. It had been airy and pleasant, and the residents had seemed cheerful. Perhaps after a while, his mother might even find it agreeable. She had no quality of life cooped up in the apartment on Rue des Trois Rois. Regardless, he would still feel like he was abandoning her. He had broached the subject numerous times, but she was adamant. 'Never!' she said. 'When I leave this apartment, it will be in a box!' Then she would start sobbing like a child. 'Albert, *Albert*, why are you trying to get rid of me?'

Gorski took a sip of wine. 'I know,' he said.

He topped up their glasses. Then, in order to change the subject, he glanced around the room and asked if Chez Gervaise was a regular haunt of hers.

'I've never been here before.' Then she ran her fingers along the sticky waxcloth and whispered, 'And I'm not sure, I ever will again.'

'Oh, I rather like it,' Gorski replied, also now lowering his voice. 'It has a certain charm. Perhaps we could join *la patronne* for a game of cards later.'

'Well, you know I really can't stay too long,' she said.

Although this statement set a limit on the evening, it constituted some kind of admission. She had not said she didn't want to stay. She said she *couldn't*. The implication was quite clear. Beneath the table their knees were touching and had been since they had sat down. Neither of them had made any attempt to move.

Madame Beck glanced down at her glass. She touched her fingers to her lips. Gorski found himself wondering what she would do if he leant over the table and kissed her, but he dismissed the thought. It was quite impractical. He would be sure to upset their glasses or tip over his chair. Instead, he took out his cigarettes.

'Do you mind?' he said. He had never seen Madame Beck smoke.

She shook her head, then said, 'May I?'

Gorski gave her a cigarette and lit it for her.

She sat back in her chair and exhaled, widening her eyes. 'I haven't smoked since I was at school.'

'How is it?'

'Good,' she said, nodding her appreciation. 'I feel a little light-headed.'

At this moment, the door opened and a stout elderly woman with a wheezing pug entered. She was wearing an enormous tweed coat and a matching hat with little feathers sprouting from one side. She negotiated the business of getting through the door with some difficulty. This achieved, she looked with some surprise at the couple occupying the table by the wall. As she passed them, she respectfully inclined her head.

'Monsieur, madame,' she said by way of greeting.

When she reached the table at the back of the room, Gervaise rose and the two women silently greeted each other with a kiss on both cheeks. The pug observed with its goggly eyes. The newcomer removed her coat and sat down with the weary air of a traveller who had come a great distance. Gervaise cleared up the cards, then fetched a glass for her companion and poured a measure of pastis, topping it up with water from the jug on the table. Then from behind the counter she produced a box which she brought to the table. This contained a set of checkers. The pieces were arranged on the board and a game commenced. All this was carried out at a laborious pace and without a word being spoken.

'That will be me in a few years,' whispered Madame Beck.

Gorski laughed.

She drank more wine. The bottle was already half-empty.

That night Gorski was unable to sleep. He got out of bed and went into the living room and sat in his father's chair by the fireplace. His mother was sound asleep.

He and Madame Beck had parted on the pavement outside the apartment. She had insisted that there was no need for him to walk her any further. She had even joked that her husband would have sent out a search party for her.

Over the second half of the bottle, they had talked about their schooldays. Madame Beck had spent her childhood in Mulhouse. On account of her lanky figure, she had always felt awkward. At high school, the boys had called her The Skeleton, and some of the teachers had even taken up this nickname. Gorski had taken the opportunity—emboldened by the wine—to tell her that he thought she had a very elegant figure. Then he had told her a little of his own difficulties at school. 'I always felt as if I was watching the other kids through a window,' he said.

'Yes,' Madame Beck had replied, 'I felt exactly the same.'

She had been only too pleased to move to Saint-Louis after her marriage. It had felt like a new beginning, but sometimes she wondered where life would have taken her if she had not married so young. She asked if Gorski ever thought about how his life might have been different if he had not married Céline or chosen to become a policeman. Gorski had replied that he was not sure he had ever *chosen* anything. He had suggested getting a second bottle, but she had looked at her watch and made her apologies.

On the pavement outside the apartment, there had been a moment when Gorski wondered if she wanted him to kiss her, but he had not acted and the moment passed. Instead, they parted with a stiff handshake and, as he watched her walk off, Gorski had been left cursing himself. He should have abandoned his reserve, caught up with her and pressed her against the wall and crushed his lips to hers, his hands around her wrists, their breath quickening. To hell with whoever might see them!

Now, though, sitting in his father's chair, he felt relieved that he had not done anything so rash. He would only have made a fool of himself. There was no evidence to believe that Madame Beck had any amorous interest in him. Such thoughts were entirely without foundation. So what if she put on a little lipstick? That meant nothing. He was glad he had not insulted her by misconstruing her motives. And yet, and *yet*, had there not been something flirtatious in her manner? In the way she had looked at him, in the self-deprecating stories she had told him of her teenage years, in the ruefulness with which she spoke about her marriage. Gorski had no way of knowing. He had never been accomplished in reading the intentions of the opposite sex. He had been only too happy to allow Céline to take the lead in every aspect of their relationship. It had been a relief to have the decision-making taken out of his hands. But, now in middle age, he was forced to conclude that it was the very willingness to relinquish control that led him to the point of sitting alone in the darkness of his parents' apartment, unable to make up his mind about whether he should have kissed the woman from the shop downstairs.

Eleven

Shortly after eight o'clock, Gorski heard the little bell above the door herald Madame Beck's arrival in the shop below. She was a little earlier than usual. He had contemplated leaving before she arrived in order to avoid discussion of their assignation the previous evening, but now the matter was out of his hands. Generally in the mornings, they exchanged no more than a brief greeting. Often Madame Beck would already be on the telephone or absorbed in her order book. Twice a week a van pulled up outside, and she would be supervising the delivery. It would be remiss, however, not to pass a few pleasantries this morning. Madame Beck would be sure to take any failure to do so as a snub. Perhaps he should even make some allusion to whatever it was that had occurred between them. The trouble was, he did not know exactly what had occurred. Perhaps they had simply been two adults sharing a glass of wine and there had been no more to it than that.

The important thing was to act naturally.

Gorski examined himself in the mirror in the hallway. Was he looking older? There were some unsightly broken capillaries on his cheeks, and perhaps the creases at the corners of his eyes had deepened. He was not in the habit of scrutinising himself. Once the business of marriage is dispensed with, men do not much concern themselves with their appearance. Their sartorial choices and matters of personal grooming immediately fall under the jurisdiction of their spouse. Set adrift from the marital regime, most men swiftly regress into a state of dissolution. Gorski had not yet entirely let himself go. He had always taken a degree of pride in his appearance and personal hygiene, perhaps unconsciously compensating for his humble origins. Now he returned to his room and changed his tie. The striped one he had unthinkingly put on was too dandyish. Did he think that just because he had shared a glass of wine with a married woman he was suddenly some sort of Don Juan?

He called goodbye to his mother, who was already installed in her chair. She had been up since five or six o'clock as usual and had made no comment about the state of the kitchenette.

Gorski made his way down the stairs, treading noisily to alert Madame Beck to his imminent arrival. That way, if she did not want to converse, she could step into the back shop or pretend to be talking on the telephone. She did neither of these things, however, and Gorski found her standing over her order book, as was quite usual. She looked up from her paperwork as he entered.

'Good morning, Georges,' she said.

Georges. Madame Beck had never previously addressed him by his first name. It could not be a coincidence that she now chose to do so. It was an acknowledgement that something had changed between them. He paused in the middle of the shop—this already a departure from his normal practice—and returned her greeting, but he could not yet bring himself to use her forename, which he knew only from the mail he saw on her counter. Gorski fancied that there was a little colour in her cheeks, but that may simply have been on account of having just come in from the cold.

She looked at him, as if puzzled or amused.

'Business ticking over?' he asked, with a gesture towards the order book. He momentarily recalled the Saturdays of his childhood when he was entrusted with the task of keeping a record of the day's transactions in his father's ledger.

'Someone somewhere always needs flowers,' she replied.

'Of course,' he said. 'Funerals and so forth.' He stepped towards the door.

Then quite quietly she said, 'My husband was wondering

where I'd got to last night.'

Gorski stopped. He had not expected this.

'Of course, I told him about the fire,' she went on.

She delivered this quite casually and then returned her gaze to her order book, but she was clearly communicating that, if only by omission, she had lied to her husband. If there had been nothing illicit in what they had done, why conceal it?

Gorski swallowed. Because he could think of nothing else to say, he muttered, 'Well, mother seems none the worse for the experience.'

Then before Madame Beck had the chance to prolong the conversation, he wished her good day and hurried out.

What a clot he was! He had not gone half a dozen steps before cursing himself. Why had he not simply said that he had enjoyed their drink together? He might even have suggested that they do it again sometime, and if he had had the nerve, added the flirtatious proviso *If your husband doesn't object.* Clémence had told him that Madame Beck thought he was a 'nice man'. And yet, instead of acknowledging her conspiratorial admission, he had brought up his mother, as if it had been she who was the sole reason for their tryst. He came to a halt on the pavement, wondering if he should, even now, retrace his steps and rectify his error. He should explain that he had not known what to say and dashed off like a nervous teenager. No, that would only make him seem even more idiotic. Women liked men who were decisive and assertive, not dithering schoolboys. They were attracted to brash loudmouths like Tarrou. Gorski stepped onto the road in front of a small van. The driver wound down his window and unleashed a volley of lurid phrases, before realising he was berating the chief of police and driving off.

Faubel's post-mortem report determined that Marc Tarrou had died of a cardiac arrest. It was clear that the good doctor had already made up his mind about the cause of death and had only looked for evidence to confirm his opinion. Gorski had not expected anything different, but just because Faubel had not done a thorough job did not mean that his conclusions were wrong. There was, he reminded himself, no indication that anything more sinister had occurred. Yet something continued to niggle him. It normally took Faubel a week or more to carry out such an examination and file his report, yet this one had arrived with a great deal more speed. Was there any connection between that and Keller's presence at the scene? It was hard to believe that the two things were not linked.

Gorski drummed his fingers on the desk. He lit another cigarette and re-read the report. It was not that he thought he would find some detail that didn't add up. He was not, after all, a medical man. He was merely looking for a pretext to call on Faubel. As he pulled on his raincoat, the telephone on his desk rang. He ignored it.

The doctor's practice was a few minutes' walk away on Avenue de Bâle. As he left the station, Schmitt told him he had had a call from an Annie Petrovic, or something like that.

'You too high and mighty to pick up the phone these days?' he asked.

Gorski grimaced at him. He would call her back later.

It was cold. Exhaust fumes adhered to the tarmac of the road. Gorski folded the Manila envelope containing the post-mortem lengthwise and slid it into the inner pocket of his coat.

The receptionist informed him that Faubel was with a patient. Gorski took a seat. The waiting room was every bit as dreary as those of the various veterinarians he had visited a few days earlier. There were the same moulded plastic chairs with tubular metal frames. The torn posters on the wall were similar: warnings about lurking ailments and measures that might keep them at bay. There is no call for the medical professions to make their premises comfortable or appealing. They are not hairdressers. No refreshments are offered. No chit-chat is made.

Three women waited. Two turned the pages of the dog-eared

magazines provided. The third had brought knitting, and the clack of her needles provided a not unpleasant soundtrack. None of them looked ill. Gorski had once attended a burglary at the home of the knitting woman. She lived in an apartment on Avenue de la Marne, near the railway station. Some cash and a few items of jewellery had been stolen. The woman—Gorski could not recall her name—had been apologetic about calling the police. The jewellery was of no great value. Gorski assured her that she had done the right thing, but it was unlikely that her items would be recovered. He suggested visiting any pawnbrokers in the area. She now showed no sign of recognising Gorski. Even if she had, she would have no wish to reveal that she had had dealings with the police.

Ten minutes passed. When the door to Faubel's office opened and a woman came out holding the hand of a tearful child, Gorski stood up. No one protested that he was jumping the queue. The sick have nothing better to do.

Faubel was scribbling notes and, without raising his eyes, instructed Gorski to take a seat.

'Ah, Inspector,' he said when he looked up. 'Feeling poorly?'

'I'm quite well, thank you,' Gorski replied. He held up the Manila envelope. 'I appreciate you discharging this with such alacrity.' Why, he wondered, did he feel the need to use such pompous turns of phrase when addressing members of the professional classes?

'But you don't agree with my conclusions?' the doctor replied wearily.

'I just had one or two questions.' He took out the report.

'Want a drink?' Faubel asked.

As Gorski did not object, Faubel fetched a bottle of cognac from the cabinet at the side of the room and handed him a generous measure.

'Here on page two you note some "fatty tissue" around the arteries,' he said. 'Would that in itself have been enough to cause cardiac arrest?'

'No,' said Faubel, 'but I did not suggest it had. I noted it merely as a potential contributory factor.'

'And how common would that be?'

'In a man of Tarrou's age, habits, et cetera, perfectly normal. I'd find the same if I opened you up.'

Gorski turned to the final page of the report. 'And these abrasions to the back of the skull?'

'Clearly caused by the fall onto the glass table. As noted, they were superficial and should not be considered significant, at least as a cause of death.'

'And you noted no other external injuries?'

'If I had, I would have mentioned them. There's nothing mysterious here, Georges.'

'If that's the case,' asked Gorski, 'why did you feel the need to call Mayor Keller?'

Faubel looked at him questioningly.

'You called Keller from Tarrou's office.'

Faubel shook his head. 'Why would I do that?'

'That's what I'm asking,' said Gorski.

'I didn't call Keller or anyone else,' said Faubel.

Gorski pursed his lips. 'Then there seems to have been some misunderstanding. While I'm here, I wonder if I might ask you about another matter.'

Faubel indicated with a gesture of his hand that he should go ahead.

'Is a Madame Duymann of Rue Saint-Jean a patient of yours?'

'She is,' he said wearily.

'And—' He did not have to finish his question.

'Physically there's not a lot wrong with her. Low blood pressure, anaemia, nothing serious. Mentally, she's all right, some loss of memory function.'

'Nothing more serious than that? Paranoia, delusional thinking, for example?'

'Not that I've observed.'

Gorski stood up and apologised for taking up Faubel's time.

He had purposely not finished his cognac, as if to demonstrate to the doctor that he was capable of a modicum of self-control.

'It'll be the usual malingerers out there,' said Faubel. He walked Gorski towards the door, taking him gently by the elbow. 'Speaking of elderly ladies,' he said, 'you know that the current situation with your mother cannot continue indefinitely.'

'Yes,' said Gorski. 'I'm aware of that.'

'I think we both know what needs to be done.'

Gorski looked at him for a moment, unsure of what he meant.

'Given your situation,' the doctor went on, 'the arrangements can be made with, as you might say, all alacrity. There's nothing to be gained by postponing the inevitable.'

Gorski assured him that he would speak to her.

'Good man,' said Faubel.

If Gorski now called again on Madame Duymann, it was not because he had any real reason to do so. Robert Duymann received him with mild annoyance and repeated his joke about not yet having murdered his mother.

Gorski found the warm and over-scented atmosphere of Madame Duymann's bedchamber strangely soothing. Their conversation was accompanied by the faint clacking of the typewriter below. He now insisted that Madame Duymann call him Georges. She suggested that Robert would be happy to bring them some tea, but Gorski went downstairs and made it himself, returning a few minutes later with the things set out on a tray.

'How very kind you are, Georges,' she declared. 'If only my own son was so obliging.'

Gorski told her about his father's pawnbroker's shop. He described the special smells of dust and leather and varnish, and how on Saturdays he had been charged with recording the day's transactions in the great ledger. Even then he had known this to be an onerous responsibility, but his father never looked over his shoulder or checked his work.

Madame Duymann remembered the shop on Rue des Trois Rois, but had never been inside. It had always seemed so dingy. Gorski explained that the low lighting had been intentional. He repeated his father's dictum: *People are ashamed of entering a pawnbroker's shop. They do not wish to be illuminated when they do so.* Madame Duymann expressed the view that this seemed very wise.

'Your father sounds like a very agreeable man,' she said.

'I sometimes think,' Gorski confessed, 'that I could have done worse than to take over the business.'

'Then who would I have to call on me?' Madame Duymann had responded.

The room was warm, and Gorski felt his eyelids drooping. He collected the tea things and took them back downstairs on the tray. Duymann looked askance at him. Gorski understood his perplexity. If challenged, he would have been hard pressed to explain why he had paid this visit.

Clémence did not appear for their weekly dinner. Gorski had neglected to visit the grocer's on Rue de Mulhouse, so unless he went out again there would be nothing to eat. More importantly, he had been planning to raise the subject of the nursing home and had felt this would be easier in Clémence's presence. He could never quite banish the nagging feeling that when there was no one else around, his mother acted up more. With Clémence present, it would seem as though the decision was not solely his responsibility, but had been reached collectively for his mother's own good. In any case, he planned to say that he had spoken to Doctor Faubel and it was *he* who insisted on this course of action. Not that such nuances would make any difference to his mother.

As he awaited Clémence's appearance, he sat in his father's chair drinking a glass of wine. His mother was calm. She was mumbling a song from her childhood under her breath. When seven o'clock passed and it became clear that Clémence was not coming, Gorski got up and searched through the kitchen cupboards. There were only a few packets of powdered soup and some stale bread. What did it matter? His mother barely ate anything. If he went to the trouble of preparing proper meals, it was really only for his own benefit; for the sake of something to do.

Nevertheless, he set the table as usual and cajoled his mother from her seat.

When he placed her bowl in front of her, she asked, 'What's this?'

'A nice bowl of asparagus soup, Maman.'

Madame Gorski banged her spoon on the table with surprising force. 'I don't want soup,' she said. 'I want a cutlet. I want a cutlet and potatoes.'

'You'll have a cutlet once you've eaten your soup,' Gorski replied mildly.

He tore off a hunk of bread, dipped it in his soup and made some appreciative noises.

Madame Gorski then placed her left hand to the right of her bowl and, keeping her eyes fixed on Gorski, swept it off the table, upsetting the cruet set on its way. The bowl smashed against the windowsill. The contents sprayed the wall and dripped onto the rug beneath.

'I don't want soup,' she repeated. 'I want a cutlet.'

Gorski took a number of slow breaths. He could not help feeling that his mother was behaving maliciously. She would not have done such a thing if Clémence had been there. When Clémence was there, she softened. She was no more gaga than he was. Her aberrations were a sham, motivated by nothing other than a desire to torment him. He glared across the table at her. She stared back, defiantly it seemed. Gorski put his napkin on the table, rose and fetched a bucket from beneath the kitchen sink. Kneeling at his mother's feet, he put the pieces of the bowl in the bucket and began mopping up the spillage, which had splashed over a surprisingly wide area. Some of it had spattered onto his mother's legs. He didn't care if she had burned herself. She only had herself to blame. When he had finished, he wrapped the broken crockery in newspaper and placed it in the kitchen bin, before swilling the contents of the bucket down the sink. He resumed his place at the table and replaced the items of the cruet set on their little saucer. He started to eat his soup, which was now cold. His mother started to cry.

'Where's my soup?' she sobbed. 'Why don't I have any soup?'

Gorski took his own bowl into the kitchen, lingered for a few moments then brought it back out and placed it in front of his mother.

'Thank you, Albert,' she said. She picked up her spoon and started to eat at a slow but methodical pace. Gorski watched her impassively. Soup dribbled from the corners of her mouth.

When she had finished, he wiped her face with a napkin. In the kitchenette, he washed and put away the dishes, before putting on his jacket and leaving the apartment.

Twelve

To those passing through, Saint-Louis may seem a drab and unremarkable place. Here there are no majestic boulevards or handsome civic buildings. There are no Belle Époque brasseries, thronging theatres or museums. There are no statues, fountains or cathedrals. There is nothing, in short, to give visitors cause to linger. But those hastening on to more glamorous destinations are missing out. For lurking behind the tired store frontages and the voile curtains of the modest dwellings, there is life; or at least some semblance of it. And though at first glance, it may appear a much-of-a-muchness sort of place, like all towns, Saint-Louis has its tribes. It has its proletariat; it has its middle class; and it has its grande bourgeoisie.

Those fortunate enough to find themselves in the upper echelons of Saint-Louis society do not care to question how they arrived there. In all likelihood their position was not earned by any merit of their own, but instead by the enterprise or malfeasance of some long-buried forebear. This does not, however, prevent them from looking down their noses at those below. These tinpot Brahmins despise the middling folk who account for the bulk of the town's population, and keep their interactions with them to a minimum. They despise their vulgar taste in décor, the recent construction of their houses and the orderliness of their pitiful gardens. They despise their tolerance for mediocre wine, their acceptance of synthetic fabrics and their mania for labour-saving devices (for the middle classes have no maids). Most of all, they despise their servility. They despise them for not reciprocating the contempt in which they are held.

The poor, on the other hand, these small-town patricians do not despise. The poor are there to be pitied. Just as the grande bourgeoisie have done nothing to merit their position, so the poor have done nothing to merit theirs. These downtrodden creatures are not responsible for their own misfortune, for the poor have no free will, and were they to be granted this power, they would only squander the opportunities it brings. In the eyes of their betters, the poor exist solely that they, the affluent, may demonstrate their largesse. The poor may not be welcome in the homes of the rich, nor even in the leafy avenues in which they dwell (such infractions being liable to result in a call being placed to the local constabulary), but from time to time donations are made for the schooling of orphans, the relief of the indigent or the re-housing of battered wives. Munificence is an effective balm against the niggling awareness that deep down one is no better than the drunk propping up the counter of the Café de la Gare. Munificence buries the guilt.

As for the middling folk—the petite bourgeoisie—they neither despise nor pity the poor. These middling folk fear the poor. They fear that they will burgle their houses, violate their daughters and lure their sons into indolence, crime and addiction. They fear that they will piss on their manicured lawns or maliciously key the paintwork of the top-of-the-range Citroën they have scrimped so hard to acquire. As they pass certain hostelries, respectable bourgeois women fear the crude remarks that emanate from the doorway, even as these comments cause a quickening in their groins. In a similar way, the male of the species will cross the road to avoid the slurs on their masculinity that cause them to lower their heads and quicken their step, inwardly cursing their lack of mettle.

These mediocre individuals, however, do not reciprocate the scorn of their betters. Rather, they gaze upon what passes for the town's aristocracy with veneration. They admire their idleness, their patched-up clothes and ramshackle mansions. They envy their loose morals and the offhand manner with which even their womenfolk employ certain epithets. But more than anything, they envy their charm, a quality to which no middling plodder can ever aspire.

Then, finally, at the bottom of the heap, there is the hoi polloi, the ne'er-do-wells who inhabit the streets around the railway station, yet have likely never set foot on a train. This is the happiest of Saint-Louis' tribes. The poor aspire to nothing but inebriation and sexual gratification. They care nothing for those above them in the town's pecking order. These higher castes barely enter their consciousness. Better to confine their brawling, robbing and fucking to their own breed. It's a lot less trouble that way. The poor accept their just measure of violence and larceny with good grace. Such things are part of life and if you don't like it, go blub elsewhere. Certainly, there is no cause to trouble the authorities about such matters.

None of this rich tapestry is apparent to those hurrying onwards to the A35. And nor should it be. They have more pressing things on their mind. But it was apparent to Georges Gorski. It was apparent to Gorski because he had no tribe. Thanks to his progress through the ranks of the police force, he had made an outsider of himself. Saint-Louis takes a dim view of those who abandon their tribe. Those with a yen for self-improvement are best advised to go elsewhere to satisfy their urges. The same is true of those on a downward trajectory. The wife of the mayor is not welcome in the Café de la Gare or Le Pot. She would be thought by one and all to have gone to the dogs; her presence an embarrassment to all concerned. And conversely, the son of a pawnbroker should not become the chief of police. It upsets the natural order of things.

Like Gorski, Marc Tarrou had belonged to no tribe. But unlike the chief of police, he was accepted by bourgeois and ne'er-do-well alike. He was accepted because he had charm, or at least he had enough effrontery to pass as charm. He also had money, and money has a strangely emollient effect on even the most deeply-held prejudices.

Those gathered for his funeral reflected this.

The municipal cemetery in Saint-Louis is situated at the junction of Rue de la Gare and Rue de Mulhouse, a short walk from the Hôtel Bertillon. It is enclosed by a whitewashed wall topped with clay coving, and can be accessed via gates at both the front and rear. Here, if nowhere else in the town, the rich mix freely with the poor. Above the surface, the graves of the well-to-do are distinguished by ostentatious mausoleums bearing the family name. But below, the worms make no distinction between the flesh of the rich and the flesh of the poor. It all goes the same way.

From every point, the water tower with the large sign bearing the name of the town is visible. The cemetery is bounded to the rear by railway tracks. The chapel within the grounds is an understated affair. Like Saint-Louis itself, it is functional rather than spiritual. Gorski had bidden farewell to his own father in this building. On that occasion, aside from himself and his mother, the congregation had consisted of Maloin, a handful of his father's customers, Marie and Pasteur, and a few regulars from the Restaurant de la Cloche. Ribéry had sat at the back of the chapel respectfully observing proceedings.

Gorski liked funerals. There was an authenticity to them. Aside from immediate family or the occasional close friend, those present do not much lament the passing of the individual in the box. There is no need to indulge in excessive displays of grief. Showing up is all that's required. The ability to say that there was a 'good turnout' is a comfort to the bereaved and as fulsome a tribute as most Ludovicians can hope for. Family members are seated in the front row so that they are unable to see those behind smirking and passing boiled sweets to one another. Undertakers know what they are doing. As soon as the buffet is served, the deceased is forgotten and conversation turns to other matters.

Weddings, by contrast, are a charade. Guests feel obliged to feign joy for the betrothed couple, while simultaneously making wagers on how long the union will last. Then there is the pantomime of the exchange of vows. At Gorski's own marriage, Céline had pulled a comic face and traded looks with her maid-of-honour as the vows were recited. Gorski acted as if he was in on the joke, but keenly felt his humiliation in front of the assembled worthies of the town.

Now, many of these same worthies had turned out for Tarrou. Despite the drizzle, the mourners loitered around the steps of the chapel. Among those present were Keller, bedecked in his mayoral chains; several members of the town council; the solicitor Gustave Corbeil of what had once been the firm of Barthelme & Corbeil; the up-market estate agent Henri Martin; Arsène 'the Satchel' Susselin; and, naturally, Doctor Faubel, who made a point of attending the interment of all those he dissected. There was also a huddle of workers from the concrete factory, short barrel-chested men with thick fingers, looking ill at ease in the presence of their betters. They had not dressed up for the occasion and satisfied themselves by clutching their caps to their chests as the coffin was carried in. No doubt they would have thought Tarrou a good sort. Gorski could imagine him effortlessly engaging in the sort of coarse banter that men employ to win acceptance from those below them on the social ladder.

Behind this cluster of men Gorski spotted the transparent dome of Anna Petrovka's umbrella. He had not yet returned her call. She was not alone: even aside from the wives of the local worthies, there were a large number of women in attendance. Given what he had learnt of Tarrou's habits, this was probably to be expected, but Gorski was surprised to see Céline there. Most likely, he supposed, she knew Tarrou through her father. There was also an attractive woman of around forty, who, though she was not dressed in mourning, must have been the widow, as the funeral director ushered her to the front of the chapel. Tarrou did not appear to have spawned any offspring, at least none that were officially acknowledged. Also present was Lucette Barthelme, widow of Betrand Barthelme, the lawyer killed when his Mercedes left the A35 and collided with a tree.

She was dressed in a neat black suit with a pillbox hat and veil. Gorski nodded a greeting in her direction. She smiled ruefully at him. After the investigation into her husband's death, Gorski had considered coming up with a pretext to call on her, but his nerve had failed him.

The service was perfunctory. Afterwards, Gorski waited while the congregation filed past the priest.

As she passed, he touched Anna Petrovka on the arm. 'You wanted to talk to me,' he said.

She shook her head like a child that doesn't want to eat its greens. Gorski followed her out. Her knee-length white boots were spattered with mud. She put up her umbrella.

Gorski apologised for not returning her call.

'It wasn't important,' she said.

Gorski clasped her lightly by the elbow and led her to the side of the path. She looked around, as if concerned that they might be overheard.

'It was important enough to call me,' he said. If she was in possession of some information, she was obliged to share it with him.

She insisted that she had to leave. Gorski let go of her elbow. He had her address. He would call on her at the first opportunity.

'She's a little young for you, don't you think, Georges?' Céline had joined him at the side of the path. 'Or maybe you're making up for lost time.'

'She's a witness,' said Gorski.

'Sure she is.' She nudged him playfully with her elbow and winked theatrically. 'You got a cigarette?' she asked.

He took a packet from his coat pocket and they lowered their heads into a brief huddle to light up. Gorski caught her familiar scent.

'I thought you'd given up,' he said.

'No fear,' she replied. 'Cancer, pah!'

It was an archetypal Céline response. Cancer was for lesser mortals. She formed her lips into an O and slowly exhaled a stream of smoke. Gorski felt an unwelcome pang of desire.

If pressed, Gorski would have struggled to put his finger on the moment that he knew their marriage was over. He had been aware from the start—when, as a young cop, he had walked into the ladieswear shop where she worked—that she was too good for him. It was etched in the vocabulary she used; her disdainful attitude to rules; the offhand way she spoke to waiters; the quality of her clothing; her utter lack of shame about the sexual act. The difference, back then, was that Gorski thought he could raise himself up: that somehow through hitching himself to the daughter of a local bigwig, his humble origins would be erased. Also—and it helped—he was quite besotted by her.

It was perfectly possible, he found, to learn what cutlery to use and to put down his fork between mouthfuls of food. It was possible, with a bit of effort, to drop certain plebian turns of phrase from his speech. He even managed to affect an interest in fine wine and the theatre. Gorski allowed Céline to upgrade his wardrobe and accepted the ridicule of his colleagues as a price worth paying. But despite his efforts, there were certain traits—certain traces of his low breeding—that he found it impossible to eradicate. He could never bring himself to allow a waiter to pick up his dropped napkin. He could not sit at the vast dining table in the Keller family home without feeling like an imposter. He had never been able to rid himself of a creeping feeling of guilt after sexual intercourse. It was not even possible for him to get sozzled in Le Pot without secretly trying to ingratiate himself into Yves' good graces.

The first time Céline had gone on holiday without him—the third year of their marriage—it had come as a relief, but he had been unable to admit this to himself. For the first few days after his wife's departure for Nice, Gorski wandered aimlessly around the house. He left ashtrays unemptied and allowed coffee cups and glasses to pile up in the kitchen sink. One evening, after questioning a witness, he stayed in a bar in Mulhouse and got so drunk that he had had to be accompanied to the nearest hotel.

None of this brought him any pleasure however, and as he could think of no better use for his freedom, within a week he began to miss Céline. When, on her return, he told her this, she cheerfully told him not to be so silly.

And perhaps that had been it. The realisation that while for him the sight of a tennis coach's hand on the small of his wife's back was enough to incite feelings of jealousy, if he had confessed that he had spent a week in Strasbourg carousing with whores, she would have laughed it off and told him to be sure to take some penicillin.

They fell in behind Tarrou's coffin. Keller was one of the pallbearers; Corbeil another. Weak winter sun cast the drizzle in a peculiar yellow light. The shingle path was uneven and Céline's heels were unsuited to the terrain. With her free hand she balanced herself on Gorski's arm.

'I didn't know you knew Tarrou,' he said.

'*Everyone* knew Marc,' she said archly. 'But what brings you here?'

Clearly Gorski was not included in the category of 'everyone'.

'I'm here in a professional capacity.'

'I thought he had a heart attack.'

'So everyone thinks,' he said. He couldn't resist trying to give the impression that he was in possession of some privileged information.

Céline flicked her half-smoked cigarette into the mausoleum belonging to the Barthelme clan. 'Clémence said that your mother is not doing well.'

'No,' he replied, 'she's not. Things can't go on as they are.'

'It must be difficult.'

Gorski nodded his assent. 'I didn't see Clémence yesterday.' As Céline made no response, he added, 'Is she all right?'

She shrugged. 'How would I know? You know how teenagers are. She's hardly likely to come running to mummy with her problems.'

They were nearing the freshly dug hole.

'This is where I peel off,' she said. 'I don't do graveside.'

Gorski gave a little laugh through his nose. He still liked her. He couldn't help it.

He watched as the coffin was lowered into the ground. Keller was the first to step forward to drop a handful of dirt into the grave. He did so with studied solemnity, before carefully brushing the soil from his gloves.

'Still sniffing around, Georges?' he whispered as he passed.

It was only now that Gorski spotted the Slav standing by the wrought iron gates at the exit onto Rue de Mulhouse. There was no reason to think there was anything untoward in that. His hotel was nearby and if Gorski ever found himself in the Republic of Yugoslavia, he would certainly pause to observe a passing funeral. Such rituals reveal much about the traditions of a place.

Thirteen

After midnight something in the atmosphere of Le Pot changed. It was as if the room contracted and grew darker. It became claustrophobic. Those who continued to converse did so in hushed tones, as if wary of being overheard. By this hour, the casual tipplers and neophytes had left the stage to the serious boozers: those for whom the business of drinking oneself into a stupor was a nightly task, carried out with the solemnity of a rite.

Aside from Gorski, the former schoolteacher who had been forced to leave his position after a pupil made some unsavoury allegations was in his usual place by the door. Two men Gorski had not seen before occupied the stools at the counter. From their earlier conversation, it was apparent that one was a salesman dealing in agricultural feed. Now, however, they were drinking mostly in silence, exchanging only sporadic remarks to ensure that the other did not leave.

At this time of night, whether they knew it or not, those left in Le Pot were in cahoots. It was a point of honour to Yves that he would never close up as long as a single customer remained. But it was equally an unwritten rule that the last man standing should finish the drink in front of him and order no more. Thus, the final patrons were locked in an unspoken contract. In order to keep drinking, they needed each other. It was not that anyone who found himself in Le Pot in the small hours did not have a stockpile of booze at home or a half bottle of hooch stashed in his suitcase, but that was not the same. Drinking alone in one's apartment or hotel room is injurious to a man's self-respect. No matter how plastered a guy gets, how incapable of coherent speech or self-conveyance, as long as he is sitting in a bar, the illusion that he is engaged in a socially acceptable activity can be maintained.

The two fellows at the counter were now engaged in an earnest debate about whether to have another round. Their foreheads were only inches apart. Yves looked on impassively, already sure of the outcome. The salesman, sitting on the right of the two, was wavering. For the last half hour or so, he had kept the toe of his right shoe planted on the floor. His left hand was clamped on the shoulder of his drinking companion, his right flat on the bar. He resembled a condemned building prevented from collapse only by the scaffolding encasing it. If he now agreed to his pal's proposal to have 'one more for the road', it was only because he could not currently be confident of making it as far as the door. What was required was a pick-me-up. That was indisputable.

When Yves replenished their glasses, Gorski felt that this was a suitable juncture to empty his bladder.

The WC in Le Pot was situated behind the coat stand to the left of the bar. It was so small that in order to close the door one had to place one's feet on either side of the pan, which had been without a seat for as long as anyone could remember. On the door was a humorous but redundant sign reading, *Usage limité à 5 min*. Gorski had once heard one of the regulars ask Yves when he intended to get the toilet fixed. 'If you want to take a dump, there's a gutter outside,' had been his response. As if in support of this policy, the establishment provided no lavatory paper.

Gorski was inebriated enough to leave the door ajar, but not so much as to be unembarrassed by the splashing sounds or by the urine that spattered his trousers. Thankfully he was wearing a dark suit. To the left there was a tiny wash hand basin and Gorski twisted round to run some water over his hands. An encrusted grey towel hung on a hook, but Gorski satisfied himself with wiping his palms on the seat of his pants.

He emerged, zipping up his flies. For a moment he was confused. It appeared that he had already returned to his place on the banquette. It was as if time had shifted forward and he had slipped a few seconds behind. Then he noticed the flattened nose of the individual sitting in his place. It was not himself, but the Slav.

Gorski sat down next to him. He was not averse to having some company. He bid him good evening.

The Slav returned his greeting. Yves placed a measure of clear spirit in front of him.

'Vodka?' Gorski asked.

'*Šljivovica*,' said the Slav.

Gorski looked blankly at him.

'Perhaps you would call it plum brandy. Or *eau-de-vie*.'

'Another one for you, Inspector?' Yves asked. As Gorski was barely halfway through his beer, it was clear that Yves' motive was solely to alert the newcomer to the fact that he was in the presence of a cop.

Gorski felt suddenly self-conscious about drinking beer. Beer was what teenagers ordered the first time they got up the nerve to enter a bar. It was not a drink over which serious men conversed into the small hours of the morning. On his first visit to Le Pot, he had felt the need to demonstrate that, despite being the chief of police, he was not above drinking a glass of beer at the counter of a working men's bar. From then on, it was unthinkable that he could drink anything else. To change his regular order would reveal him to be a phoney, jeopardising the acceptance he had worked so hard to earn.

Nonetheless, on an unchecked impulse, he now indicated that he would have whatever the Slav was having. Yves shrugged. It made no odds to him by what means his customers chose to get sozzled. The Slav said something in his own language, then knocked his shot back with a sharp tilt of his head. Gorski felt obliged to follow suit. The spirit burned the back of his throat. The Slav indicated with a sideways movement of his index finger that they would take two more.

As he poured out the measures, Yves asked him, 'Did you

box?' He briefly touched his nose to indicate that it was this feature that had prompted his question.

'A little,' the Slav replied. 'Not professionally. Yourself?'

'Only in the army, but I was pretty useful.'

Yves put the bottle down, adopted a fighter's stance and threw a few punches into the air above the table, exhaling sharply with each blow. He danced back a couple of steps, unexpectedly nimble, feinted left and right, then advanced on his toes with two sharp jabs and an uppercut with the right. The former schoolteacher observed the spectacle from his table by the door.

The Slav applauded briefly.

Yves retrieved the bottle from the table. 'It can come in handy in this line of work,' he said, before returning to his place behind the counter. In his many visits to Le Pot, Gorski had never witnessed any incident that might have required Yves' pugilistic skills. The clientele was too docile to cause any trouble, but perhaps that was only on account of the tacit threat of violence Yves carried.

In order to prevent a silence descending on them, Gorski asked if the Slav had visited the bar before. 'I haven't seen you in here,' he added.

The Slav made a non-committal expression.

'Of course,' Gorski ploughed on, 'it's hardly the most salubrious establishment Saint-Louis has to offer, but it does have one distinct advantage—' At this point his little speech fizzled out. He had suddenly lost his train of thought. He took a swallow from the glass of beer that was still on the table.

'And what would that be?' said the Slav.

'What would what be?' said Gorski. He turned to face his companion, who was regarding him curiously, a faint smile playing on his lips.

'Its one distinct advantage. You were saying that the establishment has one distinct advantage.'

'Ah yes, its distinct advantage!' said Gorski, remembering what he had been going to say. 'The distinct advantage of Le Pot is that no one can see you in here.' He gestured towards the two oblong windows high in the wall, which were for the purpose of ventilation only.

The Slav nodded thoughtfully at this. 'That sounds more like the outlook of a fugitive than a policeman. Who would you be hiding from?'

'It's not that I'm hiding from anyone,' said Gorski. 'It's just that sometimes one prefers to be invisible.'

'So you feel that people are observing you? That you are, so to speak, under surveillance?'

'No, it's not that.' The Slav had a habit of twisting his words against him. Or of drawing inferences he had not intended.

'In that case, let me ask you a question: if you did believe yourself to be under surveillance, how would you alter your behaviour?'

The truth was that Gorski already felt himself to be constantly under surveillance. He could not leave his mother's apartment without passing through Madame Beck's shop and although she never questioned his movements—why should she?—he often felt compelled to furnish her with an explanation of where he was going. He could not walk along Rue de Mulhouse without being greeted by the travel agent Vinçard or one of the other business owners. At the police station, Schmitt was there keeping tabs on his comings and goings. Gorski had the option of using the rear entrance, but he disliked doing so. It made him feel furtive, and that by avoiding Schmitt's attention he was tacitly admitting that he was bothered about what he thought. When he had lived with Céline in the house on Rue de Village-Neuf, had he not always felt that his wife was observing his every move, and that he went about his own home in fear of committing some transgression? Even now, he felt that his mother—gone in the head though she was—was passing judgement on his every act. And it went without saying that in the various hostelries he frequented, his presence never went unnoticed, and whenever possible he sat in an inconspicuous corner.

When these things were considered in totality, Saint-Louis assumed something of the nature of a penitentiary in which one was perpetually visible. It was only here in Le Pot that he felt a sort of relief from this relentless scrutiny.

The question, therefore, was not how Gorski would alter his behaviour if he thought he was under surveillance. The question was how he would alter his behaviour if he was *not* under surveillance.

He did not say any of this, however. Instead, he said, 'Why would I change my behaviour? One would only change one's behaviour if one was engaged in some kind of wrongdoing.'

'But if you haven't done anything wrong, why do you feel the need to be invisible?'

'I don't,' he said, aware that he was contradicting what he had said only moments before. He felt bamboozled; that the Slav was purposefully bamboozling him. In an attempt to change the course of the conversation, he suggested they have another. The Slav nodded his assent, but it was he who gave Yves the sign to refill their glasses. He then instructed him to leave the bottle on the table.

This taken care of, the Slav slid himself a little along the banquette, so that their shoulders and thighs were touching. An image of Siamese twins Gorski had once seen in a children's encyclopaedia flashed into his mind.

The Slav kept his eyes directed forward, but he spoke in a semi-whisper. 'And how is your investigation progressing?'

Gorski, drunk as he was, had the feeling that it was this that the Slav had all along been working up to. He turned his shoulders so that he was facing his drinking companion. They were close enough to kiss. 'What investigation would that be?' he said, though he knew perfectly well what he meant.

'Your investigation into the death of Monsieur Tarrou.' He swirled his *eau-de-vie* around the glass.

'As I said before, there is no investigation.'

'Really?' The Slav gave a little shake of his head, as if mystified.

'A man drops dead for no apparent reason and the police see no reason to investigate.'

'Monsieur Tarrou died of natural causes.'

'And you believe that, do you?'

'What I believe is neither here nor there,' said Gorski. 'That was the conclusion of the post-mortem report and there is as yet no evidence to suggest anything different.'

The Slav gave a little laugh. 'I admire your strategy,' he said.

'Strategy?' said Gorski. 'I don't have a strategy.'

'Come come, Inspector. It's clear that this pretence that there is no investigation is just a ruse to lull the culprit into a false sense of security, so that he will think he's off the hook and commit some error.'

Not for the first time, Gorski wondered if the Slav might himself be some sort of investigator.

'It's not a pretence,' he said.

The Slav ignored him. 'Or perhaps you think that by giving him—the culprit, I mean—enough rope, he will be lured into a confession; that he will want to take credit for a deed that you are dismissing as an accident.'

'Nonsense!' said Gorski.

'Is it?' said the Slav. He paused, refilled their glasses from the bottle that Yves had left on the table. 'So, what would it take for you to open an investigation? What if, for example, some new evidence was to come to light?'

'It would depend what that evidence was.'

'So you admit that such a thing is a possibility, that there may be an alternative explanation for Monsieur Tarrou's demise.'

'I always keep an open mind. I am governed by whatever evidence is available to me.'

'But if this new evidence was to exist, how could it come to light if there is no investigation?'

'Investigations cannot be undertaken on a whim. There has to be some basis from which to proceed.'

The Slav knocked back his glass of spirit. 'What, say, if a witness was to come forward with some fresh piece of information?'

'Naturally, I would be obliged to consider it.'

'So, what if I told you, hypothetically speaking of course, that I had got talking to a fellow in a bar—just as you and I are talking now—and that this fellow told me he had murdered Tarrou?'

He adopted a breezy tone, as if to give the impression that he was merely talking off the top of his head.

'And why would this fellow-in-a-bar do that?'

'It's a perfectly common occurrence, or so I hear. A criminal feels compelled to confess, to unburden himself of the guilt he feels. And who better to confess to than a stranger in a bar? You must have come across this many times, Inspector.'

'I can assure you I haven't,' Gorski replied.

'Nevertheless, my point, or rather my question, remains. If such evidence was to come your way, what would you do?'

Gorski looked at him. Even before the Slav had appeared, he had drunk too much. What was it? Five, six beers? More than that? Now the *eau-de-vie* was making his head swim.

'I would attempt to ascertain if there was any truth in this fellow's story.'

'Feel free,' said the Slav with an open-handed gesture.

Gorski saw no harm in playing along. 'Well,' he said, 'for a start, where did this fellow claim to have carried out this act?'

The Slav did not miss a beat. 'In Monsieur Tarrou's office.'

'And at what time?'

'Around ten o'clock in the morning. But these questions would not get you anywhere, Inspector. All this was mentioned in the newspaper reports.'

'Yes,' Gorski replied, feeling he was now on firmer ground, 'but one must proceed methodically. One must establish the facts, the basic facts. That done, I would ask him how he had killed Tarrou.'

The Slav nodded. 'Of course, I asked him the same question. After a brief struggle—so this gentleman claimed—he injected him with a substance that induced a cardiac arrest. Tarrou then staggered backwards and collapsed onto a glass coffee table.'

Gorski felt suddenly sober. He could not be sure, but he did not think there had been any mention of the coffee table or the position of Tarrou's body in any of the newspaper reports.

'And this *substance*: what was it?'

'Ah, yes, I also asked him that,' said the Slav, as if searching his memory. 'What was it he said? Potassium something … potassium sulphate, I believe, although I couldn't swear to it.'

Gorski made every effort to commit the name of this chemical to memory. 'No marks were found on the body,' he said. 'Nor did the post-mortem identify any toxic substances.'

The Slav cheerfully dismissed these objections. 'Of course, I'm no expert, but I would have thought such a substance would only be detected if the proper tests were carried out. As for the mark of a hypodermic syringe, I imagine that would be quite easy to miss, particularly if the pathologist in question was close to retirement and had already made up his mind about the cause of death.'

Gorski looked at him. He was beginning to feel nauseous. He massaged his temples between his thumb and forefingers.

The Slav suddenly started laughing.

'No need to look so serious, Inspector. You understand, of course, that I have been speaking only hypothetically. Obviously I met no such fellow in a bar. I was only curious to know what it might take for you to open an investigation.'

The Slav put his arm around Gorski's shoulder as if they were long-standing drinking buddies. He filled their glasses, then raised his in a toast.

'*Nazdrovje*, Inspector!'

Gorski attempted to repeat the word, but his tongue stumbled over it. He was having trouble following his own train of thought. Certainly, there was one point on which he agreed: the Slav had not heard any of this from a fellow in a bar.

'Perhaps you're now wishing that you had kept up your surveillance of me,' the Slav suggested.

‘How do you know I haven’t?’ said Gorski.

‘Well, I haven’t seen your horse-faced boy lately.’

‘I have other resources at my disposal,’ said Gorski.

‘Then you’ll know whether there’s any truth in what I’ve told you,’ the Slav said jovially. He jabbed his elbow into Gorski’s ribs as if this was an excellent joke.

Despite the fact that he continually felt the Slav to be getting the better of him, Gorski had taken something of a liking to this curious foreigner. He wondered whether, under different circumstances, they might have become friends.

They were now the last customers in Le Pot. Gorski had not noticed the others leave. Yves stood behind the counter with his arm folded across his chest. He must have overheard every word of the conversation.

Gorski excused himself and got up to use the WC. This time he did not trouble to close the door. When he returned, the Slav was gone. Gorski knocked back his final shot while standing at the table. He could get a taste for this stuff. He approached the counter to settle the bill, but Yves told him it had been taken care of.

Outside, he emptied the contents of his stomach into the gutter, steadying himself with one hand on the bonnet of a parked car. When he had finished, he had a good look around. It did not appear that anyone had witnessed his undignified behaviour.

Fourteen

The following morning Gorski had a thick head. He had passed out in his father's chair and awoken around six when his mother started pottering around the kitchenette. He had wordlessly taken himself to his childhood room and slept face down on the divan for a further hour or so, dreaming vividly. He was roused for a second time by the sound of a van pulling up outside Madame Beck's shop, followed by the usual kerfuffle of the delivery. He got up, showered, shaved and dressed and was now drinking a cup of coffee at the table. There was a gnawing feeling of anxiety in his gut. He told himself that this was merely on account of having drunk too much, but he suspected it had a deeper cause. His mother was in her chair, gazing at the sideboard. Now and again her lips moved, but no sound was emitted.

He struggled to remember the details of the conversation in Le Pot. One thing was for sure: he was a clever fellow, this Slav. *Hypothetically speaking*. That was the phrase he had kept using. And yet there had been no need even for this precaution. All he would have to do was deny that the conversation had taken place, or claim that he had been speaking in jest. It was clear that he had never spoken to some 'fellow in a bar', but regardless, the conversation had no evidential value. It was worthless. Even so, he had displayed a knowledge of the scene that strongly suggested he had been there. Gorski's mind returned once more to the unnatural posture of the body, the kicked-off shoe that was suggestive of a struggle. What was the chemical he had mentioned? Sodium something. No, it had been potassium … potassium something. He cursed his poor memory. He should have written it down. Still, it would be a simple enough matter to find out if such a chemical existed and could be used in this way. Perhaps this was a task he could entrust to Roland.

Then there was the question of the Slav's motivation for his hypothetical admission. Gorski had no time for the notion that criminals were driven by some irresistible urge to confess. In his experience, quite the opposite was the case. Even in the face of the most irrefutable evidence, the criminal will stubbornly maintain his innocence. The idea of the murderer compelled by feelings of guilt to give himself up had been invented by those who had no experience of such things. It was based on the misconception that crooks are subject to the same diktats of conscience as the average law-abiding citizen. They aren't. If they were, they would not be able to function in their chosen profession.

In any case, Gorski did not think for a moment that the Slav was responding to a guilty conscience. There had not been anything spontaneous about his remarks; nothing emotional. Even if Gorski were to apply to have Tarrou's body disinterred—something which would, in any case, never be permitted—it was unlikely that any evidence to corroborate the Slav's story would be found. His position was unassailable. And perhaps he had, after all, just made the whole thing up. Yes, he had recounted some details which had not been mentioned in the papers, but as soon as Gorski had concluded his questioning of Anna Petrovka, she had been surrounded by her colleagues to whom she would have described exactly what she had seen in Tarrou's Portakabin. And then, in turn, each of these workmates would disseminate this information around the bars and cafés of the town. It was perfectly possible that the Slav had simply overheard this gossip. Had he not even once told Gorski that he had a weakness for eavesdropping? As for the chemical he had mentioned, in all likelihood he had just made that up too. Whatever the truth, or otherwise, of what he had said, it was clear that his motivation was to toy with Gorski: to demonstrate that it was he who was in control and that Gorski, the small-town chief of police, was entirely impotent.

Well, what of it? No one, except perhaps Yves, need ever know the conversation had taken place. Gorski could not even be sure that it had done. Perhaps it had been a dream. Certainly it had something of the quality of a dream. He had not seen the Slav enter or leave the bar. He had just appeared, then vanished. Then Gorski remembered that he had paid the bill. Or perhaps that had just been part of the dream too. Gorski supposed that he could ask Yves, but that would only make him look more ridiculous than he already did.

He finished his coffee. He smoked a cigarette to settle his stomach. His mother's presence needled him. She had not said a word and yet he felt she was admonishing him. He looked at her. Maybe it was all an act that she was putting on. Maybe she knew precisely what was going on around her and was also engaged in some kind of game. He returned to the bathroom and brushed his teeth for a second time to try to get rid of the acrid taste in his mouth.

Downstairs, Madame Beck was sweeping some leaves from the vestibule of her shop. When she saw Gorski, she stopped and leant on her brush in a way that accentuated the curve of her slim hips.

'You're late this morning,' she said. 'I thought you must already have left.'

Normally Gorski would have derived some pleasure from the fact that he had even crossed Madame Beck's mind, but today it only reinforced the feeling that his every move was being scrutinised; that he was constantly being called to account for his most trivial actions.

'And what of it?' he replied.

Madame Beck was taken aback by his curt tone. She made a face and resumed her sweeping, stepping back from the door to allow him to pass.

He had only gone a few yards along Rue des Trois Rois before he regretted his rudeness. Without pausing for thought, he turned back. Madame Beck must have known he had returned because the little bell above the door sounded, but she did not look up. He stood in the doorway for a few moments formulating a suitable expression of contrition in his head. Eventually she looked in his direction.

'Did you forget something?' she said blankly.

She must have known that he had come back to apologise, but she was not going to make it easy for him.

'I'm sorry,' he said. 'I … I had a bit too much to drink last night. I think this business with Maman is beginning to get to me.'

How despicable to use his mother's condition as an excuse for his ill-mannered behaviour.

Madame Beck was not impressed with his explanation. 'Georges,' she said, 'you're under no obligation to engage in conversation every time you pass through the shop, but if you're hungover or in a foul temper, don't take it out on me.'

Then, although the floor was spotless, she resumed her sweeping. He muttered a second apology and retreated into the street.

He bought a pain au chocolat from the boulangerie on Rue de Mulhouse. He was not in the mood to face Schmitt's wisecracks, so he took the alley to the car park at the back of the police station where his 504 was parked. He ate his pastry in the driving seat, dropping crumbs on his lap. He wound down the window and smoked a cigarette. Then he drove to Tarrou's concrete factory on the outskirts of the town.

Anna Petrovka had not arrived at work. No matter. Gorski had taken down her details. She did not live in Saint-Louis, but in Sierentz, a village a few miles to the north.

The countryside in this corner of the Alsace is untroubled by points of topographical interest. The land is divided into geometrically regular fields in which potatoes, asparagus and grain are grown. Those given over to cattle are bounded by jerry-built electric fences, though the bovine residents exhibit no signs of wanderlust. Why should they? They are not concerned about the monotony of the landscape. They don't know anything different. And, in any case, the pasture is excellent: succulent, green and in plentiful supply.

Due to the flatness of the land and the uniformity of the fields, the roads between settlements are dead straight. No need for corners here. If, therefore, an ambulance is idling in a field of cows with its blue lights rotating, it will be visible from a good distance in any direction.

Gorski spotted the lights soon after he turned off the A35. The appearance of an emergency vehicle is rarely an augury of good tidings, and it was with a familiar sort of dread that he approached the scene.

The inhabitants of the field in question had retreated to the farthest boundary of their territory and were observing events from a safe distance. About a hundred metres into the field, a car had come to rest on its roof. It had left two tracks at an angle of roughly thirty degrees from the road. Aside from the ambulance, two police cars were parked on the verge. Gorski pulled his Peugeot up behind them. A black Opel had also come to a halt, nosed diagonally into the field. Gorski wondered if the driver had taken some sort of avoiding action.

Roland was among those present.

'The call came in twenty minutes ago,' he said.

Gorski trudged towards the vehicle. Fifteen or twenty metres before it had come to rest, the furrow it had cut in the turf came to an end. The car must have careered through the field, then catapulted into the air. The bonnet was concertinaed and the cabin completely collapsed. The passenger-side door had flown off and was lying twenty metres away. The paintwork on the driver's side of the vehicle was marked with deep horizontal scratches. The wheels were splayed outwards. Incongruously, the engine was still running and the front wheels continued to turn wonkily. The car was a white *deux chevaux*.

Two paramedics were standing by the vehicle.

'Nothing we can do,' one of them said. 'We're waiting for the fire brigade to come and cut her out.'

Gorski got down on his hands and knees and pressed his cheek to the ground to get a look inside. Amid the tangle of metal, he could make out a mass of blonde hair, matted with blood. He walked round to the passenger side and repeated the exercise, but the car had been so compressed by the impact that he could see nothing more of the occupant. He didn't need to. He had known since he had seen the ambulance lights illuminate the morning sky that it was Anna Petrovka.

He straightened up. Three or four hundred metres in the direction of Saint-Louis was a farmhouse. A similar distance to the north, a small copse marked the boundary of the field. To the east, the factory chimneys of Basel were visible on the horizon. Other than that, nothing but flatness. Roland appeared at Gorski's side.

'The gentleman who reported it is in the car.'

They set off back across the field.

The man's name was Antoine Lutz. He was thirty-five years old and also lived in Sierentz. He worked as a book-keeper for a pharmaceutical firm across the frontier in Basel. His hands were shaking. Gorski gave him a cigarette and had him get out of the car to describe what he had seen. He had not witnessed the accident but had seen the vehicle in the middle of the field as he made his way to work. He had slept in and had not left home until 9.15, so it must have been about 9.20. He pulled over and ran across the field to see if anyone was inside. He had recognised Anna Petrovka's car at once. She lived a few doors down from him. She was a nice girl, very friendly. At this point he started to cry.

'She was such a terrible driver,' he said though his tears. 'I was always telling her she would have an accident, but she just laughed. She was always laughing.'

Gorski ignored these remarks and asked if he had seen any

other cars on the road, either ahead of him or passing in the opposite direction.

'Well, I don't think there was anyone immediately ahead of me. Because I was late, the road was quieter than usual.' Lutz gave some thought to the latter part of the question, then shook his head. 'In all honesty, I couldn't say. I mean, why would I have noticed?'

'If someone had been driving erratically, perhaps in a manner suggesting they had been involved in an accident, you might have noticed,' Gorski said.

'Yes, I suppose I would. I didn't see anything like that.'

Gorski motioned for him to continue.

Lutz had tried to open the driver's door of the car, but it was useless, so he had run to the farmhouse—he gestured towards it—and called for an ambulance. And that was that. There was nothing more to tell.

Gorski told Roland to take down the witness's details and drive him home. He would go and speak to the residents of the farmhouse. Roland asked if he could accompany him, but Gorski refused. Events were overtaking him. If he had acted with more urgency, things would not have taken the turn they had. And regardless of what may or may not have caused the 2CV to leave the road, a young woman was now crushed to death, a fate she could hardly have expected and had done nothing to deserve.

It started to rain but Gorski did not quicken his pace. He felt a prickling sensation on his forehead. His breathing came in short unsatisfactory gasps. He unconsciously flexed and unflexed his knuckles. He paused to light a cigarette. There was plenty of time to smoke one before he reached the farmhouse. A lungful of smoke did not help. Then he realised what it was: he was angry.

Generally speaking, Gorski made it his business not to get angry. His instinct was always to try to defuse a situation. How often had he pretended not to have felt a slight or offence? He prided himself on his self-control. But now there was no mistaking it: he was furious. He was angry with Keller. He was angry with the Slav. He was angry with Anna Petrovka for not telling him whatever it was she knew when she had the chance. But more than any of that, he was angry with himself. He smoked his cigarette to the filter and tossed the butt onto the verge. If there had been a tree close to hand, he would have punched it, but there was not. The nearest one was on the other side of the road, and he would have looked foolish if he went to the trouble of crossing the road for the purpose of punching a tree.

He loitered in the cobbled yard before knocking on the door of the farmhouse and smoked another cigarette. Maybe they would offer him a drink.

Gorski recognised Madame Fourneau from the weekly market. She and her husband were in possession of the third pitch from the entrance on Rue de Huningue. Among the farming folk of the area, this made them minor aristocracy. They sold cheese and other dairy products. Madame Fourneau was a ruddy woman, dressed in a man's shirt, dungarees and short rubber boots. When Gorski appeared at the kitchen door, she greeted him warmly and offered him a glass of milk. He accepted. It was not what he had been hoping for, but it might settle his stomach. They sat down at the kitchen table. The little door of the range was open, and a warm glow emanated from within. The room smelt of manure. Madame Fourneau's boots were caked in the stuff. Once when he was a teenager, after they had made love in a field not so far from where he now sat, Marthe Gelsen had scooped up handfuls of fresh cow dung and smeared it on her breasts, which she then proceeded to rub over Gorski's torso, laughing uncontrollably as she did so. Gorski had become aroused, and she had slathered his sex in more dung and manually brought him to a climax. Afterwards, she cleaned her hands on Gorski's cheeks and hair and they had lain on their backs in the sun until everything dried to a crust.

Madame Fourneau watched approvingly as Gorski drank his milk. It did not do with these sorts of people to get down to business too soon. In any case, he knew in advance that his visit would be no more than a formality. And so it transpired: Monsieur Fourneau had been hosing down the byre; Madame Fourneau had been here in the kitchen, chopping vegetables. The evidence for this was on the wooden worktop, next to the sink. Gorski was about to leave when Fourneau himself appeared in the doorway.

'A nasty business,' he said. But despite this, he behaved as if a fatal car accident on their property was not an occurrence of any great note. The livestock had been startled, he observed. The milk yield would be poor tomorrow.

Gorski stood up and thanked Madame Fourneau for the milk. She disappeared into the adjacent larder and returned with an enormous cheese. Gorski at first refused. He made a weak joke about accepting backhanders, but she waved away his objections.

'Take it for your wife,' she said. 'It'll be good in a month or so.'

It was easier to relent than to explain that he and Céline were no longer together. The cheese was heavy and required both hands to carry it back to his car. He and his mother would never get through it. He would offer some to Madame Beck. She had once mentioned that she was partial to a piece of cheese. Perhaps it could serve as some sort of peace offering.

Fifteen

Gorski was making his way slowly along Rue des Trois Rois. It was six o'clock in the morning or thereabouts. The streets of Saint-Louis were deserted. Outwardly, aside from the fact that he was not wearing a tie or overcoat, he did not appear very different from normal. On closer inspection it might have been noticed that his eyes were red, and he was blinking more frequently than usual, but to someone happening to catch sight of him from the window of their apartment, there would have been little to excite their attention. Inwardly, however, Gorski did feel different. He felt utterly numb. He had just killed his mother. This done, it had been unthinkable to remain in the apartment and now, having left, he could hardly just loiter on the pavement outside Madame Beck's shop. So he placed one foot in front of the other and found himself walking. He turned right into Rue de Mulhouse. An icy breeze blew from the direction of the railway station, stinging his eyes.

He could not have said when he had decided to kill his mother. Actually, 'decided' was not the right word. It was an idea that had presented itself and which he had then acted upon. He had not *decided* anything. If the idea had taken up residence in the back of his mind some time ago, he had resisted acknowledging it. To have done so would have been to somehow make acting upon it inevitable. But that was what had happened. He had become less and less capable of ignoring its presence. For—aside from those acts carried out in the throes of passion—no one commits any deed, however insignificant, without having first conceived of it. And if one conceives of something, then the corresponding action in the world becomes a possibility. Without the thought, there can be no act.

And, certainly, the thought of killing his mother had not occurred to Gorski only in the moments before he acted. No, it had been lurking there for some time, but like a troublesome fly flitting into his peripheral vision, he had swatted it away. The question was when this thought had begun to squat in his mind. The other night when his mother had pushed her bowl of soup onto the floor, had he not muttered the words, *I could kill you*, under his breath? Or had it been the day he returned to find the kitchen on fire? The following day, when Faubel had said, *I think we both know what needs to be done*, Gorski could not help wondering if he was insinuating something. But he would hardly have interpreted Faubel's words in such a way had he not already been harbouring such thoughts himself. Could he claim that it had been Madame Duymann's accusation that her son was trying to kill *her* that had planted the thought in his head? No, the roots were more deeply established than that. Perhaps it started when his mother's mental lapses could no longer be dismissed as old age; when she continually mistook her son for her long-dead husband. It was impossible to say with any certainty. Gorski was not even sure that it would be an exaggeration to think that this outcome had been inevitable since the moment, forty years before, when he had placed his foot on the little mustard spoon and purposefully pressed downwards. It had not been the act of breaking the mustard spoon that was important, malicious though it was. It was the fact that his mother knew he had done it. Had she accused him at the time, he would have admitted everything. But she had kept her counsel, perhaps hoping that her son would own up of his own volition, and ever since that day he had felt she was sitting in judgement over him; that he was a source of shame to her. Later, his decision to become a policeman had not—as he told himself—been a rebellion against the shady nature of his father's business, but an attempt to demonstrate to his mother that he was not the miscreant she took him for. It had not done any good, however. She could see him for the imposter he was. Or so he supposed.

In any case, it had reached the point when he had found himself sitting on the edge of his mother's bed listening to her sobbing over and over, *Albert, don't send me away. You're throwing me away like a pair of shoes.* The fact that she thought this act of treachery was being carried out by her husband rather than Gorski himself made it no more bearable. No matter how many times he repeated that no one was being thrown away, her wailing persisted. When her refrain altered to *I'd rather be dead, I'd rather be dead*, Gorski could not pretend that it was this that had planted the thought in his mind.

He had got up from the bed and returned to the living room. The wailing abated a little. Had there been neighbours, they would have heard everything. But there were no neighbours. There was only the shop downstairs. Gorski had taken a swallow of wine, then swigged what was left in the bottle from the neck. He knew what he was going to do. It was now only a question of when. Once you have fixed on a disagreeable task, it is better to get it over and done with. But still he procrastinated. He fetched another bottle from the cupboard beneath the sink. That was another sham. Maman knew very well where he kept his stash. He poured out a glass, carelessly sloshing some onto the counter. He was seeking insensibility, while retaining an awareness that if he became too inebriated, he might botch the job. It was a question of balance. Half the bottle now, he decided, the second half when the deed was done.

For a moment, standing by the stove where for decades his mother had made stock from bones freely given by the butcher on Rue de Mulhouse, and where her slippers had formed an indentation in the linoleum, Gorski's resolve failed him. His knees weakened and he had to clutch the counter with both hands to prevent himself from falling. How despicable he was, thinking of the killing of his mother as *a disagreeable task* for which he would reward himself—yes, *reward himself*—with the second half of the bottle when the deed was done. And yet it was this, the thought of the booze, that spurred him on. He even held the bottle up to the light to see how much was left. He had made a contract with himself and he was going to keep it. He was a man of honour.

He returned to his mother's bedroom. Regardless of when he may or may not have fixed on this course, he had at no point contemplated the reality of carrying it out. Had he done so, it would certainly have acted as a brake. But he had not, and once he had set out from the kitchenette, fuelled by wine and the promise of more to come, there could be no backing out.

The job had not been easy. He had sat once more on the edge of his mother's bed and held her hand. He had murmured some reassuring words. No, he would not send her away. She could stay here in her own apartment. He had even turned and looked her in the eye. Her whimpering subsided, but her eyes darted from side to side like those of a cornered animal. Then Gorski had reached to the far side of the bed and taken up the pillow. It was a generous, weighty pillow, stuffed with goose down. Fearing a moment of understanding in his mother's eyes, he had turned his head away as he placed it over her face. For thirty seconds or a minute perhaps, her body went limp. These moments were time enough for Gorski to feel a sort of grim relief, firstly, because his mother had not the strength to resist and, secondly, because, he told himself, he was in fact only doing what she had asked. Was it, morally, any different from taking a dog to the veterinarian to be put to sleep? At worst, he was only hastening the inevitable. Then Madame Gorski's body stiffened, and moments later she began to struggle against the pressure on her face. Some sort of life force kicked in. Her body convulsed under the bedspread with surprising strength. Her arms were trapped beneath the covers. An image he had once seen on television of psychiatric patients receiving electro-shock therapy flashed through Gorski's mind. There was never any question that she would overpower him, but he was forced to manoeuvre himself onto the bed to pin her down. Even so, somehow, she managed to work her right arm free of the covers and it flailed uselessly around her son's face. Gorski had not reckoned on this, but he did not allow his resolve to fail. He could, after all, hardly abandon the task halfway through. Then her bony hand grasped his wrist. The second hand of his watch progressed slowly around the face. Thirty seconds passed, then forty-five. The fingernails of his mother's hand turned white. Another twenty seconds. Then, a sudden rigidity before everything went limp.

Gorski remained on the bed straddling his mother's chest for some time. He was breathing heavily from the exertion. He did not remove the pillow from her face. He had to prise her fingers from his wrist. He tucked her arm back under the sheets. He climbed off and looked at the aftermath. There was so little to his mother that he might have been gazing at no more than a pile of rumpled blankets. He felt a sob rise in his throat, then remembering the deal he had made with himself, returned to the kitchenette and emptied the remains of the bottle down his throat.

So it was that he now found himself trudging along Rue de Mulhouse into a bitter wind without a coat. Was this also part of a plan he had formulated but not admitted to himself? Certainly he knew where he was going and what he was going to do. There was an inevitability about it. He did not feel that he was making a choice. There were no longer any other options open to him. In any case, he had had enough. He had had enough of everything.

He thrust his hands into the pockets of his trousers. How absurd to be thinking about keeping his hands warm at a time like this, but there was nothing to be gained by being cold. It crossed his mind to return to the apartment to fetch his coat, but he rejected the idea. He had to push on. For once in his life, he needed to show a bit of backbone.

At midnight, Rue de Mulhouse would have been little busier than it was now. Perhaps you might encounter a drunk weaving along the pavement or glimpse a cat skulking between bins. The occasional car might pass, driven with the over-cautiousness of the inebriated. But at this time of the morning, there was nothing.

Gorski moved with a determined gait. He had a purpose. His hands were warmer. It had been a good idea to put them in his pockets. He congratulated himself on this decision.

He approached the police station. Aside from the light in the vestibule at the top of the steps, it was in darkness. Gorski crossed to the opposite side of the road. Schmitt would be sitting on his little stool behind the front desk, eating caramels and filling out the crossword in the previous day's *L'Alsace*. He liked the early shift as it meant he could be home in time for lunch.

Gorski did not take the turning towards the railway station. It would have been a simple matter to leap from the footbridge onto the tracks, but there was sure to be a night porter who would make it his business to intervene. In any case, it was altogether too conspicuous—too *visible*—and Gorski did not want any witnesses. He crossed the road and continued for another block. He passed the cemetery where his mother would soon be buried next to his father. In the months after his father's death, Gorski had visited the grave now and again, but he had done so only for appearances' sake. Once or twice he had tried speaking to his father, but he had felt foolish and found himself looking round to make sure that no one had seen him. It now crossed his mind to pay a final visit to his father's grave, but for what reason? He did not want to think of his father in the final years of his life, wheezing in his chair in the apartment in Rue des Trois Rois. In any case, the gates to the cemetery were locked at night, this after an incident the previous year in which some graves had been desecrated.

He continued past the cemetery gates and turned into the narrow footpath skirting the northern edge of the cemetery. Beyond the reach of the streetlamps, Gorski had the sense of stepping into another world. The path was bounded on the left by the cemetery wall and on the right by undergrowth that engulfed a three-metre-high mesh fence, forming a kind of tunnel. Gorski hesitated for a few moments to allow his eyes to adjust, but to little effect. He wondered if there might be men lurking in the undergrowth waiting to spring out and demand his wallet. They would be out of luck, as his wallet was in the pocket of the overcoat he had neglected to put on.

Through the shrubbery the hulking shape of the water tower was faintly discernible. As teenagers, Gorski and Pigeon had once waited until after dark and scaled the mesh fence. They planned to climb the spiral ladder beneath the tower and spend the night on the platform. The whole thing had been Pigeon's idea and Gorski had gone along with it only because he did not want to be called a chicken. Pigeon had pilfered a bottle of wine from his parents and Gorski had brought some bread and dry sausage. When they reached the foot of the tower, they found that access to the ladder was blocked by a padlocked gate. They were discussing how they might surmount this obstacle when a caretaker with a flashlight appeared and shouted at them to scram. They ran off, Gorski feeling a trickle of urine filling his underpants then moistening the inner thigh of his trousers. Pigeon suggested climbing into the graveyard to drink the wine, and Gorski had agreed as it was dark there and his friend would not be able to see the stain on his trousers.

A fox emerged from the undergrowth a few feet ahead. It stopped and looked at Gorski, its eyes glinting like coins. Then, as if deciding that Gorski was of no interest, it ambled across the path and disappeared into the vegetation at the foot of the cemetery wall. The path curved gently to the right, towards the railway tracks. Here, the mesh fence barred Gorski's way. There was a gate, but it was fastened by a thick chain. Gorski's plan was no better thought through than Pigeon's had been all those years before. He tilted his head and assessed the barrier separating him from the tracks. He had no appetite to climb it, but there was no alternative. Those bent on self-destruction cannot give up at the first obstacle.

Without further hesitation, he took four or five steps back, then ran at the gate and leapt, attempting to grasp the uppermost part of the structure. He succeeded only in throwing himself against the fence and falling backwards onto his behind. He got up hastily, as if trying to give the appearance to any unseen onlooker that this was precisely what he had intended. He brushed the dirt from his clothes, leaving a smear of blood. He had cut the base of his thumb on the mesh. He pressed his hand against his thigh to stem the flow of blood, but perhaps on account of the cold he did not feel any pain.

A faint sliver of light was now visible on the horizon to the east.

Gorski stood by the gate and assessed his options. A diagonal strut was attached to the vertical post of the gate. It was on the other side of the mesh, but it would be sufficient to provide some purchase. He gripped the fence above his head and pushed the toe of his left shoe through the mesh. Céline had given him these shoes for his birthday a few years before and had made a point of telling him they had come from an expensive store in Strasbourg. From this position he succeeded in pulling himself halfway up the fence. Awkwardly, he brought his right foot to the top of the metal strut. He pushed upwards and grasped the top of the gate. His left shoe remained trapped in the mesh. Blood dripped from the wound in his hand. He would have to haul himself up one more time and throw his leg over. The mesh at the top of the fence was jagged. Gorski thought about the potential consequences for his genitals, but what of it? They had not been put to any good use for some time.

He successfully manoeuvred himself onto the top of the fence and sat awkwardly straddling it. His scrotum was intact, but the leg of his trousers was torn at the thigh. He sat for a few moments astride the gate, one hand in front, one behind. Then he hauled his left leg over and lowered himself to the ground. He landed on his backside and sat in the scruffy grass catching his breath. He felt he had achieved something.

The first of the four sets of tracks that carried trains from Saint-Louis to Basel and Strasbourg and beyond was only a few metres ahead. Gorski had no idea in which direction the next train would be travelling, but it did not matter. He could not remember the last time he had taken a train.

The tracks were raised above ground level, the sleepers supported by large rocks. Gorski approached the tracks and knelt down. He must have looked like he was about to pray. Then he lay down on his belly so that his neck was on the rail. The metal was cold against his skin. His position was awkward and he wriggled forward so that his shoulders pressed against the side of the rail. He turned his head to the left, facing in the direction of Basel, and placed his hands on the rail. This was relatively comfortable. He recalled the joke about the condemned man who places his hands beside his head on the block of the guillotine, only to be told by the executioner, *Mind your fingers.* It was a good joke and it brought a smile to his lips. Nevertheless, the prospect of having his fingers severed was disagreeable, so he spread his arms out on either side, as if he was imitating a bird or an aeroplane.

Due to the position he had adopted, his wristwatch was now directly in his eyeline. It was twenty to seven. This watch had been a present from his father on the occasion of his twenty-first birthday. No doubt it had been an item brought into the pawnbroker's shop, but even to this day it kept good time. He would have liked Clémence to have it. He took it off and placed it in the pocket of his jacket.

It was very cold. It had been a mistake not to bring his overcoat, but he could hardly return to the apartment to fetch it now. After a few minutes, his back began to hurt. He had no idea what time the first train would pass. He should have checked the timetable. He realised too that when a train did approach, he would prefer not to be facing it. He wondered if there would be time to turn his head in the opposite direction.

Birds were beginning to twitter in the undergrowth, but other than that there was silence.

Some time passed. The sky behind the factory chimneys in Basel glowed pink. Gorski became anxious that someone might pass along the path on their way to work and see him. It would be difficult to explain what he was doing.

Then, before he heard anything, he felt a vibration in the ground. Gorski remembered reading as a boy that snakes discerned sound through vibrations in their underbellies. His heart began to palpitate. This was it. Was this what he wanted? It was too late for questions like that. He thought of Maman at rest on her soft mattress, her body growing cold. His eyes were moist. The vibrations grew more intense and were now accompanied by a sound akin to the roar of a distant waterfall. Very rapidly it grew thunderous. Gorski realised he no longer had time to change his mind. He closed his eyes and drew in as deep a breath as he could muster. He wondered what his final thought would be. He pictured his father in his brown store coat and himself as a boy hunched over the great ledger in which the shop's transactions were recorded. He liked that image and tried to hold it in his mind, but it flickered away. He saw Clémence leaning against the doorway of the kitchenette, watching him quarter a bulb of fennel. What would she think of her father if she could see him now? The noise grew deafening. In defiance of the executioner's advice, he reached his hands forward and gripped the rail. Then silence.

Clémence Gorski awakes with a start. The first morning light has begun to sneak through the gap below the blind. She turns over. It is too early to get up, but she has a feeling of anxiety in her stomach. The previous evening, Raymond Barthelme invited her to his house, a shabby mansion on the outskirts of the town. They went upstairs to his room, which was painted entirely white. There was nowhere to sit aside from a straight-backed chair in the middle of the floor. They listened to some records, then she had lain next to him on the bed and they had kissed for a while. He asked if she had any brothers. When she replied that she did not, he asked if she would like it if they were brother and sister. She left shortly after that. Unable to sleep, she gets up and raises the blind. Her room is at the back of the house on Rue de Village-Neuf and overlooks the small garden, which is tended by a gardener, Monsieur Guizot, who is supposed to come once a week but is there on an almost daily basis. He's already standing on the patio trying to get his pipe going.

The little park by the Protestant temple is deserted. An icy breeze blowing from the direction of the railway station rattles the few leaves still clinging to the branches of the chestnut trees.

The travel agent Eugène Vinçard stares at the clock by his bed. It is around half past six. He has already been awake for an hour or so. Since the death of his wife, he sleeps only fitfully. He misses the warmth of her body beside him and dreads the empty hours before he can open up the shop downstairs. He gets up and looks through the gap in the curtains onto Rue de Mulhouse. The cop with the funny name is passing on the opposite pavement. He is not wearing a coat. Vinçard shakes his head to himself: the guy will catch his death of cold.

Dejan Vukašinović clicks the brass clasps of his suitcase shut. There is no need to formally check out. He has paid in advance, so he can just leave his key on the counter as he departs, but it is early yet and the weaselly proprietor keeps the front door of the hotel locked until seven. No matter. He is not in any hurry. He stretches out on the bed, not troubling to remove his shoes.

In the apartment above Le Pot, Yves Reno lies snoring, his tattooed arm draped over his wife Titou's chest. She stirs a little and, without waking, snuggles closer into her husband's chest.

At the front desk of the police station on Rue de Mulhouse, Willy Schmitt has spilled coffee on his crossword. He gets up and fetches some paper towels from the dispenser by the sink and mops up the mess. He has a caramel in his mouth. He likes to suck a caramel while drinking his coffee. His wife scolds him for the slurping noises he makes when he does this.

Emma Beck is making coffee. Upstairs, her husband is still asleep. She does not normally rise so early, but she was upset by an exchange with the cop who is living in the apartment above her shop. She has developed a fondness for him and had to fight back tears when he spoke curtly to her the previous day. The situation has left her feeling quite unsettled.

Ivan Baudoin is asleep next to the dog he now calls Charlot. They are nose to nose, like a pair of lovers. On the first night, when the dog tried to climb onto his bed, Ivan shooed him away, but when he woke up in the morning, the dog had clambered up next to him anyway. Now Charlot sleeps there every night, making grizzling noises as if he is dreaming. If, at some point, Monsieur Baudoin happens to run into Charlot's real owners, he will of course be obliged to give him up, but he will be heartbroken to do so.

Sixteen

Gorski's first thought was that his fingers had not been severed. Likewise, his head remained attached to his shoulders. This realisation led him to conclude that he was not dead. The train had passed on an adjacent track. The noise had been deafening and continued to reverberate in his ears. He raised himself to a kneeling position. He felt foolish, but there had been no one around to witness the farcical spectacle. Perhaps the train driver had caught sight of him as he flashed by. What of it? Even if he had glimpsed a figure by the tracks, Gorski would not have been recognisable. The important thing was that he was still alive. There was no question of waiting for another train. It was not so much that this too might pass on the wrong track, rather it was that Gorski realised he was glad he was not dead. He could not, he reflected sardonically, even do away with himself. Had he been serious, he could have checked the timetables displayed on the station platforms without arousing suspicion. And instead of placing his head on the track, he would have thrown himself in front of a moving train in the customary fashion. As suicide attempts went, it had been pretty shoddy—laughable really. He had, in effect, left it to chance.

He stood up and brushed himself down. He remembered that he had left one of his shoes in the fence. It was still there. He climbed back over. It was easier this time as the diagonal strut was on the railway side of the mesh. He retrieved his shoe and put it on. It was scuffed and bent out of shape. His suit was filthy and torn, and the wound on his hand seeped blood. He looked like a tramp.

As it was now beginning to get light, he took the route behind the cemetery, emerging at the junction of Rue de Mulhouse and Rue de la Gare. He walked briskly, anxious not to be seen in his dishevelled state. There were now a few more cars on the road, but as yet no pedestrians. It was only when he turned into Rue des Trois Rois that he properly recalled what awaited him. He was suddenly seized by a fear that his mother might not be dead; that she had only lost consciousness. In the aftermath of his act, he should have checked for a pulse, but he had not been in a sound state of mind. It was understandable, given the circumstances, that he had failed to take this precaution, but what if Maman was now sitting up in bed awaiting his return? What if she remembered that he had tried to smother her? Well, it would be simple enough to dismiss any such memory as an aberration of her disordered mind, but it was, nonetheless, an eventuality he would prefer not to face.

As he let himself into the shop, he reflected on his good fortune that he had returned before Madame Beck arrived at work. Had she already been there, it would have been difficult to explain where he had been and how he'd come to be in such an unkempt state.

He climbed the stairs, straining his ears for any sound from above. Madame Gorski was an early riser and would normally be up and about by this time. Gorski pushed open the door, which he had not thought to lock. He stood for a few moments in the little hallway, holding his breath. Silence. The door to his mother's room was ajar. Had he left it that way? He couldn't remember. There was no one in the living room. He went into the kitchenette and washed his hands. The cut on his palm had almost stopped bleeding. It was not particularly deep, but at some point someone was sure to ask about it. He dried his hands on a dishtowel, leaving a smear of blood. He shook his head: he was not behaving rationally.

The bottle of wine with which he had rewarded himself now stood accusingly on the worktop. He rolled his head on his shoulders. He must proceed methodically. He stuffed the bloody dishtowel in the kitchen bin. That was no good. That was the first place an investigator would look for evidence. It was the first place *he* would look. He removed the dishtowel from the bin and put it into a discarded grocery bag. He looked at the wine bottle. There was nothing incriminating about that. Experience had taught him a valuable lesson: what is absent from a scene can constitute evidence every bit as much as what is present. When inspecting a crime scene, Gorski made a point of looking for what should have been there but was not. What might have been removed? An excessively tidy crime scene only suggested that someone had tried to straighten things out before the cops arrived. So, the wine bottle stayed where it was. A person *in extremis*—someone who had just found his mother's body—would not think to tidy the kitchen.

Tentatively Gorski pushed open the bedroom door. The first thing he saw were his mother's feet, protruding from beneath the crocheted bedspread, the right hanging over the side of the bed. The pillow still covered her face. He remembered now. He had left it there quite deliberately. That had been a mistake: it would have made it obvious to whoever discovered the body—Madame Beck most likely—that she had not died of natural causes. That had not been a consideration at the time, but the situation had changed.

Gorski sat down on the edge of the bed. He removed the pillow and let it drop to the floor. His mother's eyes were open, staring blankly into the space above his head. Gorski closed them with his fingertips. He let out a long slow breath. He drew the bedspread over his mother's feet. That way it looked less like there had been a struggle.

Then he went into his own room and undressed. He balled up his torn trousers and pushed them, along with his suit jacket, into the back of the wardrobe. He would dispose of them as soon as possible, along with the bloodstained dishtowel.

He left his underwear in a heap on the floor and put on his

pyjamas. He threw back the covers of the bed and rucked them up. He scrunched up the pillow, but the bed did not look slept in. The sheets were too crisp. He lay down and pulled the covers over himself. He turned over a few times and kicked his legs about. He got out. It looked a little better, but no one was going to be inspecting his bed. Why would they?

He went into the bathroom and examined his face in the mirror. He was unshaven. His eyes were bloodshot. That was good. It looked as if he had been crying. He brushed his teeth. When he woke in the mornings, his breath had a sour tang, but because he had not been asleep, this was absent. If questioned, he would say that he had brushed his teeth before finding his mother's body, for what sort of person would think to brush their teeth after discovering that their mother was dead?

It was only then that he stepped into the hallway and called Faubel.

How long had he taken to arrive? Fifteen minutes? Certainly no more than twenty. Gorski felt a rising anxiety, but he did not permit himself to smoke, imagining Faubel before the examining magistrate saying, *When I arrived, he was cynically smoking a cigarette*. For similar reasons he did not get dressed, and he even went downstairs to greet the doctor in his bare feet. They shook hands awkwardly in the little vestibule of the shop before Gorski ushered him in. It was Faubel who led the way up the narrow staircase. He had, after all, visited the premises on numerous occasions. As he examined Madame Gorski, first lightly grasping her wrist before nodding solemnly to himself, Gorski stood in the doorway. Maman looked quite peaceful, just as if she was asleep.

'I was the one that closed her eyes,' he said, before immediately regretting it.

If his mother had died in her sleep, wouldn't her eyes have been closed anyway? Gorski was not sure. It was, furthermore, a curious turn of phrase. If he had to speak, why not just say, *I closed her eyes*? Even if Faubel had assumed that someone had closed her eyes, it could only have been Gorski. The phrase he had used suggested that there had been someone else present. Either way, Gorski's mistake to say anything. That was how the guilty behaved. They felt the need to fill silences with inane prattle.

Faubel did not make out a death certificate. Until a post-mortem examination was carried out, he was unable to determine the cause of death. Gorski asked if that was strictly necessary. Faubel reminded him that he of all people should understand the need for procedure to be followed.

Despite Gorski's silly remark about closing his mother's eyes, Faubel had gone about his business with no sign of suspicion. It was, Gorski reminded himself, a routine matter for a doctor. An elderly patient had died in her sleep. Such things happened all the time and Faubel was, moreover, hardly a model of diligence.

Madame Beck arrived to find an ambulance blocking the street. She proceeded directly to the apartment, only to meet the paramedics manoeuvring the stretcher down the stairwell. Gorski and Faubel followed behind. She retreated into the shop and held the door open. The paramedics nodded their thanks, before loading their cargo into the back of the vehicle.

Faubel shook Gorski's hand on the pavement and walked off. He did not bother with any words of condolence. His Citroën was blocking the narrow pavement a few metres along the street. Gorski found himself wondering if he would now go directly to his surgery on Avenue de Bâle or first return home for breakfast. He decided the latter was more likely.

Madame Beck joined him on the pavement.

'Oh, Georges,' she said, as they watched Faubel's car lurch off the kerb. 'I'm so sorry.'

He nodded in what he imagined would seem a sad but resigned fashion. 'Maybe it's for the best,' he said.

She started to cry. She had been fond of his mother and, aside from Gorski, was the person who saw her most. He placed his hand on her upper arm and she took this as an invitation to embrace him. Her cheek touched his. Her skin was soft and warm, as if she was not long out of the bath. She smelt of lavender or rosewater or something similar. Gorski had never had much of a nose for such things, but the scent put him in mind of the little bags of potpourri that hung in his mother's wardrobe.

The ambulance pulled away. They must have seemed an odd pair, embracing on the pavement. He had avoided doing anything to suggest that he had, at this moment of crisis, been concerned about his appearance, but now standing in front of Madame Beck, he felt quite mortified. He had thrown a raincoat over his pyjamas and was wearing a pair of shoes with no socks. He had purposefully decided not to tie the laces and, as they moved inside, Madame Beck noticed this and advised him to be careful not to trip. This was good. If, later on, questions were to be asked, details like this could take on some importance.

He was so distraught, he hadn't thought to tie the laces of his shoes!

The florist accompanied him upstairs. Gorski closed the door of his mother's room, then put on some coffee. While it brewed, he excused himself and went to his room to get dressed. Madame Beck sat at the table by the window.

Gorski returned and served the coffee. There was a bottle of cognac in the sideboard and Madame Beck did not object when he poured some into both of their cups. It was then that she asked about the cut at the base of his thumb. He instinctively turned his hand inwards, as if to conceal it. He could not think of any plausible explanation of how it might have happened.

'Oh, that,' he said. 'I don't know. I only noticed it afterwards.'

Afterwards? That didn't even make sense. After what? Madame Beck, however, did not pursue the matter. His mother had just died. It was perfectly natural that he might not remember every detail of what had occurred. Instead of questioning him further, she stood up and reached across the table for his hand. She clasped his fingers in her palm. She ran the forefinger of her free hand along the length of the cut. It was a pleasurable sensation.

'All the same,' she said, 'you should put a dressing on it.'

Gorski nodded obediently, like a little boy. The incident seemed to have dispelled the ill-feeling caused by his brusque behaviour of the previous day.

Madame Beck had inadvertently sat at his place at the table, which obliged him to take what had been his mother's seat. It was disconcerting, like looking at a mirror image of the room. Everything was the wrong way round. He lit a cigarette and offered one to Madame Beck. She blew out a thin stream of smoke and gazed at the cruet set. Gorski had an urge to tell her the story of how he had broken the little mustard spoon, but he refrained from doing so. Instead, he explained how he had found his mother's body.

'I knew right away,' he heard himself saying, 'that something was wrong because she was always pottering about before I get up.'

Then he described how he had pushed open her bedroom door and found her. At this point he had paused and gazed out of the window, as if composing himself. He was careful not to over-embellish the story. That was an amateur's mistake: the belief that the addition of superfluous details added authenticity to their story. Madame Beck listened in silence. At a certain point she placed a hand over his and squeezed it. She did not question anything Gorski told her. Why should she?

When he fell silent, she said that she would be happy to close the shop for the day if he needed any help making what she called 'the arrangements'. Gorski thanked her but said that wouldn't be necessary. Naturally, it had fallen to him to take care of things after his father's death, and, in any case, in his line of work he was familiar with the bureaucratic necessities.

It was pleasant sitting there with her, the smoke rising languidly from their cigarettes. Perhaps later he would invite her up for a glass of wine. Given the circumstances, she could hardly refuse. On the other hand, it might be politic to allow a few days to pass. He did not wish to seem opportunistic.

With Madame Beck gone, the apartment felt empty. Gorski opened the window. The traffic on Rue de Mulhouse was faintly audible. There was a light drizzle. It was nine o'clock. Children would already be in school. Along the town's thoroughfares, traders would be raising their shutters. In his youth, Gorski had sometimes imagined throwing open the window of an apartment in Strasbourg or Paris and leaning out over a wrought iron balustrade to take in the teeming life of the city below: pork butchers and greengrocers hawking their wares from barrows; whores catcalling passers-by; men huddled in doorways dealing in assorted routes to oblivion. Instead, he now watched as an elderly woman passed on the opposite pavement with some kind of terrier. Gorski had seen her walk by countless times. The dog paused to sniff at a clump of dandelions sprouting from a crack at the base of a wall, then lifted its rear leg. A rivulet of urine trickled past its owner's shoes, which were of sturdy construction.

Downstairs Madame Beck would be leafing through her order book, the reading glasses she had lately acquired balancing on the tip of her nose. There were no sounds from below—the business of floristry is not a noisy one—but Gorski pictured her moving around the shop, calmly organising her day's activities. Nevertheless, if he felt a certain freedom or liberation in the absence of his mother, it was dissipated by the knowledge that Madame Beck was below. If, for example, he suddenly decided to forego his various duties and head straight to Le Pot, he could not do so without passing through the shop and, inevitably, having to provide Madame Beck with some explanation of where he was going. Not that he had any intention of doing so. There were things to be taken care of and, in any case, Yves did not open the bar until mid-afternoon.

He splashed some cognac into his cup and swilled it around the dregs of his coffee. He looked at his mother's chair. It was strange to think that she would never occupy it again. It was, in effect, no longer her chair. Now it was just a chair like any other. Gorski saw it as if for the first time. Although it had not been moved for decades, it sat on castors, and the curved wooden legs that clasped them were shaped like animal's feet. Gorski had never noticed this before. The castors had formed indentations in the carpet, just as his mother's slippers had left their mark on the kitchen linoleum. The chair itself was upholstered in brocade, threadbare where his mother's elbows had rested when she had still been able to spend her evenings knitting. At a certain point, Madame Gorski had added a mustard-coloured cushion to support the small of her back. Gorski had often watched her plumping up that cushion before lowering herself so hesitantly into the chair that it was hard to imagine her ever getting out of it again. On the headrest was an antimacassar with some decorative stitching around its edges. It was yellowed with age. Without thinking, Gorski stepped across the room and lifted it off. He held it to his face and inhaled. It smelt of his mother and the aroma brought a sob to his throat. It was as though a ghost had entered the room. He stuffed the antimacassar into the grocery bag containing the blood-stained dishtowel.

He went into the bathroom to shave. Although he was not particularly hirsute, shaving had always held a certain importance to him. He performed the ritual every morning, without fail. It felt indecent to leave the house unshaven. His father had been the same. *Nobody wishes to do business with a man with stubble on his chin*, he had once told his son. Similarly, Gorski could not remember seeing his father without a shirt and tie, and no matter how warm the weather, he would never set foot outside without a jacket. Gorski, too, felt slovenly, almost indecent, in an open-necked shirt. He did not own any casual clothes.

His eyes remained bloodshot, but the colour had returned to his cheeks. The episode by the railway track was already a distant memory. It was as if he had been sleepwalking. He recalled the roar of the approaching train and felt a shiver pass down his spine. What if it had been travelling on a different track? Chief Inspector

Georges Gorski of the Saint-Louis police would no longer exist. The thought did not make any sense. Was it even possible to contemplate one's own non-existence? He splashed cold water on his face, then carefully rinsed the tideline of whiskers from the sink. He felt better. Order was being restored.

It was only when he stepped back into his mother's room that Gorski noticed the unpleasant odour. She had soiled the sheets. There was not a great deal to it, but the sight of his mother's excrement shamed him. Did those who died peacefully in their sleep lose control of their bowels? He did not know, but Faubel had not appeared to notice and the ambulancemen had gone about their business with the customary indifference of those whose professions inure them to such things.

He stripped the bed. There was a brown stain about the size of his hand on the mattress. He opened the bedroom window and set about scrubbing the dark circle on the mattress. It disappeared quite rapidly.

He put the soiled sheets in the bag with the antimacassar and dishtowel. Then he remembered the suit he had been wearing. It would be best to burn the lot of it.

And there he was: planning to destroy evidence like a common criminal.

The fireplace had not been used for many years, but there was no reason to think that the chimney was blocked. Even so, it would seem suspicious if he were, all of a sudden, to break with habit and light a fire. Especially on the morning of his mother's death. No, the evidence would have to be disposed of in some other way.

It was important to act logically, to not make any errors. He returned to the living room and replaced the bottle of cognac in the sideboard. He sat down at the table and lit a cigarette. He forced himself to go over the chronology of events. Perhaps there was some detail he had overlooked. He reminded himself that to an impartial observer, there was nothing unusual in what had happened. Even so, something niggled him. Perhaps there was some seemingly insignificant detail he had overlooked, but he could not put his finger on it. Probably he was just on tenterhooks. Given what had occurred, that was understandable. But still, he must proceed with caution. If he wasn't careful, everything would unravel.

The arrangements were, in truth, taken care of in short order. When his father died, there had been a good number of acquaintances and business associates to be informed, but his mother had no friends. Latterly, her existence did not extend beyond the walls of the apartment on Rue des Trois Rois. In the afternoon, Gorski walked round to the undertakers on Rue Henner. Madame Beck offered to close the shop and accompany him, but he preferred to go alone. It would be less fuss that way. He opted for the most rudimentary plan the funeral directors had to offer. If he did not choose the very cheapest coffin, it was not due to any imagined wishes of his mother—she would have scorned the idea of spending a centime more than necessary—but to avoid the disdainful look on the undertaker's face.

Afterwards, he stood at the counter in the Café de la Gare and drank a couple of glasses of beer. No one paid him the least attention. Why should they? The news would not yet have filtered around the town.

Later, he called on the house on Rue de Village-Neuf. It would not have seemed right to tell Clémence the news over the telephone.

Céline seemed surprised but not entirely displeased to see him. 'Georges,' she said, 'what brings you here?'

He asked if Clémence was at home.

Céline shook her head, but she stood back from the door and Gorski followed her inside. There was a bottle of wine and the remains of a bowl of salad on the kitchen table. It pleased Gorski that Céline had been drinking alone.

'You want a glass?' she asked.

He shook his head. He was aware that Céline thought he drank too much. She fetched a second glass and poured him one anyway. There was no fooling her.

'Do you know when she'll be back?' He was referring to Clémence.

Céline spread her hands and widened her eyes. 'She's a teenager, Georges, I don't keep tabs.'

She had always taken a laissez-faire attitude to motherhood. It had never been something that interested her greatly.

She sat down and invited Gorski to do the same. Then she asked how his mother was.

'That's why I was calling,' he replied. 'She's gone.'

He then repeated, more or less, the story he had told Madame Beck earlier.

Céline said she was sorry. She topped up his glass.

'I wanted to tell Clémence in person,' he said.

'I think she's seeing some boy,' she said. 'Or perhaps she's at a friend's. I'll tell her when she comes in.'

Gorski nodded. This latter sentence indicated that he would not be welcome to wait indefinitely. A few moments of silence passed. Then Céline asked when the funeral would be. Gorski replied that there was first to be a post-mortem. Then he started to cry. He was not sure if he had ever wept in front of his wife before. Certainly he was not a man given to displays of emotion. He covered his eyes with the palm of his hand. It was perfectly natural to be moved by such an event. To be unmoved was unnatural, even suspicious. In any case, it didn't last long.

Céline handed him a tissue and patted him on the shoulder.

He blew his nose. 'It's for the best,' he said.

She nodded. 'Let me know about the funeral,' she said.

He finished his wine and left.

Seventeen

In the days following the incident with the little mustard spoon, the eight-year-old Gorski was overcome by a feeling of dread. He was convinced that at any moment he would be called to account for his actions. If the classroom door opened, he assumed it would be the police arriving to interrogate him. *Do you really expect us to believe, young man, that you have no knowledge of what happened to the mustard spoon?* At home, he avoided his mother's gaze, pretending to bury his head in a book or skulking in his room. In the evenings, if his father lowered his newspaper, he expected this to be the prelude to a grave talking-to. The only explanation for his father having not yet broached the subject was that he wished to prolong his son's suffering.

Gorski felt as if a quantity of some viscous black substance was pulsating inside him. At night, he lay awake feeling this oily mass rise in his chest, convinced that if he fell asleep it would seep from his orifices and engulf him. In the mornings, he was exhausted, but it was out of the question to plead off school. His mother commented on his pallid appearance, but he insisted that he felt perfectly well. It was imperative to act as if nothing out of the ordinary had happened.

If he regretted breaking the mustard spoon, he also understood that it had been no more than a momentary failure to exercise restraint. His real mistake had been not to own up there and then. Had he done so, he could easily have passed it off as an accident. No one would have doubted him. He was not a child given to wanton acts of destruction. His father would have glued the pieces back together and the incident would have been quickly forgotten. It was thus not the actual breaking of the spoon for which he chastised himself so much as his subsequent actions. How foolish he had been to dispose of the pieces in the street right next to his own. Although he had been careful to check that there had been no one in the vicinity, could he really be sure? A resident of Rue du Temple could easily have observed him from the window of their apartment. As he dropped the shards of china down the culvert, a fragment had landed on one of the slats of the drain and he had had to poke it down with the toe of his shoe. It would have been obvious to anyone watching that he was up to no good. It had, in any case, been a mistake to dispose of the evidence in this way. No doubt in the drainage system running beneath the streets there would be some kind of mesh to prevent blockages. When this mesh came to be cleaned, the pieces of the mustard spoon would certainly be found and traced back to the pawnbroker's shop on Rue des Trois Rois (his father having been sure to have mentioned the incident to his cronies in the Restaurant de la Cloche). Questions would be asked about how the pieces had come to be in the drain. The mystery would grip the entire town. Stories would be written in the newspapers. Competing theories would be expounded. Witnesses would come forward and the guilty party would be unmasked. Rather than dispose of the pieces at the earliest opportunity, Gorski should have held his nerve and thrown them into the Rhine or ground them into an unidentifiable powder before scattering them over some piece of wasteland. But he had not done so, and for days he awaited the inevitable reckoning. He even began to long for it. It would come as a release to be relieved of his burden; to be revealed as the miscreant he was. He would accept whatever punishment was imposed.

But the days passed, then a week, a fortnight and a month, and the reckoning did not arrive. The viscous substance throbbing in his gut began to drain away. When the door of the classroom clicked open or the little bell above the door to his father's shop sounded, Gorski no longer dreaded what was to come. And then one morning as he walked to school, he realised that for the first time in weeks he was thinking about something other than the mustard spoon. It had been a bright spring morning, and he paused to sit down on the low wall that bounded the little park by the Protestant temple. A woman was sitting on one of the benches, tossing scraps of bread from a brown paper bag. Pigeons teemed around her feet. As he watched her, Gorski realised he had got away with it. All his angst had been for nothing. How ridiculous it had been to imagine that the pieces of the little spoon would be recovered from the drain or that some witness would come forward to accuse him. Yes, his mother knew—he was convinced of that—but for reasons of her own, she had decided to keep her suspicions to herself. Perhaps she did not want to humiliate her son, but whatever her motive, this shared knowledge bound them together. She had made herself his accomplice.

Now, forty years later, this complicity had been broken. It was a relief. Gorski knew that the most successful criminals were those that worked alone. Ultimately, either by design or stupidity, accomplices always end up betraying one another. All it takes is a loose word after a few too many drinks or a falling-out of the type that is commonplace among villains. Thus, accomplices hold sway over each other not merely for the duration of a particular job, but for as long as they both remain in the land of the living. It is a kind of grim marriage. For no other reason than this, they grow wary of one another, and such feelings persist until one party or the other pops his clogs. But unlike these criminal associates, it was not that Gorski feared that his mother would betray him to the powers-that-be; it was that she herself was the powers-that-be.

So it was that with his mother gone, Gorski proceeded along Rue de Mulhouse with an uneasy feeling of liberation. Only a day or so had passed, but it was as if an oppressive regime had been unexpectedly overthrown.

It was an unseasonably bright morning. The sky was blue and punctuated only by a few high cumulus clouds. It was almost eleven o'clock, so what passed for rush hour in Saint-Louis was over. The air was crisp and free from the factory fumes of Basel. Gorski knew perfectly well that the thoroughfare had not suddenly become wider, and yet it seemed so. The sunlight sharpened the colours of the signs above the shops that lined both sides of the street. How many thousands of times had Gorski passed along this thoroughfare barely noticing anything around him? Today, he was alive to everything. He was conscious of the faint scuffing of the soles of his shoes on the pavement; of the stench of over-ripe bananas as he passed the greengrocer's; of the engine notes of passing vehicles and of the facial expressions of their drivers. In the window of the butcher whose name he could never remember a glistening display of offal struck him as obscene. A large fly perched on a luridly purple cut of brisket. He noticed for the first time that the V in the sign above Vinçard's travel agency was missing. For how long had that been the case? Years, most likely. Ordinarily, he scarcely raised his eyes from the pavement and, if he did, whatever passed across his field of vision scarcely registered. Today, however, everything was intense. It was vertiginous. He felt lighter. Yes, that was it: he felt lighter.

He paused at the glass-covered information board at the foot of the steps to the police station. The blue paintwork of the frame was blistered and faded, exposing the wood below. Behind the glass, the same poster advertising the Foreign Legion had been displayed for as long as he could remember. It showed a young man in a kepi gazing idealistically into the future. Beneath, the slogan *Voir la vie autrement* was written. The sentiment caused Gorski to smile wryly. He did not feel ready to re-enter his place of work quite yet, so he continued along Rue de Mulhouse. He raised his eyes and inhaled deeply. He drew back his shoulders. He reached the little park at the Protestant temple and sat down on a bench. He could feel the texture of the wood against his buttocks. He spread his arms along the splintered planks of the backrest. Above him, the last few rust-coloured leaves clung to the branches of the trees. They were large leaves with fronds like fat fingers. Through the foliage, the sun made dappled patterns on the paving stones. He lit a cigarette. What did it matter if anyone saw the chief of police sitting idly on a bench on a weekday morning? His mother had died and, at least for a time, this event granted him licence to do whatever he wanted. It was difficult to believe, sitting there in the shimmering sunlight, that such a short time before he had been lying with his neck on the cold steel of a railway line. The image seemed less like a memory than a scene from a film featuring an actor playing a character who resembled him. Had it not been for the cut on his hand and the torn suit that remained stuffed at the back of the closet, he might have thought that he had dreamt the whole thing. The scene in his mother's bedroom had something of the same quality. Had it really happened the way he recalled? He could not be sure and he had no wish to recollect the details. Instead, he replayed the version that he had told first to Faubel, then to Madame Beck and later to Céline, being careful on each occasion to modify the words he used so as not to appear over-rehearsed. Each time he repeated this version of events, he came to believe it more and more. This narrative had already begun to obliterate what had actually occurred. And as each person he had told would have then passed it on to several others, it would soon, through force of repetition, come to be accepted as the truth.

And yet, even so, Gorski still had a nagging feeling that at some point suspicion would fall on him.

Some months after the incident with the mustard spoon, a box of pencils had gone missing from the stationery cupboard at school. Although he had nothing to do with the theft, Gorski felt that it was only a matter of time before he was accused. In preparation for this, he wrote down a detailed record of his movements on the day the crime had occurred. Then he realised that this record might itself be seen as incriminating. Why would an innocent person go to such lengths to account for his whereabouts? He ripped the pages from his exercise book, before tearing them into tiny pieces and distributing them in litter bins along his route to school. The following day the headmaster addressed the school assembly. The guilty party, he said, was somewhere in the room and would sooner or later be exposed. It would be better all round for the individual in question to give himself up of his own volition. Only by an effort of will did Gorski refrain from raising his hand. As he observed his fellow pupils filter out of the hall, he was struck by the fact that none of his classmates exhibited any obvious sign of guilt.

During lunch break that day, a classmate named Jean-Claude Lantier, flanked by a couple of his cronies, cornered Gorski in the playground. He was a thick-set boy from one of the apartment blocks adjacent to the railway station. Even at that age, he already had the beginnings of a moustache. His fingernails were permanently ingrained with dirt.

'I thought you might like a pencil,' he said. He held one out. It was brand new, unsharpened at either end.

'No, thank you,' Gorski replied, struggling to keep his voice steady.

'Take it!' He jabbed the pencil into Gorski's stomach.

'I don't want it.' He was by now on the verge of tears.

Lantier shrugged. 'Up to you,' he said. 'But if anyone grasses us in, I'll know where to come.' He feigned to punch Gorski, pulling back his fist at the final moment.

After the break, Gorski was disturbed to see Lantier approach Mademoiselle Doisneau's desk. She was a pretty young woman of probably no more than twenty-three or twenty-four. When Lantier returned to his seat, the teacher announced that this was now the last chance for whoever had stolen the box of pencils to come forward. She even looked beseechingly in Gorski's direction, but he kept his eyes fixed on the desk upon which a number of his predecessors had carved their names. Mademoiselle Doisneau then asked him to come forward with his satchel. He knew he was done for. As he stood at her desk, she asked one final time if he had anything to say. His fellow pupils looked on in silence, enthralled by the unfolding drama. Gorski shook his head. Mademoiselle Doisneau then opened his satchel and brought out half a dozen pencils, unsharpened at either end.

She led him by the hand to the headmaster's office. Once in the corridor, Gorski made no attempt to staunch his tears. The teacher produced a tissue and made him wipe his eyes. Gorski half-heartedly protested his innocence. If that was the case, the headmaster asked in an even tone, then how did the pencils come to be in his satchel? Someone must have put them there, Gorski had murmured, but he did not dare to name Lantier. He was sent home with a letter for his parents. As soon as he reached the shop, he told his father everything that had happened. Monsieur Gorski remarked that he knew Jean-Claude Lantier's father and that he was a bad lot. But there was nothing to be done: sometimes such injustices just had to be endured. For his mother, however, the episode only seemed to confirm her son's delinquent tendencies. In a certain sense, he came to accept that he had stolen the pencils. Somehow it was easier not to set himself against the general consensus. He had learnt that what mattered was not what had actually occurred, but what people believed to have occurred. Later, observing the proceedings of countless trials, he saw this dynamic play out over and over again.

The elderly woman with the sturdy shoes whom Gorski sometimes saw passing along Rue des Trois Rois had sat down on a bench opposite. Her terrier jumped up and sat next to her, its tongue lolling from its mouth. Gorski bid her good morning. She returned his greeting but did not appear to recognise him. There was no reason why she should. He had only ever seen her from the window of the apartment, and she never raised her eyes above the pavement.

Eighteen

Schmitt did not greet Gorski's arrival at the police station with any surprise. The sound of the door caused him to raise his eyes from his newspaper and, as Gorski passed the counter, he offered his condolences. Gorski nodded his thanks, but he did not pause to prolong the conversation. It was only when he sat down in his office that he realised something about the brief exchange had bothered him.

What was it Schmitt had actually said? *I heard about your mother*. That was all. *I heard about your mother*. Gorski had taken this as an expression of sympathy, but it was nothing of the sort. It was no more than an acknowledgement of what had occurred. He had not said, *I'm sorry to hear about your mother*, or any of the other usual formulations. Nor had he followed his bald statement with *My condolences.* It was not that Gorski expected anything better of Schmitt. Nor did he care whether he observed the conventional niceties following a bereavement, but it would have been better for him to have said nothing at all. To acknowledge the fact of his mother's death but fail to offer even the most perfunctory expression of commiseration seemed pointed; a sort of sly insinuation. He said he had heard about Gorski's mother, but he did not say *what* he had heard.

Perhaps, after all, it had been a mistake to sit smoking in the little park by the Protestant temple a short while before. *I saw him sitting around smoking as if he had not a care in the world. And his mother not yet in the ground*. Perhaps he needed to be more circumspect. He stood up and opened the window. The room was stuffy and overheated. Water dripped from the

antiquated iron radiator beneath the window. He looked out over the car park, feeling the cold air on his face. He must not overreact to things, particularly inconsequential remarks from the likes of Schmitt, who liked nothing more than to get under his skin. He needed to keep things in check, to do nothing to give himself away. He remembered the soiled sheet, bloodstained dishtowel and the torn suit he had not yet disposed of. The thought of these items—the evidence—brought a prickle of sweat to his brow. He would deal with them later. It had been out of the question to try to smuggle them past Madame Beck this morning. She would be sure to recall, if questioned later, that he had been carrying some sort of package when he left the apartment the day after his mother's death. Perhaps, after all, it would be best to burn them.

In the meantime, police business did not grind to a halt just because his mother had died. The criminals of Saint-Louis could not be expected to respect a period of mourning.

He summoned Roland, who took up his customary stance with his hands behind his back. After a moment's hesitation, the young cop delivered himself of a speech he had clearly prepared in advance: 'Sir, I don't know if it's my place to mention it, but I wished to offer my condolences on the occasion of your mother's death.' He blurted this out while staring at the carpet, the colour rising to his cheeks. When he had finished, he glanced up at his boss, anxious to see if his statement met with his boss's approval.

'Thank you, my boy,' Gorski replied. He had never addressed Roland as 'my boy' before. It was something Ribéry used to call him, and it had always made him feel there was a special bond between them. He would have liked to ask how Roland had heard about his mother's death or what other people were saying about it, but he resisted doing so. The chief of police could not be seen to concern himself with the thoughts of an underling.

Instead, he asked if the roadblock set up on the outskirts of Sierentz had turned anything up. Roland provided a typically comprehensive account. Not only had he and two other officers questioned the occupant of every car leaving the village in the morning, but he had taken it upon himself to repeat the exercise later in the day when residents were returning home from work. Gorski commended his initiative. He did not even intervene when Roland painstakingly enumerated the questions they had put to each driver. He already knew what the result would be.

'Unfortunately,' Roland concluded, 'no one witnessed the accident or reported any unusual activity.'

Gorski thanked him for his efforts. 'But tell me,' he went on, 'what are your thoughts?'

'My thoughts, sir?' Gorski had never asked him for his opinion before.

'Yes,' said Gorski. 'You must have some ideas about the case.'

'I'm not sure.' Roland appeared confused, as if it was a trick question. 'There's no evidence to suggest that it was anything other than an accident. In fact, several individuals mentioned that Mademoiselle Petrovka was an erratic driver and that something like this was bound to happen sooner or later.'

'So you don't think it's curious that this accident occurred only a few days after her boss died in suspicious circumstances?'

He did not even mention the uncanny similarity to the incident in which the advocate Bertrand Barthelme had been killed a year or so before.

'It does seem to be something of a coincidence,' said Roland cautiously, 'but just because two incidents happen in close proximity does not mean that there is a causal relationship between them.'

Gorski had taught him well.

'You have always told me to attend to the evidence, sir,' he went on, 'and that anything else is meaningless conjecture.'

'But what if we were to allow ourselves, as a kind of experiment, to speculate a little?' At this point Gorski made an expansive gesture, spreading his palms as if releasing a dove into the air.

'What happened to your hand, sir?' Roland asked. 'It's bleeding.'

The cut at the base of Gorski's thumb was leaking blood. He stared at it for a moment. Then he took a handkerchief from his pocket and pressed it to the wound. Roland stepped towards the desk to offer his assistance.

'It's nothing,' said Gorski sharply.

Roland asked how it happened.

'I was slicing an apple. The knife slipped.' *Slicing an apple*! Where had that come from?

Roland nodded, but he did not look convinced. And nor should he. Even if Gorski had been slicing an apple, he would have been holding the knife in his right hand and would thus have cut his left. It was the sort of idiotic fabrication he would expect of the most dim-witted of suspects. Gorski did not even like apples.

He gestured for Roland to leave. The bleeding did not last for long. Why had he even felt the need to explain himself to his subordinate? The stupidity of his response was compounded by the fact that he had told Madame Beck that he could not remember how he had cut his hand. It would be clear to anyone that he was lying. And if he was lying, he must have something to conceal.

He was angry with himself. The first rule of the suspect is to keep your mouth shut. As soon as you speak, you risk incriminating yourself. The soundest policy is invariably to say nothing.

And there it was: Gorski thought of himself as a suspect. No one had accused him of anything, but he could not help feeling that people knew what he had done and were just waiting for him to crack. He stood up and paced around the room. He stood at the open window and took a few deep breaths. Would even such an innocent act as standing by the window of his office taking a few deep breaths be taken as a sign of guilt? He told himself to calm down. He was not thinking straight. It was nonsense. Nobody knew what he had done. He was allowing his guilty conscience to taint his thinking. He was seeing insinuation where none existed. It was only natural after what had happened that he would be on edge. He was thinking like a criminal. In the eyes of the law, he was a criminal. Certainly, he had committed a criminal act. And had he not, since the previous morning, engaged in a deliberate campaign of lies, repeating over and over a fallacious version of events? Was he not planning to destroy the evidence of his guilt? This was unquestionably the behaviour of a criminal. And yet Gorski did not *feel* like a criminal. He had not been motivated by any personal gain. He had only done what his mother herself had wanted. If that was a criminal act, then so be it.

He looked at his watch. Le Pot would not be open for hours. True, he could have a snifter at the counter of the Café de la Gare, which opened first thing in the morning, but he would feel conspicuous there. Even so, he should remain visible. He must not seem to be hiding himself away. He had not yet taken to keeping a stash of booze in the drawer of his desk. That would have constituted, in his own eyes, the crossing of a certain line. In any case, it was better not to drink. Alcohol loosened the tongue and he had already said too much.

He called Roland back to his office. He made no reference to the conversation about his hand. Instead, he instructed Roland to check on the garages in the area for any vehicles brought in since the morning of Anna Petrovka's death. In particular, he wanted to know of any vehicles with damage to the paintwork on the passenger-side. Roland nodded enthusiastically. He could see what Gorski was getting at.

Gorski was under no illusion that Roland would turn anything up, but it was good to occupy his mind with other matters. Even if his theory about how Anna Petrovka had died was correct, the culprit would not be so dim-witted as to make the error of bringing the vehicle in question to a garage. In the name of procedure though, the possibility had to be eliminated.

Before lunch, Gorski visited the pharmacy on Avenue de Bâle

and asked for a dressing for the wound on his hand. The woman at the counter asked if he would like her to apply it.

'Been in the wars?' she asked when he held out his hand.

'A knife slipped,' he said. It seemed better to stick to his earlier lie than to contradict what he had told Roland. The pharmacist was not to know whether he was right- or left-handed.

She disappeared for a moment, before returning with some disinfectant and cotton wool. She cleaned the wound, before applying some gauze and securing it round the base of his thumb. Gorski felt some pleasure in the touch of her fingers.

'That's better, Inspector,' she said when she had finished.

She refused any payment and Gorski did not insist. Outside he examined her handiwork. She had done a good job. The dressing drew attention to the fact that he had injured himself, but this, paradoxically, only served to suggest that he had nothing to hide.

Gorski's appearance at Restaurant de la Cloche was not greeted with any special fanfare. The lunchtime service was in full swing. Cutlery and plates clattered. The doors to the kitchen constantly swung open and closed. Diners raised their voices to be heard above the din. Gorski was glad to be there. Marie briefly squeezed his upper arm and said she was sorry to hear about his mother. Gorski did not ask who had told her. As far as he knew, his mother had never set foot in la Cloche, but that did not matter. He had not appeared for lunch the previous day and that would be enough for eyebrows to have been raised. In towns like Saint-Louis, even the most routine gossip circulates with great speed, but when something as noteworthy as a death occurs, it can be vouchsafed that within twenty-four hours the only person unaware of the news will be the deceased themselves.

Shortly after Gorski had taken his seat, Pasteur summoned the waitress Adèle and had her bring a glass of cognac to his table. Gorski raised the glass in Pasteur's direction and the proprietor responded with a brief downward movement of his head. Gorski appreciated the phlegmatic nature of his fellow Ludovicians. Yes, his mother had died, but there was no call for histrionics. Gorski would eat his lunch and drink his *pichet* of wine as usual. It was understood that the glass of cognac would be on the house, but aside from that no special dispensation would be sought or offered.

At the end of his meal, Gorski went to settle his bill at the counter in the normal way. Pasteur took his money without comment. Gorski placed his usual tip in the pewter saucer. He lingered a moment longer than normal to give Pasteur, who was at that moment distracted by the business of decanting a bottle of wine, the opportunity to utter a word of condolence. When he looked up, however, he appeared surprised to see Gorski still standing there.

'Was there something else, Inspector?' he asked.

Gorski shook his head. 'No, not at all,' he replied, but he could not help but feel that the brief nod Pasteur had earlier given him did not constitute adequate acknowledgement of his loss. The dispensing of condolences and similar sentiments was something Pasteur was happy to delegate to his wife, but even so, Gorski might have expected a tactful word or two. Indeed, he could not help feeling that these words were being deliberately withheld.

Instead, the only proper expression of sympathy came from an unlikely source. As Gorski was making his way out, Lemerre rose from his table and offered him a limp handshake. 'The death of his mother is the most profound moment in a man's life,' he pronounced solemnly. He then placed his hands on Gorski's shoulders and kissed him ceremoniously on both cheeks. It was a deeply unpleasant experience. Lemerre gave off a pungent odour of sour sweat and hair oil. Gorski extricated himself, thanked Lemerre in a perfunctory way and made a swift exit. He should perhaps have been moved by the hairdresser's words, but he was not. Instead, they shamed him.

Outside, he felt unsettled. He wondered if even Marie's expression of condolence had been somewhat half-hearted. He reminded himself that it had been the busiest part of the day. He could hardly have expected her to down tools on his account. It was not as if they were friends. He was no different from any of the other regulars and did not merit any special attention. Still, Schmitt's words returned to him: *I heard about your mother*. What exactly had he heard? Gorski reassured himself with the fact that Lemerre, at least, had not appeared equivocal. If any untoward rumours had been doing the rounds, they would certainly not have escaped the attention of the hairdresser. Even so, something niggled him. He walked slowly back towards the police station. Aside from the stupid remark about the injury to his thumb, he could think of nothing he had done that might have raised any eyebrows. And yet there was something. He forced his mind back to the previous morning. Was there something he had overlooked? Some detail that had seemed to be of no significance at the time?

The first person he had contacted was Faubel. The exchange on the telephone had been brief and to the point. The doctor had picked up after four or five rings. Was he already up? Very possibly. It was also likely that, as a doctor, he kept a telephone by his bedside, although he had not spoken in the hushed tone he might have used if he had not wished to disturb his wife. In any case, he had answered with the simple phrase, neither curt nor friendly, *Faubel speaking*.

Gorski had thanked him for answering at such an early hour, before saying, *It's Maman. I think she's gone*, or words to that effect. Had he said, *She's gone* or *I think she's gone*? It didn't matter. Either way, Faubel had replied with a single syllable: *Ah*.

It was that *Ah* that Gorski now pondered. It was this that was needling him.

It was not the word itself. It was the intonation, the *way* Faubel had said it. It had not been intended to convey surprise, but there was nothing sinister in that. For Faubel, being informed of the death of an elderly patient was a commonplace occurrence. But nor was it pronounced in such a way as to express sympathy or condolence. At this point, Gorski said the word under his breath several times, trying to capture the inflection that Faubel had given it. Then he had it. *Ah.* It had been elongated, ever so slightly elongated, but without any rise or fall in pitch. A flat monotone: *Ah.* What Faubel was communicating was that he understood what had occurred. Gorski breathed the word again. *Ah.* It was clear. Faubel knew.

Gorski looked around him. He had reached the corner of Rue de Mulhouse. Nobody was paying any attention to him, which was fortunate, as he felt that his guilt must be apparent to anyone who looked at him. He forced himself to keep walking. The action of placing one foot in front of the other was suddenly effortful. His legs felt as if he had borrowed them from someone else and they did not fit properly. He continued past the little park at the Protestant temple. It would not do to pause there. Vinçard was staring out through the window of his shop. Gorski raised his arm, but the travel agent did not return his greeting. Was Gorski mistaken, or had he deliberately turned his head away? Gorski paused to light a cigarette. He caught his reflection in the window of the butcher's shop. He did not look any different from normal. Guilt was not written across his face. He drew smoke deep into his lungs. He was behaving ridiculously. He was over-interpreting everything. He was overwrought. It was only natural. His mother had died. She had passed away peacefully in the night. He thought again of Faubel's *Ah.* That was all it was. A meaningless syllable, uttered only to indicate that the information given had been registered. There was nothing more to it than that.

Roland was awaiting his return on the pavement outside the police station. He spoke to Gorski as if nothing was amiss. A white Mercedes had been brought into a garage on Rue du Rhône. The nearside headlight and indicator were broken, and the front wing was dented and scraped.

Gorski feigned interest.

'It belongs to a Monsieur Pierre Tournier of 23 Rue de la Couronne,' Roland informed him.

Gorski told him he had done well.

Monsieur Tournier was not at home, but they found him at the shoe shop he owned on Rue de Huningue. He was a neatly dressed man with heavy-framed glasses and thinning hair. He was wearing light brown slip-on shoes with a little gold clasp. Gorski wondered if this was where Robert Duymann came to buy his shoes.

Tournier did not seem disconcerted by the appearance of two policemen. He showed them into his office. Gorski took the only free seat and lit a cigarette. He gestured to Roland to explain why they were there, which he did in a long-winded way, omitting no detail about the time at which the vehicle had been brought into the garage and the damage sustained. When he had finished, Tournier confirmed that what he had said was correct.

'And may I ask,' Roland continued, with a glance towards Gorski, 'how this damage was sustained?'

He had left his car in the street outside his house overnight and when he returned from work the following day, it had been in some kind of collision. He assumed the damage had been caused by a passing vehicle but had not reported it as there did not seem any point.

Roland asked if Monsieur Tournier had heard, or been woken by, any loud noise. He had not.

'And when you left for work in the morning, the car was undamaged?'

'I couldn't say for sure,' he replied. 'I passed by on the driver's side.'

'So the impact might have occurred after you left for work?'

Tournier agreed that this was possible.

As they walked back towards the police station, Gorski asked Roland if he had any further thoughts. Roland responded cautiously. Perhaps Tournier was right and his car had simply been damaged by a passing vehicle. Gorski contended that Rue de la Couronne was a quiet street. It seemed unlikely that such a collision would have gone unnoticed.

Gorski dispatched Roland to question Monsieur Tournier's neighbours on Rue de la Couronne. He then walked the length of Rue de Mulhouse to the Hôtel Bertillon.

He found Henri Virieu in his glass cage bent over a chess set. Gorski sounded the brass bell on the counter. Virieu emerged, removing the reading glasses which he kept on a chain around his neck.

'Ah, I didn't expect you back so soon, monsieur.'

Gorski looked quizzically at him.

Virieu squinted at him for a moment. 'Ah, forgive me, Inspector. I thought for a moment ... My eyesight isn't what it used to ... There's a certain resemblance.'

'A resemblance?' said Gorski.

'Yes, with my erstwhile guest. The foreign gentleman. A very definite resemblance. I'm surprised I didn't notice it before. But it is a pleasure to see you again. May I offer you a small libation of some sort? You would be doing me a great honour.' He rotated his small hands as if he was washing them under an invisible tap.

Gorski shook his head. 'Actually, it was this guest of yours I wished to speak to,' he said.

'Has there been some development?' Virieu asked eagerly. 'I knew there was something not right about him. When you've seen as many people come and go as I have, you develop a nose for these things. I rather think I would make quite a good detective myself, although of course I understand, Inspector, that there must be a great deal more to it than meets the eye. I don't mean to imply that I could step into the shoes of a man like yourself. A man of your calibre. Good gracious, no.'

Gorski let Virieu's speech run its course before asking if the gentleman in question was here.

'No, I'm afraid he's not,' he replied. 'He departed a day or two ago.'

'Could you be more specific?'

The little man pondered this question for a few moments.

He asked what day it was. 'It can be hard to keep track, don't you find?'

'Not really,' said Gorski.

After some further thought, Virieu stated that he had left first thing the previous morning. Yes, he was quite certain. 'So really neither one day nor two,' he added, as if to defend his previous statement.

Gorski asked if he had any record of him leaving.

'As I explained, I'm afraid I have become somewhat lax with regards to paperwork. It was my wife who—' He allowed his sentence to trail off sadly.

'I don't suppose you found out his name?'

Virieu shook his head. 'To tell you the truth, I did not find him to be a particularly agreeable fellow.'

The entrance to the hotel opened and a man in a dark brown suit with two large suitcases came in. A few of the dry leaves that littered the vestibule blew in as he manoeuvred his luggage through the door.

Nineteen

Following his visit to the Hôtel Bertillon, Gorski stopped off at the grocer's on Rue de Mulhouse and bought two bottles of wine of better quality than usual. He also bought half a dozen apples, this with the purpose of backing up his story about how he had cut his hand and also to place between the bottles in the grocery bag to stop them clanking as he passed through Madame Beck's shop. Gorski was not in the habit of buying fresh fruit, but the woman behind the shop counter made no comment on his purchases. Despite the fact that Gorski visited the store on an almost daily basis, she was not one for engaging in small talk. Most likely her mind was on other things.

Madame Beck was trimming the stems of some roses. She looked up when the little bell above the door sounded. She asked if he had had a busy day.

It was the first time she had addressed him with the informal *tu*. Gorski had himself been considering this for some time but had not quite mustered the courage to take this step. Madame Beck delivered her question quite nonchalantly, as if she attached no special significance to this abandonment of formality.

Gorski replied that the various arrangements had been taken care of.

She asked when the funeral would be. Gorski replied that it had not been possible, as yet, to set a date. He omitted to mention the reason for this.

'Of course, I would be grateful if you could supply the flowers.'

'I'd be glad to,' Madame Beck replied.

Gorski nodded, as if to suggest that he was pleased that this piece of business had been taken care of, but he did not move off and Madame Beck looked questioningly at him.

'Actually, I was wondering if you'—he here corrected *vous* to *tu*—'I wondered if you might like to join me upstairs for a glass of wine when you're finished.' He gave a little shrug, as if it was a matter of no consequence to him.

'You mean, to discuss the flowers for the funeral?'

'Eh, no.' Gorski stumbled over his words. 'I thought perhaps you might just like to—'

Madame Beck spared him any further explication.

'I don't see why not,' she said. She glanced at her wristwatch. 'In half an hour or so?'

'Perfect.' Then, absurdly, he made a little bow, like an old war veteran lowering his head to receive a medal. What a buffoon! Madame Beck looked at him with amusement.

Upstairs, he set about readying the apartment. Fearing that something of the aroma of his mother's soiled sheets might have lingered in the air, he threw open the living room window. It was, in any case, good to let in some fresh air. His mother had always kept the place oppressively overheated. It was no wonder she had spent so much time dozing in her chair. In her absence, the room felt unfamiliar. He gazed around at the decades of accumulated gewgaws. How often he had dreamt of binning the lot of them. He picked up a figurine of an ancient balloon-seller and turned it over in his hands. It was a hideous object with a thread of yellowed glue along the base where his father had once repaired it. He put it back where it came from. The mantelpiece looked bare without it. His parents' tat had now become his tat, and he felt suddenly less inclined to discard it.

The cruet set was a different matter, however. Gorski stared implacably at it, as he would at an ancient foe. He wondered how things might have been different if he had not broken the little mustard spoon. He picked it up and put it in the cupboard in the kitchen where the crockery was kept. He considered throwing it out there and then, but he could not bring himself to do so. It would, he felt, have been an act of violence; a sort of gratuitous insult to his mother.

He returned to the living room and smoothed out the tablecloth. He fetched two glasses from the sideboard and set them on the table. Then he opened the bottle of red he had bought and placed it between the glasses to breathe. Perhaps he should also have bought some hors d'oeuvres, but that would have spoken too plainly of calculation. Sharing a glass of wine could be passed off as spontaneous, but had he prepared some sort of buffet, Madame Beck would be quite justified in concluding that he was planning to seduce her. It was not that such a thing had never crossed his mind, but his mother's apartment was hardly conducive to such an undertaking. There was only the soiled mattress on which Madame Gorski had recently expired and his tiny childhood room with its uncomfortable single divan. Neither seemed an apposite setting for any amorous activities. In any case, it had been testing enough for Gorski to bring himself to use the informal pronoun. He had no wish for any further escalation in intimacy.

On the other hand, it was not out of the question that Madame Beck might expect certain advances to be made and might even feel insulted if they were not forthcoming. She was a married woman visiting the apartment of a—to all intents and purposes—single man. It was an act of impropriety. They were, after all, adults. Perhaps her sudden adoption of *tu* after all these years was intended as a signal that she wished to progress their relations. Now that Gorski gave proper consideration to this, it was as wanton as if she had unfastened a button of her blouse. He began to panic. Even if, at some point in the future, such a juncture was to be reached, he was not sure he would be capable of performing in the manner expected, let alone in the next few minutes.

He regretted his invitation. It would have been better all round to have suggested returning to the strange little bar on Rue de Huningue, but there could be no backing out now.

He was sweating heavily. There were dark circles under the arms of his shirt. He had time for a quick shower. He soaped his armpits and genitals thoroughly, then turned down the temperature and forced himself to stand under the cold water for sixty seconds. He emerged feeling invigorated. He wrapped a towel around his waist and stepped out into the little hallway.

In the living room, a slim figure stood silhouetted in the window. It was not Madame Beck, but Clémence. She was crying, but when she saw her father emerge half-naked from the bathroom, she started laughing through her tears.

'Clémence,' Gorski said.

He was aware that, regardless of his state of undress, he should step into the living room and embrace her, but he could not bring himself to do so. Instead, he muttered for her to give him a minute, ducked into his childhood room and hastily dressed in a fresh suit and shirt.

When he reappeared, she had sat down at the table. She stood up and Gorski put his arms around her. She started sobbing.

'Poor Grandma,' she said.

'Yes,' he said. He did not, at this moment, feel any guilt. It was quite as if his mother had indeed died of natural causes and he could experience a moment of mutual grief with his daughter. He waited patiently for her sobs to subside. 'Poor Grandma,' she said again.

It was a good phrase and expressed a good deal more than was contained in its three meagre syllables.

'Yes, poor Grandma,' said Gorski.

They sat down at the table. Clémence wiped her face with the sleeve of her sweater. The gesture made her seem much younger, like the little girl she no longer was. Clémence, Gorski realised, was the one person he could be sure suspected that nothing untoward had occurred.

'The room seems empty,' she said.

'It is empty,' said Gorski.

Clémence nodded. She seemed to appreciate that her father

was not attempting to assuage her sadness with fatuous sentiments.

She sat back in her chair and exhaled a long breath.

She was sorry they had missed their last dinner together.

'It's always like that when someone dies,' Gorski said. 'You always miss the last of something.'

Clémence nodded. She tipped her head towards the bottle of wine and glasses set out on the table. It was like the set of a low-budget theatrical production.

'You expecting someone, Pops?' she asked.

Gorski felt as if he had been caught in some illicit act. 'Actually,' he said, as casually as he could muster, 'Madame Beck is joining me for a glass of wine.'

He felt his cheeks colour.

Clémence's face broke into a smile. 'Aha,' she said. 'The charming Madame Beck is joining you for a glass of wine.' She gave the final words a certain playful emphasis. She nudged him on the upper arm.

'It's nothing more than that.'

'I'm sure it isn't, but I'm glad you've taken the trouble to shower.' She leant back and inspected him, then adjusted his collar, as if he was a little boy setting out for his first day at school. 'I should leave you to it,' she said. 'I don't want to play gooseberry.'

Gorski insisted that she would be doing no such thing, and in any case Madame Beck would not be arriving for a few minutes yet. He asked her if she would like a glass, but she shook her head.

At that moment, there was a light knock from the hallway.

'*Coucou*,' said Madame Beck, putting her head around the door.

Gorski leapt to his feet.

'Emma,' he said. 'Come in, please.' He had not planned to use her first name, but it had suddenly felt quite natural to do so and she did not appear to object. If they were now on *tutoyer* terms, did it not make sense to also address her by her given name? And somehow, for the first time speaking aloud the name he had so often read on the mail he had picked up from the vestibule of the shop and which he had sometimes murmured under his breath, Gorski felt a surge of affection.

Madame Beck, who was always so composed, suddenly looked a little unsure of herself. He stepped towards the little hallway and they briefly embraced. It could easily have been passed off as a simple greeting—it lasted no more than a couple of seconds—but somehow, as they made to kiss each other on the cheek, their lips fleetingly brushed. They stood back from each other as if they had experienced a minor electric shock. Gorski's cheeks coloured for the second time in a matter of minutes. Madame Beck's fingers flitted across her mouth and then onto her neck.

Clémence observed this dumbshow with amusement.

Gorski gestured for Madame Beck to join them at the table.

'My daughter Clémence,' he said by way of introduction.

The stupidity of this statement—they must have met a hundred times—made them laugh.

Clémence explained that she was just leaving.

'Please don't go on my account,' Madame Beck said, but Clémence had already collected the canvas satchel she used as a schoolbag. She winked at Gorski on her way out.

'Such a nice girl,' said Madame Beck. 'You should be very proud of her.'

'Yes,' said Gorski. 'I am.'

Madame Beck took a seat at the table. She now looked like an actress in the opening scene of a third-rate play. In the early days of their marriage, Céline had insisted on dragging Gorski to the theatre in Mulhouse and Strasbourg, but he had never been able to get over the absurdity of watching grown men and women pretending to be someone other than themselves. He now felt something of the same inauthenticity, that whatever he said would sound as if he was reading from a script.

Instead, he occupied himself with pouring the wine.

He sat down. They touched glasses and Gorski toasted their health. The wine did not taste any different to the cheaper stuff he usually bought. Whenever Céline or Keller waxed lyrical about the flavours and aromas of whatever wine had been served, Gorski had nodded his agreement, but it all tasted the same to him. Silence threatened to envelop them. Madame Beck gave a little shiver. Gorski got up and closed the window, glad of the distraction. Then he turned on the ugly electric fire which had been his mother's constant companion.

'I'm sorry,' he said. 'I didn't think to—'

'It's fine,' said Madame Beck.

'It'll warm up presently,' Gorski said. Then he apologised for not having anything to eat. 'I'm afraid I'm not very used to entertaining.'

Madame Beck told him not to worry. She said she couldn't stay too long. She threw her eyes vaguely in the direction of where she lived. The gesture contained a hint of apology, or perhaps of resignation. Either way, it suggested that if she could not stay long, it was not because she did not want to.

Although there was no need to do so, Gorski topped up their glasses.

'It's strange to be here without your mother,' she said.

'Yes,' Gorski agreed. 'Very strange.'

'I keep expecting to see her there in her chair.'

'Yes,' said Gorski.

'Will you stay on here?' she asked.

Gorski said he hadn't yet had time to think about it.

Madame Beck then commented that there was something missing from the table. The cruet set was gone. Gorski explained that it was in the kitchenette. He wondered how she would respond if he told her about the incident with the little mustard spoon. Probably she would think it outlandish that he would attach any significance to something that had happened forty years before. And yet he felt a strong desire to tell her. He had never told anyone, not even Clémence.

Perhaps the feeling of intimacy provoked by using her first name loosened his inhibitions, but he told her the story. He omitted no detail, warming to his task and even getting up from his seat to act out his parents' search of the room. He described how he had disposed of the pieces in a culvert in Rue du Temple, and imitated his father, weeks later, scratching his chin and wondering what had happened to the little spoon. He ended by saying that were it not for this incident, he might never have become a policeman. His entire life might have turned out differently. They both laughed. Gorski was pleased with the effect his story had had. Not only had it banished the awkwardness between them, but he felt unburdened. Madame Beck was right to laugh. He could now see that the whole episode was comic and inconsequential. How ridiculous it had been to attach any importance to it.

Madame Beck held out her glass. She had emptied it while Gorski was telling his story. The wine had stained her lips red. She moved her chair a little closer to his.

She then described how when her own mother died, she had found a doll in a box in the attic of her childhood home. It was an ugly thing with nylon hair and a china face, but as a little girl she had been inordinately attached to it. When it had mysteriously gone missing, she had cried for days on end. Her mother insisted that it must have been stolen, but all these years later, she discovered it hidden in the attic. Its face had been smashed. Her mother must have broken it and not had the heart to tell her.

'For years afterwards I looked out for it, hoping I would see another little girl playing with it, but it had been up there all the time in the attic. That made me so angry with my mother.'

She gave a little laugh and drank some wine.

'I don't know why I told you that,' she said. 'I've never told anyone before.'

She glanced fleetingly at her wristwatch and made an apologetic face.

Gorski did not want her to leave. He wished he could cook her sea bass with fennel and spend the evening with her, doing no more than talking.

'We might as well finish the bottle,' he said. It was now dark outside.

'I'll be drunk,' she said, but she did not object when he refilled her glass.

Gorski drew a deep breath. 'You know,' he said, 'Maman didn't die the way I said.'

Madame Beck looked towards the window. The tips of the fingers of her right hand lightly stroked the stem of her glass.

'No,' she said quietly, 'I didn't think so.'

She continued to stare out the window for some time. There was nothing to see. Only the glowing curtains of the windows opposite, behind which the occupants would be preparing dinner, dozing in armchairs or gazing blankly at the flickering screens of their television sets.

When, eventually, she turned back to Gorski, it was with a rueful smile. Gorski felt he should say something; to attempt to justify his actions. But she did not appear to require any further explanation. *No, I didn't think so.* If she already suspected that this was the case, had she not tacitly sanctioned him by coming upstairs to share a glass of wine?

Still, it had been a mistake to tell her. He had been carried away by the feeling of intimacy engendered by the childhood anecdotes they had shared. He had succumbed to a sudden urge to confess, born of a desire to feel vindicated. But now, having satisfied that impulse, what he had said could never be unsaid. He had made an accomplice of Madame Beck. Now, regardless of what may or may not happen between them in the future, they would always be bound by this knowledge. It wasn't fair on her. He should have kept his mouth shut.

He looked away. Then, in order to try to restore the convivial atmosphere between them, he asked if he should open another bottle.

She shook her head. She said in an apologetic tone that she should be going.

'But another time,' she said.

Another time. Gorski nodded. He wasn't sure if she meant it.

'Yes,' he said. 'I hope so.'

He accompanied her to the door. They kissed awkwardly on the cheek. Gorski listened to her make her way down the stairwell, then opened the second bottle.

Twenty

Keller's office on the first floor of the town hall was spacious and modishly furnished. The windows afforded a view of the Place de l'Hôtel de Ville below. When he had run for mayor, Keller had done so under the slogan *A time for renewal.* He was a man who liked to knock things down. His first order of business had been to purge his office of the flock wallpaper, Louis Quinze desk and brocade armchairs. The only items to survive were the various portraits of former mayors and local worthies, but even those had had their gilt frames replaced by brushed steel. Now everything was sleek and hard-edged. Gorski had once been part of that renewal too. Ribéry had been unceremoniously shoved out to make way for the fresh blood. His enforced retirement had little effect on Ribéry's routine. For years afterwards, he continued to make his daily tour of the town's hostelries, having a snifter or two on the house and opining on any current cases to anyone within earshot.

When, in this same office, Keller informed Gorski of his promotion to chief of police, he had made it clear that it was to him that he owed his advancement.

'I can't have my daughter married to a common-or-garden plod, can I?' he had said, before slapping Gorski on the shoulder and passing the remark off as a joke. That day, they had sat on the uncomfortable leather sofa next to the fireplace. Today, however, Keller did not invite Gorski to take a seat, nor did he offer him a drink. Instead, he obliged him to remain standing in front of his desk like a schoolboy summoned to the headmaster's office. Behind Keller were portraits of the President of the Republic and of Napoleon I, a *tricolore* and a flag bearing the six-crowned insignia of the *département* of Haut-Rhin. The function of this paraphernalia was to bestow the occupant of the mayoral office with power. When the mayor spoke, he did so with the authority of the municipality.

'I expect you know why I've asked you here, Georges,' Keller began.

It was the oldest trick in the book. Gorski had used variations on this gambit countless times to lure a suspect into incriminating himself.

'I haven't the faintest idea,' he replied.

'Really?' said Keller. He theatrically placed the index finger of his left hand on a Manila envelope on the desk. 'Do you know what this is?' he asked.

'I feel sure you're going to tell me.'

'It's Madame Gorski's post-mortem.' He paused, his finger remaining on the envelope as if to prevent it from scuttling away.

Gorski forced himself to hold Keller's gaze, but he could not prevent himself from swallowing. There was no legitimate reason for Keller to have the report. If it contained anything incriminating, it should have been passed to the examining magistrate. Post-mortems were no business of the mayor, who—officially at least—had no jurisdiction over criminal matters.

'Our mutual friend Faubel thought I might find it of interest,' Keller went on. 'And I must say he was correct. It makes for fascinating reading.'

Gorski considered a number of responses. He could laugh it off: *Why would that be of any interest to me?* He could make a derogatory remark about the quality of Faubel's work. He could protest that it would be too painful to hear any details of his mother's death, perhaps even mustering some tears in support of this. But saying nothing was not an option. That would unquestionably be taken as a sign of a guilty conscience.

'I don't see why such a report should be in your possession,' he said. 'It's most irregular.'

Keller knew Gorski to be a stickler for procedure. In any other circumstances, it would be this bureaucratic nicety he would focus on.

'Irregular or not, I think you'll find that Faubel has done us both a favour.' He now laid his palm flat on the envelope. 'Now, I hope it will not be necessary to spell out the good doctor's conclusions.'

For the time being, there was nothing else for it but to stick to his story. It was possible that Keller was bluffing. For all Gorski knew, the envelope might be empty. 'I assume he concludes that my mother died in her sleep,' he said.

Keller shook his head slowly. 'No, Georges, that's not what he says. Perhaps you would like me to read it to you after all? There are plenty of highlights, but I don't think any of them will come as a shock to you. Personally, I found the detail of the fractured clavicle to be particularly damning.'

Gorski felt nauseous. It was not just that he was done for. The idea that he had snapped his mother's collarbone as she had struggled under the pillow sickened him. How despicable he was! And what a fool he had been to think that he could get away with such a thing. Somehow he had convinced himself that the very procedures upon which he had built his career would not pertain to him. He had not thought things through. He could not even claim that he had acted on a momentary impulse. He had known in advance what he was going to do, and in order to see it to its conclusion he had banished any thought of the consequences from his mind.

Now he had his reckoning.

Keller stood up. He gestured towards the sofa by the fireplace. 'I expect you could do with a drink.'

He strode over to the sideboard on which various decanters were set out and poured two generous measures of cognac. He handed the larger one to Gorski. They sat down. Gorski shamelessly knocked back his drink. Keller produced a cigar from the inside pocket of his jacket. He lit it and sat back in his chair, savouring the nutty aroma, as if enjoying a postprandial moment in a gentlemen's club. Then as if suddenly remembering the business in hand, he shook himself out of his fleeting reverie and leaned forward.

'How rude of me!' He thrust a second cigar in Gorski's direction.

Gorski shook his head. He was sure Keller had choreographed the whole scene down to the tiniest gesture. If he now refused the mayor's cigar, he did so only as a petty act of defiance.

In the early years of his marriage, Gorski and Céline had lunched every Sunday at the Kellers. At first, Gorski had found these lunches excruciating. He cringed at being waited on by the family's maid, who was older than he was. He was conscious of his coarse manners and his ignorance of the wines and dishes that were served. These feelings of inferiority did not extend to his career, however. From the beginning he believed that he could succeed in the police force on his own merits. The more he listened to Ribéry's tired aphorisms, and watched as he pinned crimes on suspects because they had a protruding brow or their eyes were too close together, the more convinced he became that he could do better. He devoured every book he could find on criminology and forensics. After these Sunday lunches, Keller would invite Gorski to share a cigar on the terrace. He would joke about his daughter's headstrong ways and ply him with alcohol. The booze loosened Gorski's tongue and he would disloyally describe Ribéry's sloppy methods, and go on to pontificate about his reading of the latest theories of detection. Keller was not yet mayor, but Gorski was aware of his political ambitions and influence.

'Jules Ribéry may have his faults,' he once told him, 'but he has one great virtue: he knows what side his bread's buttered on.'

Gorski had not been sure what Keller had meant by this. He must have looked puzzled because the older man had added, 'Sometimes, if one wants to get on in life, a degree of pragmatism is necessary.'

Keller now gave a shrug and returned the proffered cigar to the breast pocket of his jacket. If Gorski wanted to puff away on cheap cigarettes, it was no skin off his nose.

He adopted an affectedly breezy tone: 'You've got yourself in quite a fix, wouldn't you say, Georges? But now that we know where we stand, the question is what do we do about it?'

Gorski thoroughly loathed him.

Keller then proceeded, at great length, to outline the fix in which Gorski found himself, all the time maintaining the same jovial tone. Gorski had been correct to point out that it was irregular for Faubel's report to be in his possession. Of course, there was still the possibility that the report could find its way onto the desk of the examining magistrate. Whether it did so or not, Keller asserted, was entirely in Gorski's hands.

'It's all,' he said, 'a question of pragmatism. You know, Georges, you have a lot more in common with your sottish predecessor than you think.' He got up to refill their glasses, apologising for failing to notice that Gorski had already emptied his. 'You will recall, no doubt, a certain murder that occurred I don't know how many years ago. Twenty? Twenty-five? What was her name again?'

Gorski saw no point pretending he did not know which case he was referring to. 'Juliette Hurel,' he said.

'Yes, Hurel, that's it. Your first big investigation, as I recall.'

A teenage girl had been found murdered in the woods near Saint-Louis. There were no leads and eventually a vagrant was convicted on the flimsiest of evidence. Gorski had never believed that the accused man was guilty, but he had kept his doubts to himself. At a press conference after the trial, Keller had gone out of his way to praise Gorski's efforts.

Gorski cast down his eyes. The memory of it shamed him.

'It was your conduct in this investigation that convinced me—that convinced *us*—that you were the right fellow to succeed our old friend Ribéry. We all knew that the convicted man was no more than a scapegoat. But you went along with it, didn't you,

Georges? You went along with it because it was in your interests to do so. And that was what we were looking for: someone who knew where his interests lay. A pragmatist who would not concern himself with things above his station. And I must say that, over the years, you have amply justified our faith in your mediocrity.'

He raised his glass.

'It is only recently that you seem to have drifted from your judicious ways. All of a sudden, you seem to want to stick your nose into matters that do not concern you. I'm sure I do not need to be more explicit. Suffice to say, that certain citizens—certain *influential* citizens—have been made to feel a little uneasy. But now—' He marched over to the desk and cheerfully brandished the Manila envelope. 'Now, I think I will be able to tell these good people that any concerns they may have had were quite unfounded. I feel sure we understand each other.' He spread his hands, inviting Gorski to respond.

He had nothing to say.

'I will take your silence as agreement. And as long as that remains the case, no one need know of the existence of this document.'

In the panel behind the painting of the President of the Republic was a safe. Keller spun the dial and placed the envelope inside.

Gorski stood up. In a way, it was a relief. It would be a relief to no longer have to put up with the snide remarks Schmitt made when he entered the station. It would be a relief not to be at the beck and call of busybodies like Virieu. It would be a relief to no longer feel the need to behave with the decorum expected of the chief of police. He could let himself sink into dissipation. He could drink himself into oblivion every night at Le Pot if he chose. He could even, if he so desired, pay a visit to those women offering certain services in the apartment blocks adjacent to the railway station. Freed from the burden of being chief of police, he could do whatever he liked.

He took up the decanter on the table and helped himself to another measure. 'You'll have my letter of resignation this afternoon,' he said.

Keller gave a little laugh and shook his head. 'You don't seem to have quite grasped the situation,' he said. 'Now that we have this understanding, the last thing we want is some thrusting young buck—your young Roland, for example—coming along and trying to prove his mettle. No, no, no. Much better to keep the eunuch in the harem, don't you think?' He stabbed his cigar in Gorski's direction lest there be any doubt about the identity of the eunuch. Gorski downed the measure he had poured himself.

Outside on the steps of the town hall, he lit a cigarette. The sky was overcast. A few pigeons pecked optimistically at the paving stones. There was nothing there for them. It began to rain.

Twenty-one

First thing the following morning, Gorski called Roland to his office. He allowed him to conclude his account of his enquiries in Rue de la Couronne. He had carried out his task meticulously, noting the times each of the residents had been at home, when they had gone to bed, left in the morning and so on. None of them had heard anything that might have been a collision between two cars. Roland was careful to add the proviso that that did not mean that such a collision had not occurred. It simply meant that no one had heard it.

He was a most promising young officer. Gorski pitied him. He asked if he was happy working in Saint-Louis.

Roland replied that he could not be happier.

'You might find,' said Gorski, 'that it would be advantageous to gain some experience in a different environment.'

Roland seemed puzzled. 'What do you mean, sir?

'You might want to think about expanding your horizons. In Strasbourg, perhaps. I know someone on the department there who I've no doubt would give you a chance.'

Roland responded that he did not want to work for anyone other than Gorski. His loyalty was touching.

'Just something for you to think about,' Gorski said, 'if you want to advance your career.'

Roland asked if Gorski was dissatisfied with the way he had carried out his assignment.

'Exemplary work,' Gorski said, 'but the case has been resolved.'

'Resolved? How can it have been resolved?' Roland could not hide his astonishment.

Gorski gave him a long stare. 'As there is no evidence of wrongdoing, I can't justify expending any further time or manpower.'

'But there is evidence, sir. Monsieur Tournier's car is evidence. You said so yourself.' He had never before questioned anything Gorski had said. He covered his mouth with his hand and apologised.

Gorski creased his face into a thin smile. 'There's no need for that,' he said, 'but the matter is closed.'

Roland looked crushed. Gorski understood his feelings, but he said nothing to temper his disappointment. It was his first lesson in humiliation. Better for him to acquire a taste for it sooner rather than later.

On the way to the station, Gorski stopped off at the Café de la Gare. The tiny bird-like woman with the tight curls was already at her table in the corner studying the day's horse racing cards. She spent every day flitting between the PMU counter and her table, never drinking anything stronger than tea. Gorski suspected that the proprietor never charged her for these beverages. Whatever the weather, she wore little red sandals, like a child's. Once, as she was passing, Gorski had acknowledged her with the kind of upward nod of the head that serves as a perfunctory greeting between habitués of the same establishment. She had haughtily turned her head in the opposite direction and loudly tutted, as if he had crudely propositioned her. Since then, Gorski had avoided making eye contact with her. Perhaps in her younger days, she had earned a living by disreputable means and had developed an aversion to the attentions of the police.

Gorski drank a glass of beer, leaning his elbows on the counter. There was a stool right next to him, but he did not sit on it. He did not wish to get comfortable. All the same, he ordered a second beer. He already knew he would. The function of the first beer is only to whet the appetite for the second. The second beer is an inevitability. A single beer produces no effect, unless, that is, one is thirsty, but men standing at the counters of bars at half past ten in the morning are not there because they are thirsty. They are there because the colours of the world are too vivid and the edges of objects are too sharp. They are there because there are decisions to be made and an excess of caution can be a hindrance to the desired outcome. Better to act impulsively, then later shrug and say, *I was a bit drunk*. That way, all is forgiven.

But while the second beer follows inevitably from the first, the third does not inevitably follow the second. For the drinker knows that if a third is taken, it will be followed by a fourth, a fifth and so on. Once the third is downed, the shackles are off. Restraint is no longer an option, and if there are decisions to be made or actions to be taken, they will most likely be abandoned in favour of getting sozzled. The time spent drinking a second beer is thus mostly spent contemplating whether to have a third. And so it was with Gorski at the counter of the Café de la Gare. On the one hand, what could be the harm in it? After a third beer he would no longer care who saw him propping up a bar in the middle of the day. But that was not what he had intended. He had only meant to stop off for a quick one en route to the station, so if he was to stick to his plan, there could be no third beer. There would be plenty of time for that later.

The postman who Gorski often saw on Rue des Trois Rois came in. He must have finished his round. The proprietor set a glass of white wine on the counter. Gorski looked at his watch. It was just after eleven. Gorski was rarely in the Café de la Gare at this time in the morning, but the postman recognised and greeted him affably, as if his presence was perfectly commonplace. Gorski made a banal comment about the weather. Both the postman and proprietor nodded in agreement, then engaged in an exchange of views about the likelihood of rain later. Gorski was pleased that his remark had initiated this conversation. He wondered if the little bird-like woman had witnessed it. He stole a glance over his shoulder, but she was absorbed in the study of the day's racing pages of *L'Alsace*.

Once he had made the decision not to have a third beer, Gorski took his time over his second. He was in no hurry, but if he delayed too long, things were more likely to go awry.

He paid up and left.

It was, as Gorski had pointed out in the bar, a cloudy day, but there did not, contrary to the view expressed by the proprietor, seem to be much prospect of rain. Gorski walked the short distance to the station. The two beers he had consumed gave him a feeling of well-being. There was a lightness to his tread and he paused to help a young woman who was struggling to manoeuvre a pram through the entrance of an apartment building.

Gorski entered the station. He ignored the ticket office and purposefully did not look up at the departures board, proceeding instead directly to the underpass that led to the various platforms. He did not want to know where he was going. He would get on the first train to pull in and buy a ticket on board. He emerged onto Platform 3 just in time to see a train pull away. Never mind. He would get the next one. He sat down on a bench and lit a cigarette. A few passengers waited on the opposite platform. None of them paid him any attention. Why should they? He was just a man waiting for a train.

Naturally, he wondered what his destination might be. Paris, Strasbourg, Nancy, perhaps. It didn't matter. Wherever it was going, he would get on it. The important thing was not to exercise any choice. Even if the train went no further than Mulhouse, he could simply travel onwards from there. Perhaps that would even be for the best. Changing trains would introduce a greater degree of chance. The point, after all, was to disappear. Wherever he ended up, he imagined installing himself in a cheap hotel in a narrow backstreet, adjacent to some proper drinking dens. Establishments where no one would know he was a cop and where he would be completely anonymous. *Invisible.* His mind returned to those alleyways of Nice with their air of debauchery and the heady aroma of marijuana and rotting vegetables.

A train pulled into the opposite platform and departed in the direction of Basel. Gorski ground out his cigarette with the sole of his shoe. He got up from the bench and walked to the end of the platform. At this time of day, the station was not busy. Perhaps, after all, he did look conspicuous. Perhaps a train was not due to arrive at this platform for hours and the station staff would wonder why he was loitering there. He began to feel a tingling in his stomach. That was all right. It was natural to feel edgy. He just had to hold his nerve. Maybe he should have had that third beer after all.

When he reached the end of the platform and turned back, a man had appeared on the platform. That was good. A train must be imminent. He was wearing a dark brown suit and had placed two large suitcases on either side of his feet. A cigarette protruded from his mouth. As Gorski drew nearer, he recognised him as the salesman who had arrived at the Hôtel Bertillon while he was speaking to Virieu. A short time later a harassed young woman with a baby cradled in one arm emerged from the underpass. She looked anxiously up and down the platform, as if she expected at any moment to be apprehended. Gorski wondered if she too was making some sort of escape. After a few minutes, a man in his twenties joined her. He kissed her and took the baby from her. He handed her a paper bag and she took out a croissant and began to eat it.

Gorski realised he too was hungry. He had not had breakfast. That was nothing to worry about. If the train was going any further than Mulhouse, there was sure to be a restaurant car. If not, he could have breakfast at the café at the station there. He resisted the temptation to look up at the board above the platform. When he boarded the train, he did not want to know his destination. When the conductor came round, he would simply ask for a ticket to wherever the train terminated. Of course, the conductor would find this behaviour odd, suspicious even. Who, other than a fugitive, gets on a train without knowing where it's going? But Gorski realised he was not concerned about what the conductor would think, and this in itself was a kind of liberation: he no longer cared. Maybe he had become a sort of fugitive.

The previous night, he had been sitting in Le Pot, nursing a beer, without having noticed that he was the last customer. He must have been trying Yves' patience, but he finished his beer at his leisure and left without apologising. Yves had not seemed the least bit put out. He likely respected Gorski more for behaving in this offhand manner.

As he had strolled back towards the apartment, a little unsteady on his feet, Gorski realised he no longer had any reason to remain in Saint-Louis. There was only Clémence, but in a few months she would be studying in Strasbourg. Perhaps for the first few months she would return now and again to see her dad, but her visits would soon dwindle. That was as it should be. He did not want her to come back. He wanted her to make good her escape, unburdened by anything that might claw her back to Saint-Louis.

A few more travellers were now distributed along the platform. There was a minor commotion, then a murmur of general discontent, followed by some expressions of annoyance. With an air of resignation, people began to take up their luggage and drift back towards the underpass. There had been an announcement of some kind, but Gorski had been lost in thought and missed it.

He approached the man in the brown suit and asked him what was happening.

'Some joker chucked himself in front of the 10.45 from Basel. No more trains until further notice.'

Gorski gave a little snort through his nose. No doubt it would fall to him to break the news to the bereaved relatives.

Robert Duymann had left the door to the house on Rue Saint-Jean unlocked. Gorski let himself in. He stood in the hallway for a few moments, before stepping into the living room. The house was in silence. Duymann's typewriter remained in the corner, but the various papers on the desk had been cleared away. There was no note. There almost never was. Those at the lowest ebb of life rarely think to commit their thoughts to paper.

From upstairs, there came a faint cry. Gorski stepped back into the hallway.

'Robert?' It came again a little louder, plaintively: 'Is that you, Robert?'

Gorski did not reply. He would wait a few minutes before going upstairs and breaking the news. He poured himself a whisky from the decanter on the sideboard. It could not do any harm to allow the old lady to believe for a little longer that her son had returned.

It is a slow night in Le Pot. The only customer is the former schoolteacher who left his post after a pupil made some unsavoury allegations. Yves Reno has no idea if these allegations had any basis in truth, but it is no business of his. He turns off the hotdog boiler and pulls himself a beer. Earlier that afternoon, he installed a toilet paper dispenser in the WC. Lately he has been letting the place go to the dogs.

In her tiny apartment on Rue de Sauvage, Aude Poiret is reading *Madame Bovary* for the twelfth time.

The newest occupant of the nursing home on the outskirts of Bartenheim is sobbing loudly in her room. A nurse, Angélique Martin, pauses in the corridor outside and listens at the door. There's no point intervening. They're all like that at first. She'll get used to it.

Emma Beck gazes at her husband, Paul, across the kitchen table of their house on Rue de la Couronne. When she was nineteen and at the point of leaving Mulhouse for university in Lyon, she fell pregnant. Although there was some doubt about the identity of the father, Paul immediately offered to marry her. Shortly after their honeymoon, she suffered a miscarriage. Last year they celebrated their twentieth wedding anniversary. Paul sets aside his plate and asks what is for dessert. Emma has stewed some apples from the tree in the garden. In the last two months, they have eaten so many stewed apples it has become a joke between them.

Georges Gorski is sitting in his father's chair in the apartment on Rue des Trois Rois. He wonders where he might now be if that morning he had not drunk a second beer in the Café de la Gare.

It's probably for the best. This is where he belongs. He has poured himself a glass of wine and picked out *The Fortune of the Rougons* from the bookshelf in the alcove next to the fireplace.

As is customary on a Thursday evening, Pasteur joins Lemerre and Cloutier at the table by the door of the Restaurant de la Cloche. On their table is a carafe of red wine, three tumblers, two packets of cigarettes, an ashtray and Lemerre's reading glasses. The waitress Adèle begins wiping the waxcloths of the other tables, pushing the crumbs onto the floor that she will later sweep. Lemerre absentmindedly shuffles the cards. Without Petit, they are a man short for the weekly game. Pasteur juts his chin towards the fellow sitting by the window, a commercial traveller who passes through Saint-Louis once or twice a month. Cloutier is dispatched to ask if he would like to make up the numbers. He readily agrees. His participation does not provide a permanent solution to the vacancy created by Petit's death, but it is better than nothing. Without him, there will be no game.

Afterword

When *Une affaire de matricide* appeared in 2019, veteran critic Antoine Dutacq was to pronounce in *Le Monde* that 'Raymond Brunet cannot be regarded as a major writer—his canvas is too narrow for that—but he is a major minor writer.'

It's a fair assessment, and one which the author himself might have reluctantly embraced. Despite its many allusions to the work of Émile Zola, Brunet's trilogy is not the Rougon-Macquart cycle, either in scale or in range of setting and character. While there might be a certain commonality in his satirising of the petty corruption of Saint-Louis or in his preoccupation with the impossibility of transcending one's roots, Brunet's oeuvre stands in relation to that of Zola as a doll's house does to the Louvre. It is a miniature. But it is none the worse for that. Brunet is a writer more interested in the fidgeting hands of a drunk at the counter of a bar than he is in grandiose themes. And despite choosing to clothe his novels in the conventions of the crime genre, he is less interested in the evidence a witness might provide than in what his detective might do with the gift of a block of cheese. In the same scene, Gorski is distracted from his ostensible purpose by the farmhouse aroma of manure and its attendant memories. Brunet is incapable of keeping his mind on the narrative business at hand.

In the preface to *Thérèse Raquin* (which enthrals the teenage Manfred Baumann in *The Disappearance of Adèle Bedeau*), Zola wrote, 'I have chosen people completely dominated by their nerves and blood, without free will ... Thérèse and Laurent are human animals, nothing more.' Georges Gorski's struggle throughout Brunet's trilogy is to escape the path he is expected to follow. As a teenager, he rebels against his father's desire for him to take over his pawnbroking business by becoming a policeman. *A Case of Matricide*, however, reveals the young Gorski's act of rebellion to be bogus, to be an instance, one might say, of bad faith. As the series progresses, Gorski reverts more and more to paternal type, to the point where he finds himself sharing a bed with his mother and, at the very end, settling into his father's chair by the fireplace to read the work of his favourite author.

Each of Brunet's novels features a surrogate character engaged in a similar struggle. In *The Disappearance of Adèle Bedeau*, the maladroit outsider Manfred Baumann has rejected the course of the law represented by his oppressive grandfather. He struggles to throw off the consequences of an act carried out in his youth, but his existence is irresistibly determined by it. In *The Accident on the A35* (and more fleetingly in the current volume), Raymond Barthelme is engaged in a mutiny against the bourgeois values of his family, comically declaring, 'I mean to become a nihilist.' He is as yet too young to have been defeated by 'nerves and blood'. In the final instalment, Brunet's proxy, Robert Duymann,* has tasted a life elsewhere but been drawn back to Saint-Louis by familial obligations. Brunet's characters aspire to forge their own identities; to assert their free will, but whether any of them ever achieve these goals is questionable. As Zola puts it in the preface to *The Fortune of Rougons*, the novel Gorski settles down with at the conclusion of these pages: 'Heredity, like gravity, has its laws.'

However, despite this strong thread of determinism that runs through his work, while Zola views his characters as 'human animals', Brunet does not. Brunet cannot help but eke out a moment which reveals a degree of empathy with his characters. Even the most briefly glimpsed characters—whether the malodorous hairdresser Lemerre or a solitary man who finds

* His name, of course, being an anagram of the author's.

companionship with a stray dog—are invested with a degree of humanity. These moments of sentimentality reveal Brunet to be less of a misanthrope than he probably believed himself to be. Even if his characters are trapped in circumstances from which they are unable to extricate themselves, they are deserving of compassion. While Zola can never resist moralising about his characters, Brunet's approach is more akin to that of Simenon, whose most famous creation, Inspector Maigret, tells a suspect, 'I'm not judging you, I'm trying to understand.'

For myself, the process of bringing Raymond Brunet's work to an English-speaking audience has become a great deal more than a run-of-the-mill translation job. The first task of the translator is to interpret the work. What, we continually ask ourselves, does the author mean? Why has he or she chosen this word over that? Over the course of three novels, one begins to inhabit the mind of the author; to understand how he or she thinks; to know before one turns the page what word or phrase might be coming. In the case of the current project, I have come to feel a kinship with Raymond Brunet that I have not felt with any other author. Perhaps it springs from the similarities in our small-town backgrounds. Perhaps from the feeling of being an observer of life rather than a participant in it. Perhaps I relate a little too strongly to the obsessive overthinking displayed by his characters. Like Brunet, I am an admirer of the work of Georges Simenon and the existentialists of the mid-twentieth century. At the beginning of *The Accident on the A35*, the description of the seventeen-year-old Raymond Barthelme reading Sartre and fantasising about a life somewhere less dreary than Saint-Louis might have been a snapshot of my own younger self growing up in the industrial town of Kilmarnock in the west of Scotland in the 1980s. In short, I came to feel a fraternity with Brunet; that he was my Gallic doppelgänger if you will.

As translators we are expected to remain behind the curtain, but if I am here stepping beyond the usual constraints of my role, it is not for egotistical reasons. As I worked on *Une affaire de matricide*, I became increasingly uneasy. Certain words or turns of phrase in the French edition struck me as incongruous or uncharacteristic of the type of vocabulary Brunet had previously employed.* At first, I dismissed these misgivings. All authors' styles evolve over time. Some become more loquacious. Others, like Beckett, more spare. Moreover, Brunet, I reminded myself, must have been in a state of turmoil when he was working on the book. It seemed reasonable to assume that this state of mind would have had an effect on what he was writing.

Nevertheless, my reservations persisted and, recalling Christine Gaspard's unguarded remark about the manuscript, I emailed her office to ask if it would be possible to have access to Brunet's manuscript. It was an unorthodox request and, not wishing to seem to be casting aspersions on the fidelity of the French edition, I explained that I was writing an article to accompany the UK publication and thought that the original document might provide some insight into the author's writing process. I received a reply the following day, not from Mademoiselle Gaspard herself, but from her assistant, Auxane, who merely asked me to let her know when I was planning to be in Paris. Whether her boss had even read my email, I do not know, but as I booked my flight I felt that I was engaging in a great subterfuge.

A few days later, I was pushing the buzzer of the inauspicious offices of Gaspard-Moreau on Rue Mouffetard in the 5th arrondissement. It was Auxane herself who let me in. I introduced myself, feeling that she was somehow my accomplice. For her part, she did not seem to remember either who I was or why I was there. If I had imagined that this august pillar of the French

* For example, in chapter seven, Jean-Marie Keller tells Gorski, '*Tu vas pas nous chier une pendule*.' This crude but splendid phrase, literally means, 'Don't shit a grandfather clock.' I rendered it somewhat freely as 'Don't get your knickers in a twist.'

literary establishment would be housed in grand oak-panelled offices, I was disappointed. The furniture and bookshelves were a hotchpotch of flea market chic and Ikea utilitarianism. The ceilings were strip-lit and lined with polystyrene tiles. Auxane led me along a corridor with a series of glass-panelled offices, each more chaotic than the next.

'Did you want to see the boss?' she asked.

I shook my head. The less I had to explain about my reasons for being there, the better. As it happened, Christine Gaspard emerged from her office as we were passing. She was a tall, willowy woman with a long neck and implausibly black hair cut like a schoolboy's. Her eyes were heavily made up with what I chose to believe was kohl. She looked about forty, but she must have been a good deal older as she had taken over the running of the company from her father Eugène thirty years before. Auxane introduced me as Raymond Brunet's English translator. She looked at me for precisely long enough to calculate that there was no benefit to be gained from making my acquaintance and asked Auxane to bring her some contracts to be signed.

I was shown into a windowless room at the end of the corridor, if anything even untidier than the various offices we had passed. At the foot of one of the bookshelves was a mousetrap, thankfully unsprung.

'*Les archives*!' Auxane declared. She shifted a few box files from the desk onto the floor and then asked me to remind her what it was I wanted to see.

'The manuscript of *Une affaire de matricide*,' I said. 'And anything else you have by Brunet,' I added, chancing my arm.

The title did not appear to mean much to her. She was about twenty-five and it was four years since the book had come out. It was unlikely that she had even worked there at the time. She rummaged in a filing cabinet and produced two tatty manuscripts tied up with brown string. My heart was pounding.

She dropped the bundle on the desk with a thud.

On top of the pile was a title page:

Une affaire de matricide
Raymond Brunet

The title was underlined in blue pencil. I felt as if I had stepped into Georges Gorski's shoes. Unlike my fictional counterpart, however, I would have the opportunity to peruse the manuscript at my leisure. I may have put my hand to my mouth.

'Is that what you're after?' Auxane asked.

'Yes,' I said. 'Yes, it is.'

She asked if I would like a coffee. I shook my head. She told me to come and find her if I needed anything.

Still standing, I untied the brown string securing the bundle. Beneath the title, written in the same blue pencil, was a note:

Cher Georges,
Vous devrez vous débrouiller avec ça. *

The 'Georges' here was Georges Pires, Brunet's former editor at Gaspard-Moreau who had been dead for a good fifteen years by the time the manuscripts were delivered.

I turned the first page.

Il n'y a pas de villes maudites et la mienne, en tout cas,
est un modèle de petite bourgeoisie étriquée.

I pulled up a chair and sat down. My first impression was that the manuscript was, as Christine Gaspard had let slip, *un cauchemar*. Almost every page had been heavily annotated in Brunet's pencil. Words and phrases had been scored out or replaced, or replaced and then reinstated. Networks of arrows indicated that sentences or paragraphs were to be rearranged. Whole passages had been scored out and the words *À couper!* (Cut!) or *De la merde!* (Shit!) scribbled in the margin.

It was thrilling to observe almost in real time the thought processes of the author whose mind I had inhabited for so long. In stark contrast, the manuscript of *L'Accident de l'A35* was

* You must make of this what you will.

almost pristine, with only the most occasional interventions: the indication of a paragraph break here, the addition of a comma there. It was a complete and polished document, while that of *Une affaire* was no more than a work-in-progress and was, moreover, a draft that exuded frustration, even anguish. Leafing through these pages with their increasingly baffling marginalia and aggressive scorings-out, I felt as though I was witnessing the mental disintegration of the author. I had to remind myself, however, that Raymond Brunet's state of mind was not my concern. The purpose of my visit was solely to ensure that my translation was as faithful as possible to his intentions.

To this end, I took out my laptop and opened the PDF I had been working from. It was soon apparent that there were two main issues with the Gaspard-Moreau edition. The first problem was that several passages which Brunet had indicated should be cut had been left intact. One lengthy passage, describing Gorski cleaning up the aftermath of the fire in his mother's apartment, had been marked as 'boring'. On my initial reading of the French edition, these paragraphs did not strike me as bad or obtrusive, but Brunet had scored through every line and scribbled the words *À dégager!* (Get rid of this!) in the margin. For whatever reason, the French editor had chosen to include this passage, but I felt that, in accordance with Brunet's wishes, it could be excluded without any impact on the subsequent narrative. On the same basis I also cut several shorter passages, which Brunet had marked as redundant, repetitive or simply as *merde*.

The second and perhaps more problematic issue was that a number of chapters ended more abruptly in the manuscript than they did in the French edition. On occasion, Brunet had written *À développer* or *À creuser* (Dig deeper) but had never got round to doing so. In the French edition, however, these chapters included a few additional lines, usually the sort of incidental observation, such as an elderly lady passing with her dog, with which any reader of Brunet's work would be familiar. Towards the end of the book, the scene in which Gorski and Roland question the shoe shop owner, Monsieur Tournier, is sketched in the briefest possible way. This scene as it appears in the French edition had clearly been written almost in its entirety by another hand. I had to applaud the French editor. These additions were so consistent with Brunet's style that I had passed over them without a second glance.

I quickly realised that a proper inspection of Brunet's manuscript would take a good deal longer than I had planned. Lunchtime was approaching. Glancing towards the door, I bundled the manuscript into my laptop case. I spread some pages from *L'Accident de l'A35* across the desk to make it look as if this was what I was working on, then strode out. Auxane was at work behind a glass partition.

'Just going to get some lunch,' I told her.

She didn't bother to respond.

As I strode along Rue Mouffetard with what felt like contraband in my possession, I felt I had transcended my role as Raymond Brunet's translator. I had become his custodian.

Google Maps directed me to a copy shop a few blocks away. I handed over the manuscript and went to the bar next door, drank two beers and ate a croque monsieur.

The copy cost me €235. When I expressed surprise, the young assistant explained blankly, 'It's in colour. The blue pencil. One euro per page.'

I paid up and returned the original to the archives of Gaspard-Moreau.

I do not think it necessary or desirable to provide a detailed account of the editorial decisions I have taken, but a few points are worth mentioning.

Neither the chapters nor the pages of the manuscript are numbered, but I have retained the order followed in the French edition. I have chosen not to indicate where I have removed text included in the French edition, as these excisions—whether of a single word, phrase or whole paragraph—were very large in number and it would have been obtrusive to continually draw attention to this. Readers should be assured, however, that these cuts in all cases followed the author's instructions and were not down to the whim of a maverick translator.

Perhaps more contentiously, I have retained most of the supplementary material added to Brunet's manuscript, firstly because these additions conform to Brunet's notes, and, secondly, because they had been so skilfully executed by the French editor. I have even, in the same spirit, added a small number of embellishments of my own. My guiding principle in all this was to be as true as possible to Raymond Brunet's wishes and to create a seamless and readable text. I am satisfied that I have done this to the best of my ability.

There being no reason to return to the offices of Gaspard-Moreau, the following day I caught an early morning train from Gare de l'Est to Mulhouse. Mulhouse is the small city twenty miles northwest of Saint-Louis that provides the setting for significant parts of *The Accident on the A35.* The offices of *L'Alsace* newspaper are located in a red brick building on Rue de Thann. I explained that I was a writing an article for a British newspaper and asked the receptionist if they had a file on the author Robert Duymann.

'Duymann?' she repeated hesitantly.

It was only as I was spelling his name that I realised my mistake and corrected myself. She returned with a slim file of clippings on Raymond Brunet. The articles were precisely as described in chapter eight of the current volume. As I examined the photograph of Brunet in the Paris nightclub with Claude Chabrol and Emmanuelle Durie, I felt a twinge of sadness. Here, at the zenith of his short-lived success, he looked bewildered, as if he had woken from a dream in an alien environment.

The final interview, dated 16 May 1992, was conducted 'at Brunet's insistence' while walking the streets of Saint-Louis. He had not, the journalist Sylvie Kaplan reports, wanted to meet in any of the town's cafés or bars.

'You see,' he explains as they strolled along Rue de Mulhouse, 'I am not well-liked here. People do not like it when you hold up a mirror to them. They sometimes find that they are not as pretty as they supposed.'

If he dislikes Saint-Louis so much, Kaplan asks, why does he choose to write about it?

'What else would I write about?' he replies. 'I have no imagination. I can only write about the things before my eyes. In any case, I don't dislike it. I love it. But just because you love something doesn't mean you shouldn't write about it with honesty.'

The article is by no means as hostile as the impression given in *A Case of Matricide*. Indeed, the journalist seems well disposed to Brunet, whom she describes as gentle, polite and softly spoken. 'I often,' she says, 'have to lean in close to hear what he is saying.'

I couldn't help wondering if this was a trick Brunet used to engender the intimacy he lacked in his life.

'Despite his familiarity with his surroundings,' Kaplan goes on, 'he often seems lost.' He refuses to reveal where he lives, on the pretext that he does not want his mother to be bothered. He avoids eye contact with passers-by, 'keeping his eyes fixed on the pavement, as if expecting at any moment to be confronted'. In the two hours they spend together, no one recognises him. 'He does not appear,' she writes, 'to be quite as famous as he thinks.' She does not use the word paranoid, but that is the impression she creates. At the end of the interview, she asks when another novel might be expected.

'I'm afraid,' he replies cryptically, 'that I cannot foresee that in the current circumstances.'

When she presses him on what circumstances he means, he declines to elaborate.

It was late afternoon by the time I caught the train to Saint-Louis. The journey was no more than twenty minutes, but as we passed through the villages of Bartenheim and Sierentz, I felt a tingle of anticipation. There on the outskirts of Saint-Louis was the water tower with its large yellow letters announcing the name of the town. A surprising number of passengers alighted at the station, many of them with backpacks and suitcases. It was not, I soon realised, that Saint-Louis had suddenly become a tourist destination, but because it was from here that the shuttle bus to the nearby EuroAirport departed.

I remained on the platform until the crowd had dispersed. Here I was, standing where Manfred Baumann, Raymond Barthelme and Georges Gorski had stood. And, of course, where Brunet himself must have not only waited many times but had eventually taken his own life. I swallowed hard. I felt as though I had stepped onto the set of a film I had seen many times. I took everything in: the railway tracks glowing in the last rays of a feeble winter sun; the outline of the factories and chimneys of Basel across the frontier; the art deco station building with its incongruous pastel-coloured lettering; and, beyond, the low-rise post-war apartment buildings.

A station employee approached and asked if I needed assistance. Perhaps he thought I was myself contemplating stepping in front of a train. Roused from my minor reverie, I shook my head.

I emerged from the station onto Rue de la Gare. Not wishing my experience of reading Brunet's work to be mediated in any way, I had always resisted the temptation to consult Google Street View. It was my duty as translator, I thought, to picture the town not as it really was, but as the author wished to portray it. I need not have worried. Despite the passage of thirty years, everything was very much as I had imagined it. After two or three hundred yards I passed the Café de la Gare with its PMU kiosk. A couple of smokers sat muffled against the cold at one of the pavement tables. Inside, two or three customers could be seen hunched over the counter.

I checked into the Hôtel Berlioz at the intersection of Rue de Mulhouse and Rue Henner. After briefly freshening up, I set off along Rue de Mulhouse towards the town centre. It was, as Brunet had described, a mishmash of post-war buildings and traditional half-timbered dwellings. The former gendarmerie had fallen into disuse. I turned into Rue des Trois Rois. On one side was an apartment block of recent construction. There was no pawnbroker's or florist's, but on the left there was a vacant shop with an apartment above it. The *À vendre* sign in the window had clearly been there for some time.

The little park by the Protestant temple was smaller than I imagined. It was no more than a square of grass, perhaps thirty metres long, separated from the street by a low wall. There were half a dozen chestnut trees and four benches. I sat on one of these for a few minutes and looked at the trees. A few yellowed leaves clung stubbornly to the branches. Next to the church was a dingy kebab shop. An old woman passed by with a wheezing pug. She eyed me suspiciously while her dog relieved itself against the leg of the bench. I bid her good evening and she responded with a brief nod.

From there, I turned left into Rue de Huningue and two or three minutes later I was at the Restaurant de la Poste. I resisted the temptation to stop and take photographs. Such an activity might, I thought, attract unwanted attention. Inside, it was clearly recognisable as the Restaurant de la Cloche of Brunet's novels, although to my disappointment, it had undergone some renovations. The blackboards displaying the menus were gone, as was the hulking dresser where cutlery and napkins had formerly been kept. The banquette along the far wall was intact and I took a seat at the table I imagined might have been Gorski's. I asked for a beer. While I waited, I perused the menu, but I did not order any food. I have always hated eating alone. The sight of a man eating alone in a restaurant is never anything other than wretched.

I drank my beer too quickly and indicated that I would take another. I felt on edge. The room seemed cavernous. The lighting was too bright and although no one had given me a second glance, I felt self-conscious. If asked what I was doing in Saint-Louis, I would be hard-pressed to know how to respond.

The truth: that I was Raymond Brunet's English translator and I had come to the town on a kind of pilgrimage (I could think of no other word to describe it) seemed implausible. Perhaps my imagined interlocutor—naturally I imagined Lemerre in this role—would not even know who Brunet was.

'A pilgrimage,' he would repeat incredulously. 'To Saint-Louis?'

And it would be thought that I was lying and must have some ulterior motive for being there.

I drank my second beer with no less haste, paid up and left.

I ate a kebab standing by the window of the kiosk next to the Protestant temple and drank another beer. I asked the proprietor, a burly guy with tattoos on the back of his hands, if he could tell me where a bar called Le Pot was.

He shook his head. He'd never heard of it.

Despite Brunet's mania for using street names, he had never provided a precise location for this particular drinking den, but I had formed a fair idea of where it should be.

I crossed Rue de Mulhouse and passed through a pedestrianised area with a couple of bars, one of which was brightly lit and looked quite lively. That was of no interest to me. I emerged into the Place de l'Hôtel de Ville, where the new police headquarters was housed in a bland contemporary building.

Rue Théo Bachmann was a narrow backstreet leading towards the railway station. It was dimly lit and even at this hour (around half past seven) entirely deserted. It did not seem a promising spot for a bar, but I reminded myself that the very appeal of Le Pot was its anonymity. I walked the length of the street until it emerged among the apartment blocks in the vicinity of the station. There was no sign of Le Pot or any other bar. I doubled back along a parallel street, Avenue de la Marne, which skirted the railway tracks. Nothing. I retraced my steps along Rue Théo Bachmann. Perhaps I had somehow missed it. There were a couple of unlit alleyways that had seemed to provide no more than access to the back of residential buildings. Perhaps it was down one of those. I navigated these lanes using the torch on my phone. Some kind of animal stirred among some bins near my feet, causing my skin to prickle.

I was inexplicably disappointed. I realised I had come all the way to Saint-Louis just to drink a beer in a pub that did not exist. The trip to Paris had been no more than a prelude to this; a pretext. Then I realised it was more than disappointment I felt. It was anger. I felt as though I had been deceived. If Le Pot was not real, what else was made up? I had to remind myself that Raymond Brunet was a novelist. What had I expected? To walk into Le Pot and find Gorski and the former schoolteacher who has left his post after some unsavoury allegations sitting in their places on the banquette? The idea was ridiculous. And yet, I recalled Brunet's assertion in his interview that he had no imagination; that he could only write about what was in front of his eyes. Had that all been part of the fiction? One way or another, I felt I had been duped.

I shook my head. I was behaving irrationally. It was, after all, more than likely that even if Le Pot had ever existed, it would have long since gone out of business.

In any case, I needed a beer. I remembered the lively, brightly lit bar on the other side of the square and headed in that direction.

I picked up my pace and, as I rounded a slight bend in Rue Théo Bachmann, my eye was caught by a pair of figures smoking in the shadows. High on the wall above them were two gently glowing narrow rectangular windows. Clearly they were for the purpose of ventilation only. Behind the smokers was a glass door covered entirely in yellowed advertisements and posters. On the wall next to that was a small sign, almost impossible to read: Le Recoin—the nook. My heart was pounding. I pushed open the door and stepped inside.

I knew at once that I was in Le Pot. At the back was the counter and to the left of that, the WC. The lighting was very dim, but a tatty banquette ran the length of the wall, in front of which a number of Formica tables were bolted to the floor. There was no longer a hotdog boiler, but this absence had made space for more stools along the bar. Two of these were occupied by large men in overalls and boots caked in pale clay-coloured mud. They were drinking half-litres of beer or cider. At the table to the right of the door, a man in a suit was reading a newspaper. He did not look up.

I took a seat on the banquette in precisely the place where I imagined Gorski had sat drunkenly conversing with the Slav. From behind the bar, a stocky man of about sixty emerged and asked what I would have. His hair was reddish-brown. His features were heavy, like those of a horse, but he had narrow sparkling eyes and a little goatee. He was still handsome. I asked for a beer, a large one. He nodded and returned to the counter, where he poured it with great care, using a palette knife to skim off the head. He returned and placed it in front of me. He had large powerful hands. He was wearing a short-sleeved dark-blue shirt, the pocket of which bore the name of the bar. As he turned away, I noticed that the back of his collar was embroidered with his name: Dédé.

As I was ordering my second beer, an elderly lady came in, pulling a wheeled shopping cart. She could not have been more than four-and-a-half feet tall, and it was with some difficulty that she climbed onto one of the vacant stools at the bar. No words were exchanged, but Dédé placed a glass of pastis, two cubes of sugar and little jug of water before her. The tiny woman dropped the sugar into the pastis and stirred it slowly before topping it up with water. It was some minutes before she took a sip.

I took a long swallow of beer. Nobody paid me any heed. It was as if I was invisible. I felt at home there and experienced a great surge of satisfaction, as if the pieces of a puzzle had finally clicked into place.

Acknowledgements

To my great friend and fellow traveller, Victoria Evans: thank you for saving this one from the fire.

To my publisher, Sara Hunt, and my agent, Isobel Dixon: deepest gratitude for your unwavering support for the completion of this decade-long project. Sincere thanks also to my editor, Craig Hillsley, for your meticulousness and many improvements to the text, and to Angie Harms for invaluable final tweaks. Thanks to Dan Wells for your feedback on an earlier draft, and to Michael Heyward and Jane Pearson of Text Publishing for your continued support.

Warmest thanks to Fred Bilger for your friendship, generosity of spirit and for your invaluable assistance with the French language used in the book. Thanks also to Howard Curtis, Katia Gregor and Julie Sibony for generously answering my questions on this topic.

To Jen, thank you for being there since the very conception of this trilogy. I couldn't have done it without you. Thanks also to Catriona Duggan for your steadfast encouragement during the writing of this book.

The final word must go to Raymond Brunet, without whom these books would not exist. It has been a privilege to bring his work to an English readership, but any inaccuracies in the portrayal of the town of Saint-Louis and its inhabitants are entirely his responsibility.

MANFRED BAUMANN IS A LONER. Socially awkward and perpetually ill at ease, he spends his evenings quietly drinking and surreptitiously observing Adèle Bedeau, the sullen but alluring waitress at a drab bistro in the unremarkable small French town of Saint-Louis. But one day, Adèle simply vanishes into thin air.

When Georges Gorski, a detective haunted by his failure to solve one of his first murder cases, is called in to investigate the girl's disappearance, Manfred's repressed world is shaken to its core and he is forced to confront the dark secrets of his past.

The Disappearance of Adèle Bedeau is a literary mystery novel that is, at heart, an engrossing psychological portrayal of an outsider pushed to the limit by his own feverish imagination.

'This is a crime novel, but it is so much more than that.'
—ARNOLD TAYLOR, *CRIME REVIEW UK*

THERE DOES NOT APPEAR TO BE anything remarkable about the fatal car crash on the A35. But one question dogs Inspector Georges Gorski: where has the victim, an outwardly austere lawyer, been on the night of his death?

The troubled Gorski finds himself drawn into a mystery that takes him behind the respectable veneer of the sleepy French backwater of Saint-Louis.

Graeme Macrae Burnet returns with a literary mystery that will beguile fans of *The Disappearance of Adèle Bedeau.* Darkly humorous, subtle and sophisticated, *The Accident on the A35* burrows deep into the psyches of its characters and explores the forgotten corners of small-town life.

If Roland Barthes had written a detective novel, then this would be it." —PHILIP WOMACK, *LITERARY REVIEW*

GRAEME MACRAE BURNET was born in Kilmarnock, Scotland, and now lives in Glasgow. *His Bloody Project*, his second novel, was shortlisted for the Man Booker Prize 2016, won the Saltire Society Fiction Book of the Year Award 2016, and was shortlisted for the *LA Times* Book Awards 2017. His fourth novel, *Case Study*, was longlisted for the Booker Prize 2022 and was included in the *New York Times* 100 Notable Books of 2022. *A Case of Matricide* is his fifth novel, the third featuring Chief Inspector Georges Gorski.